Owen Douglas, Sacramento's first out battalion chief, is grievously injured in the line of duty. When Brad Sundstrom finds out that Owen's been noncompliant with his physical therapy due to depression, he pushes Owen into the Capital City Rowing Club's adaptive rowing program.

Adam Lennox, a former collegiate rower, escapes an abusive relationship and makes his way to CCRC and quickly finds himself dragooned into helping out with adaptive rowing.

Owen, much to his surprise, finds both rowing and Adam much to his liking. When he realizes that Adam returns his interest, the sparks fly and they start a relationship. But even Eden has its snake, and Adam's ex, Jordan, comes looking for him, willing to do anything to make Adam and Owen pay.

BURNING IT DOWN

CalPac Crew, Book Three

C. Koehler

A NineStar Press Publication

www.ninestarpress.com

Burning It Down

Printed in the USA

ISBN: 978-1-64890-147-8

First Edition, November, 2020
Originally Published in December 2012

Also available in eBook, ISBN: 978-1-64890-146-1

WARNING:

This book contains sexually explicit content, which may only be suitable for mature readers, homophobic slurs, attempted suicide, domestic abuse, animal cruelty/death.

While he's too young to read this, Burning It Down is dedicated to my son, even though by the time he's old enough to read it, he may no longer be interested. Nonetheless, this book is for him.

Author's Note

Domestic violence is a serious issue. One in four women and one in seven men will be victims of domestic/intimate partner violence. If you don't feel safe in your relationship, please reach out. Make a plan. Get out when you can.

Call the National Domestic Violence Hotline at 1-800-799-SAFE (7223) or reach them online at thehotline.org (last accessed 9/1/20)—as the webpage notes, *computer use can be monitored*. If you're not sure your computer is safe, use another computer (perhaps one at a public library or one belonging to a friend) or call the toll-free number instead.

The LGBT+ community can experience domestic violence in ways that are sometimes specific to our community, and the National Domestic Violence Hotline recognizes this. Please check out www.thehotline.org/is-this-abuse/lgbt-abuse (last accessed 9/1/20)

Men, this affects you too. The Gay Men's Domestic Violence Project maintains a twenty-four-hour hotline at

1-800-832-1901. You can reach them online at gmdvp.org/gmdvp (last accessed 9/1/20), although the same cautions apply as with the National Domestic Violence Hotline's webpage—*computer use can be monitored.* If you think your computer is being monitored, use another computer.

All web pages accessible as of 9/1/20. Please note that links can change even if projects and resources continue. If the link is broken search for the resource by name.

Chapter One

Late summer, approximately a year and a half after the start of Rocking the Boat.

Four months into his new job as battalion chief for Sacramento City Fire's second battalion and Owen Douglas still couldn't sit still. Sure, he knew the job from a theoretical standpoint, and every day he learned more from a practical standpoint, but he couldn't ignore the niggling discomfort he felt when he saw those bugles on his collar. Like his new uniform didn't fit quite right, and perhaps from a certain point of view, it didn't. No matter how he squinted or how many times he turned it this way or that, he couldn't see all that much light between his investigation into the arson at the Bayard House at the beginning of the year and his promotion to battalion chief. More to the point, neither could the men and women under his command.

Not to mention every time he opened his mouth, unicorns crapping glitter and rainbows popped out. At least, that was what people seemed to be waiting for. He liked to think he was discreet, that nothing at work proclaimed him Big Gay Owen, no snapshots of boyfriends, no photos of him shaking his ass on a Mardi Gras float, no matter how much fun he'd had in Sydney, just a subtle rainbow on his battered 4Runner, a bar no bigger than the head of a toothbrush. He tried not to play the gay card, but he was the first out battalion chief in the fire department's history, and well he knew it. More to the point, the people under his command knew it. Maybe he was just making too big a deal out of it or felt guilty for being promoted over the heads of more senior firefighters.

His intercom buzzed with his secretary on the other end. "Yes?" Owen said.

"Prissy Morrain to see you."

"Oh! Send her in, please." He dashed to his office door. He didn't expect her until tomorrow.

Owen routinely left his office door open, but he quickly got out from behind his desk to greet his visitor, and not just because she outranked him.

"Chief Morrain! I'm so sorry! I must've made a mistake in my calendar. I wasn't expecting you until tomorrow—"

Prissy Morrain waved a manicured hand. "Retired Chief, and I'm a day early. We both have better things to do than make small talk over hors d'oeuvres over at some white-tablecloth restaurant. Did you bring your lunch today?"

Owen nodded. Since he was a "first" for the department, he'd sought out the advice of another "first," the first woman battalion chief, now retired from active firefighting and promoted off to one side to do something less dangerous involving paperwork. "I'll grab it out of the fridge. There's a nice park a block away. We can eat there."

"That'll do fine."

Prissy Morrain was a handsome woman, Owen thought; really, she could've been one of those older models, the ones with silver hair and flawless skin who pitched vitamins to women of a certain age. Her wrinkles weren't so much age lines scoring her face with years but delicate lines of character radiating out from her eyes and around her mouth to accentuate a ready smile. How she'd managed that with a career spent fighting fires and sexism, he'd never know.

He spent the short walk to the park rehearsing what he wanted to say, but when Prissy asked, "So what's the problem?" Owen could only blurt, "I'm just not clicking with the people under me. This station, sure. My office is here, but the other stations in this battalion not so much, and there's one station that when I walk in everything stops for a few minutes while I walk back to talk to the captain on duty, and that's just creepy."

"Have you talked to human resources?"

"Don't be absurd" slipped out before he could stop it.

Prissy laughed. "Smart man. You don't want this on your record."

And that was why he'd contacted her. "Team-building exercises aren't my thing at this point and are just a waste of time. I'm not in a burning building with these guys. They simply need to function with each other and work in coordinated groups, and they do. But I don't like getting the stink eye either."

"Look, hearts of gold, most of these guys, but it's a conservative profession. The younger ones are yours," Prissy said, arching one eyebrow, "maybe even literally. There's more than one gay man among the recruits, and you're a fine-looking specimen yourself." She peered over the rims of her mirrored sunglasses, holding up one hand when Owen opened his mouth to interrupt. "Of course, you know better than that, but you know what I mean. It's the ones who've been around a few years, the ones who're your age and older, you may have to prove yourself to, the ones who might've even been up for your job. They're the ones thinking 'fag' behind their smiles."

"Or not, some of them," Owen grumbled. "A few of them don't even bother to smile."

Prissy chuckled. "They'll soon learn the stupidity of that. They may be comfortable for A or B shift, but if they're dumb enough to piss in the battalion chief's Wheaties, then they'll have plenty of time to learn the errors of their ways on C shift, or better yet, transfer to someone else's command. Too bad for them you've got just about the best battalion in town."

It was true. Since he'd captained one of the downtown stations, when he'd been promoted, the fire department put him into an entirely different battalion so he wouldn't be in immediate charge of his old buddies. The open battalion encompassed Midtown, East Sac, and part of the Pocket, named for the land inscribed within a bend in the Sacramento River. Sometimes he wondered if it was a coincidence that the city's first out battalion chief also oversaw the gayborhood. He shrugged mentally. Oh well, easier relations during fire inspections, right? "That just seems so petty."

"And the frat boy antics aren't?"

Owen sighed. "True enough."

"It's not something you want to do often, because you *will* hear from their union reps about that, and about anything else if they develop an axe to grind," Prissy said, "but used strategically, it can make your point quite nicely, and the best part is, it's hard to prove."

Owen nodded his head slowly. "One hundred and sixty-eight hours in a week, and five stations to staff twenty-four seven in three shifts."

"Exactly. If you need to, you can always find something miserable for someone to do for a shift or two." She ate some of her sandwich while she thought. "One more thing, and I hesitate even to mention it, but it was something a few—a very few—of my own firefighters used against me." At his quizzical look, she said, "Sexual harassment."

Owen sat back, tossing his own sandwich down. "Oh, that's just what I need."

Prissy patted his hand. "Don't go borrowing trouble. It hasn't happened yet, but you need to be aware of the possibility. You're an out gay man, and you supervise a lot of men, some of whom are, by your own admission, not very happy right now. If they can't pin anything else on you, they may try that."

"Did that happen to you?" Owen asked, no longer hungry.

"Oh yes. I was a by-the-book chief, and when they couldn't come up with anything else, some union rep had the bright idea of sexual harassment. Male firefighters, female chief. It was a situation rife with possibilities. Too bad for them and their credibility none of it was true, which quickly emerged when it came to a hearing. The judge laughed them out of court. It may be the same with you. You'll be a by-the-book battalion chief, but some of them won't like you just because you're you, and the only thing they'll come up with is that you 'looked at 'em funny'." She snorted. "Like you'd go for their stringy asses." She stood up. "You know how to reach me, so do it if you need to. If you'll excuse me, I'm going to go sculling.

One of the advantages of seniority and a desk job is that you can take off more or less at will and no one will miss you. Of course, that's one of the disadvantages too."

Rowing. Brad. "Does *everyone* in this town row?"

"Only the best people. You should come check it out. The Capital City Rowing Club's adult learn-to-row camps are about done for the summer, but there are still learn-to-scull lessons available."

"Thanks for the talk. I really appreciate you taking the time," Owen said, remembering a time he had been anything but by-the-book. The Bayard House. The second floor. Brad. He shivered at the thought of what they'd done. Unprofessional as it had been, it had also been damn hot.

And just the kind of thing people looking to take him down would eat up with a spoon. Fortunately, Brad didn't seem like the kind to tell tales out of school. He was just too nice a guy. Brad had spent their one encounter thinking of someone else, someone who'd dumped him, and still the big sweetheart had pined for that other guy, even with Owen's lips wrapped around his cock, and hadn't that ever done wonders for his ego.

Owen wanted that, wanted that kind of devotion, he thought, sitting there in the leafy green silence of the park. Instead, like that time in the still-smoldering Bayard House, he was just the hookup. He got Brad off and sent him home and then followed up to make sure Brad called whatshisname. He liked to think he was more honorable than most, always the nice guy, always finishing last.

Then he heard the sirens and that was it, no more lunch. That was fine. He'd parted company with his appetite around the time Prissy had mentioned sexual harassment. The park was barely one block from the station, but he jogged back. "What's going on?" Owen asked the dispatcher when he got back.

"A small grass fire at Cal Expo, sir. It doesn't sound like anything to get excited over."

Yet. In Owen's experience, *all* fires were worth getting excited over, at least until proven otherwise. But maybe that was why he was a firefighter. He liked suiting up in his turnouts and racing to a fire in an engine running hot. He shook his head to clear the rising tide of adrenaline. He'd given some of that up to become battalion chief.

Then the radio went off. He picked it up. "Douglas."

"I need four more alarms. This thing's bigger than we were told. Much bigger, and it's heading for structures."

"On our way." He put the radio down. "You heard Captain Chin. Get those trucks moving and notify Arden-Arcade," he told the dispatcher.

"Beaufort!" he yelled for his driver as he ran for his office and his turnouts. *A huge grass fire at Cal Expo that's heading for the pavilions, and the state fair in less than a month. Why do I always end up involved in political fires?*

He wore his turnout pants over his uniform. Sure, he'd sweat like a thoroughbred in moments in the heat once they arrived at the fire. It certainly wouldn't be the first time. The rest he chucked in the backseat of the command SUV with the communications equipment. Then he checked his watch as he climbed into the passenger seat. Less than five minutes. Not ideal, but at least he beat his driver.

Beaufort came running up seconds later. "Damn, sir. How do you do that?"

"Because I'm a firefighter."

"Ha ha," Beaufort replied, climbing behind the wheel and flicking the sirens and lights on. But it was true. After earning his bachelor's in biological sciences at UC Davis, Owen had gone to the Fire Academy at Sierra College. Beaufort studied communications and joined the department in that capacity, along with driving Owen's now important executive-level ass to big fires.

Owen glanced out of Beaufort's side of the SUV. "Look—!"

All he could tell was that it wasn't one of his, and then the enormous fire truck smashed into them, tossing the SUV aside like a rag doll. He lost consciousness as the airbags deployed with a thunderclap.

*

The nurse looked down at her patient, her brow creased with concern. She was new to the night shift, and it left her eyes smudged with fatigue. In the background, life-support machines beeped their mindless rhythm into the darkened room.

"How's he doing?" her replacement asked as he entered for the changing of the guard. He was early, in part to give her a break.

"He's fighting the sedation."

"They always do," he sighed.

"If he doesn't stop this stupid thrashing, he's going to reinjure...just about anything."

He nodded. "It could happen." He checked the patient's charts. "It looks like he's about due for more, so that could be part of it. I'll take care of it, but it's actually a good sign, you know."

"That he's a fighter?" she asked wearily.

He nodded. "It means he'll have the strength to get through all of this. Injuries like this, they don't heal overnight. He's got a lot of PT ahead of him, and even more rehab after that. Any luck on next of kin?"

She shook her head. "Not according to the fire department. He apparently never filled out that form or whatever. They've asked us to let them know if we hear any names."

"That's just great. The only name I've heard clearly is Brad," he said, rolling his eyes. "Brad Sunstorm or Sunstrong. Something like that." He frowned. "I've been checking the phone book, but no luck. I figure it's a friend or a boyfriend."

"Right. Maybe when the police clear his personal effects there'll be something in his wallet that'll make it clearer." She looked down at her patient, even as her end-of-shift thoughts turned to sleep and seeing her kids before they went off to school, and her colleague left to check the other ICU patients before getting the morning meds from the hospital pharmacy. "You're not making it easy for us to help you, are you, Mr. Douglas?"

*

"Renochuck, Brad Sundstrom speaking," Brad said. He listened for a few moments, a growing frown marring his otherwise jovial face. "This is St. Charles Design and Renovations, yes... I see. I'm not sure what to tell you, to be honest. I worked briefly with Captain Douglas—oh, it's Chief Douglas now? Huh—when the Bayard House was vandalized while we were renovating and restoring it, but that's about the extent of my acquaintance with him."

Across the double desk Drew grunted, a sour expression ruining his otherwise handsome face, but even then, his dimples showed. Despite Drew's sometimes difficult temperament, Brad was more spellbound by Drew than ever. The feelings Drew had aroused in him more than a year ago, the ones that led the deeply closeted college grad to explore feelings he'd never realized he had? Those were chump change compared to now. Brad met his eyes and smiled. Then he ran his tongue over his lips. Slowly, like the threat and promise it was.

Drew rolled his eyes, but he laughed too. He couldn't help it. "What was that all about?" he asked when Brad hung up the phone.

"Okay, don't get upset, but remember that story about the fire trucks colliding a week or so back? That mysterious firefighter who was so gravely injured, the one whose name they wouldn't release?"

"Yeah?"

"It was Owen Douglas."

Drew's face went flat. He got the mask-like look Brad hated, the one Brad knew perfectly well meant he was in deep shit but was usually accompanied by the word "fine." "You mean the one you fucked? That Owen Douglas? Suddenly you're his next of kin?"

The last thing Brad wanted was to rehash this with Drew. Again. Would that make it re-rehashing? Okay, he was stalling and he knew it.

Brad gritted his teeth. Looked like it was going to be one of *those* discussions. "Okay, first of all, we didn't fuck. Second of all, I thought of you the entire time and he could tell. He even asked, 'What's his name?' Third, he spent a whole lot of time after pretty much ordering me to keep trying to call you. Fourth, why are you still hung up about this?"

"I don't know." Drew crossed his arms over his chest. "Why're you still hung up on him?"

"I'm not," Brad said patiently, or as patiently as he could at this point. It was the funniest thing. Drew seemed like the most confident man in the world, master of the local real estate market, a man who saw what he wanted and went for it, whether it was a gutsy bid to remodel the historic Bayard House or a certain deeply closeted former varsity rower, i.e., him. But in this one area, he let his freak flag fly, like he was afraid Brad was going to abandon him and all they'd worked for together for a hookup that had taken place while each thought the other had hated him. "Honestly, hon, of the two of us, I'm not the one who's hung up on him. I haven't thought about him in a couple of months, if only," he said, getting up to squat next to Drew's chair and laying his head in his partner's lap, "because a certain tyrant of a partner in Renochuck works me like a slave driver"—he looked up with a wicked gleam in his eyes—"here and at home."

"Oh, I do, huh?" Drew replied, an answering gleam slowly dawning in his eye.

"Yeah, you do. I barely have the energy to get through the day, let alone do things like this," Brad said, turning his head so his mouth was right over his partner's stiffening cock. He allowed himself a smug little grin as he bit the zipper with his teeth and pulled it down. Not a freshman maneuver, but he'd had plenty of practice.

"Brad!" Drew hissed. "Right here in the trailer?"

"You going someplace?" Brad said, working Drew's pants down.

"At least take your hard hat off."

Brad reached up and knocked it off with one hand, the other helping itself to the goodies.

"Someone could walk in," Drew protested, but not very strongly, Brad noted. He was getting better at this. Usually Drew resisted longer.

"No one's gonna walk in. They know better than to disturb us. Besides, what're you afraid of?" This time, Brad looked positively feral as he stood up, looming over his lover. "This, maybe?"

"Brad..."

Brad swept everything off Drew's desk, papers, lunch, and all, and then picked his partner up to set him gently on the desk with the chair's cushion under him. He pushed Drew's ankles over his head, exposing that succulent, firm ass. Damn, he loved that ass. He loved doing all kinds of things to that ass too. There were just so many options. Brad leaned down and bit one cheek.

"Ow!" Drew yelped.

But then Brad soothed it with his tongue, straying down to flick his hole, just enough to tease. Then he bit the other cheek and repeated the process. At the very least, the pain from the bites would give Drew something to think about all afternoon besides the phone call.

Or maybe, Brad thought as he got to work, this was why Drew wouldn't let it go...because every time he grumbled about Owen, Brad fucked him silly.

Chapter Two

"You would pick the hottest day of the summer to move." Steven laughed as he wiped sweat off his brow.

"I'm sorry," Adam said automatically, somehow managing to make his tall, lanky frame look small and cringing.

"Dr. Johansson, that was a joke," Steven said. "It's okay to laugh."

"It's Dr. Lennox, now." Adam shivered, and never mind the heat. "And it...it hasn't been. Not for a long time."

"I know," Steven said softly. "That's why we're doing this. Do you need to take a break?"

Adam looked at him gratefully. "Thanks, but if this is going to work, we need to hurry. Jordan's supposed to be gone until tomorrow, but who knows if that's really true? He could easily check up on me, or even have his friends spying on me."

"He really did a number on you, didn't he?"

Adam looked at his younger clinic volunteer and lately friend. "You have no idea, and I hope you never do. Let's get moving. Literally and figuratively."

Adam had called the Gay Men's Domestic Violence Project four times and hung up before he'd summoned the courage to speak to one of the counselors. It had taken a lot of time to gather even that much courage, but they'd been great, listening through his long, doubt-filled silences, patiently explaining that kisses don't come with fists.

Or black eyes.

Or trips to the emergency room.

They took even more time to explain to him that none of it was his fault. That didn't mean he could accept it then, or even now.

"Uh... Doc? Is that guy the one we're supposed to watch out for?"

One of Steven's friends, co-opted into helping him move, interrupted Adam's reverie. Derailed, really, and thank goodness for that. Of course, he could do without his heart slamming into his ribs. He whipped his head around.

No. It wasn't Jordan.

He could breathe again.

"No."

Steven's friend—what was his name? Joey? Jamie?—looked at him strangely for a moment and then smiled shyly. "Just wanted to be sure."

"Thank you," Adam said stiffly.

"Uh, Doc? Is it all just books?"

Adam shrugged, embarrassed. "I'm sorry they're so heavy. Books and clothes. Nothing else matters."

"C'mon, Joey, no chatter! You can cruise later," Steven barked.

Joey turned bright red and all but ran back into the house for another box. Adam snorted. He'd totally missed it that time. He had so much to relearn, he thought as he followed Joey back into the house for more books, but really, he should've seen it for the ruse it had been. Steven's friend Amanda was the lookout.

He still felt guilty for what he was doing. The last time he'd tried to leave, Jordan had threatened to kill himself. "I... I can't live without you, babe," Jordan had stuttered between sobs. "I mean, my life... Without you, I'm nothing. I should just end it."

By that time, Jordan had worked him over long enough that Adam just about collapsed like a soufflé. "No, Jordan, don't—"

Then Jordan had run out of the house, leaving a distraught Adam in his wake. He hadn't even put his shoes on. Naturally, it had been raining. For long agonized minutes, all Adam could do was sit, frozen and panicked. Jordan was the one who made decisions. Pain and bruises and bone injuries had taught Adam that decisions weren't his to make, not at home. He knew that. But he also knew it was raining and cold and the man he still on some perverse level loved was out in it.

But for the first time in a long time, Adam recalled in that summer heat, he'd felt something else. He'd been angry at Jordan, too, and guilty for feeling it. Not "nice" feelings, for sure, and alien-seeming on top of that since it'd been so long since he'd felt much at all, but the novelty was a relief. For too long, he'd felt like an actor playing himself. During the day, he'd played Dr. Alexander Johansson, healer of sick critters, who deflected the worried glances and concerned words of his animal health technicians and clients at the clinic, but sometime on the drive home, he'd become a block of wood, feeling what Jordan wanted him to feel. Jordan had made the cost of independence too high.

Almost against his will, and muttering to himself, he pulled on his rain boots and parka, grabbed the same for Jordan, and headed out into the wet night to find his partner. They lived near a park, and Adam had no idea where to begin to look. It was a big park. At least the pool was closed for the season, but that left the shade gardens, the rock-climbing walls, and the play structures. In the dark and the rain. He grabbed the battery lantern from the back of his SUV, just in case, his mind racing like the clouds overhead.

How the hell was he supposed to find someone in the park at night? He called Jordan's name over and over, but of course Jordan didn't answer. That would've been too easy. He was supposed to find him, to prove his love and worth, although he knew he never could.

He trudged through the wet grass, anger replacing worry with each step as he walked aimlessly through the dark. He'd give up if he knew Jordan wouldn't make him pay later, was about to give up and pay the price, since he would anyway, when he noticed something.

His footprints remained behind him in the sodden grass, still bent down from his weight. He shone the battery lantern back the way he'd come, and there they were, every last one. That meant somewhere in the park Jordan's own footprints would be visible. True, Jordan had run off in his bare feet and he wasn't as tall as Adam, but there ought to be something to look for.

Sighing again, he made his way back to the edge of the park closest to the house and started over, this time looking for footprints. It took work, squinting through the rain on his glasses, and one close call with a police patrol. He told them he was looking for a lost cat, but was "Boots" really the best name he could come up with? He was a vet, for pity's sake. It struck him as pathetic, but then, Jordan struck him from time to time, telling him how pathetic he was. Adam shivered miserably in his parka.

Finally, near a cluster of evergreens, Adam found footprints leading into the bushes, along with bent and broken branches, their leaves trampled, as if someone had rushed headlong through them. Adam flashed the big lantern's beam into the bushes, half expecting to see the smudged face of a homeless person huddled in his camp. Instead, he saw Jordan, his eyes wild.

"Took you long enough," Jordan muttered.

Adam's shoulders slumped. "I'm sorry, it's a big—"

"You could've come sooner," Jordan said, fiddling with something Adam couldn't quite see. "I thought you didn't care."

"You know that's not true. It just took me a while to find you—"

"This'll teach you to hurry." With that, Jordan pulled out a small knife and cut one wrist.

Adam gasped as blood spurted from the veins on Jordan's left wrist. In retrospect, he realized Jordan had most likely been waiting for him and had deliberately cut shallowly across the tendons, nicking only superficial blood vessels. He hadn't been serious about hurting himself. But there amongst the trees and bushes of the shade garden with the rain coming down, it had made a pretty show and had the desired effect.

He swooped in to disarm Jordan. Jordan might've been stronger, but Adam was taller, and propelled by horror and adrenaline, he powered past what he only later realized had been Jordan's token protestations to knock the knife away and grab the wrist. Looking back, when he met on the sly with a therapist paid for with a secret bank account, Adam figured out that Jordan had managed to make the entire thing about himself and not about Adam leaving. Clever, really. The therapist told him it wasn't his fault, that he wasn't responsible for Jordan's faux suicide attempt or all the rest of his actions, especially his abuse, but he didn't—couldn't—believe her. He couldn't take that chance.

When Jordan found out about the secret account, the beatings had only grown worse. "What, I'm not enough for you? I'm not good enough? Don't I provide well enough for you? You have to hide it from me? What else are you hiding, you worthless piece of shit? You paying for someone else? Someone else paying for you? That's rich."

That had landed Adam in the emergency room. Again. He practically had a standing appointment. Even with going to different ERs each time, they still knew him, at least on the night shifts. Jordan only ever beat him at night. Adam was safe at work during the day.

He couldn't meet the nurse's eyes. He told him he'd fallen down the stairs. It sounded lame even to his ears. The nurse, an otherwise unremarkable-looking man, cupped Adam's chin to look in his eyes. There in the emergency department of an inner-city hospital, Adam experienced more tenderness than he'd felt in years. "Who did this to you?"

"No one," Adam had repeated. "I told you, I fell—"

"What you said, and what's physically possible, are two different things. It's virtually impossible to break two ribs and crack your cheekbone from falling down a flight of stairs."

Adam didn't say anything. There was nothing to say.

"You're staring into space again," Steven said.

Adam looked up into Steven's eyes, dark with worry. They were dark with worry a lot these days, he'd noticed. Adam heaved himself up. "Sorry. I seem to do that frequently."

"Joey's worried about you."

"Joey wants into my pants," Adam said, laughing.

Steven smiled. "Yes, he does. I'm honestly surprised you noticed. Maybe there's hope for you yet."

"No, I'm pretty much hopeless. I mean, you've seen that menagerie I keep, right?"

Steven laughed, a little uneasily, Adam thought. Fear of his future? It seemed to happen to everyone in veterinary medicine sooner or later. Right now, his critters were all locked on the sun porch with lots of ice bottles and the fans turned on high. It was about time to put them in crates. He hadn't done it sooner because he didn't want to stress them, and it was too hot to put them into the cars until they'd been running with the air conditioners on max for a good ten minutes. Summer in Sacramento and pets in cars weren't a good mix. "Joey looks like he's got the boxes of books under control, and all those muscles of his are pretty to look at. Want to help me with the beasties?"

Steven smiled. "You know it."

The ribs had healed, the cheekbone had knit. The seeds of doubt continued to grow, sending roots down deep into his subconscious, pushing at the rocky, barren ground of his emotional landscape. Things went reasonably well with Jordan after what Adam privately referred to as suicide theater—since that was all it had been—but then, sending Adam to the emergency room had seemed to sate him for a while.

Sate him. That was how he'd known it was time to go, when he no longer believed Jordan's apparently heartfelt

"I'm so sorry, babe. I don't know what came over me. It's just... I get so crazy when I think of you leaving me. I promise, it'll never happen again. You have to believe me."

Except it had always happened again. He wanted to believe otherwise, wanted to believe this apology would be the last apology. That time, he remembered, the apology had accompanied a new Range Rover, courtesy of Jordan's trust funds and job as a commodities trader. He and Steven were about to load it full of animals. After it was cool, of course. When they were done, Adam planned to trade it in for something untainted by Jordan. It was the Achilles heel in his escape plan. If he'd done it any sooner, Jordan would've known something was up, but it meant Jordan might be able to trace him through the sale.

"I'll be right back," Adam said. He jogged out to the Rover and turned it on, cranking the AC to max. "It was the animals that did it, you know."

"Did what?" Steven asked as they slipped onto the sun porch.

"Made me leave."

Steven stopped dead in the middle of the room as a chocolate Labrador jumped off the sofa to greet them both. "Are you kidding? The animals? Not, oh, I don't know, self-preservation?"

Adam chuckled. "I know that look. It means you want to throttle me. But no, that was long gone. I came home from work one day, and my Pomeranian, Butterscotch, was dead. Remember Butterscotch?"

"She was the blind one, right?"

"Right. I think that was right after you started at the clinic as an intern. I couldn't prove it, but the doubt would always be there. I'm sure that was Jordan's intention all along, but I got the message all the same."

"Message?"

"'You're next.'"

"Jeez."

"I've got her ashes at work to remind me in case he ever finds me and starts sweet-talking me again," Adam said.

"Don't worry, if he does, I'll sit on you before I let that happen," Steven promised.

Adam carefully picked up a cat, scratching her behind the ears, and was rewarded with an ear-piercing meow from the lilac-point Siamese. "Let's get the beasties in their crates. You really have no idea how anxious I am right now, tranquilizers or no."

"Right."

They worked well together and had almost since Steven started his first summer internship at Adam's clinic between his freshman and sophomore years at UC Davis. Now about to start his senior year, he was almost as knowledgeable as any animal-health technician and was paid for his labor. Adam counted Steven as a friend and not just an employee, which was why when Adam needed to bolt, he'd allowed Steven to organize a few trusted friends to help. The reality was that Adam had alienated a lot of his own friends over the years, only some of whom had understood when he'd told them he was leaving Jordan and needed help. He didn't blame them. They'd heard it before. How did they know this time was any different? He felt the same way the counselors at the Gay Men's Domestic Violence Project told him he might well feel. But at least he felt something. It was a start.

But this time was different. He'd prove it to them. This time, Adam had a plan, as thorough a plan as he could make. The one benefit to Jordan's controlling asshole tendencies was that he paid for everything, including setting up Adam's veterinary clinic. Adam was literally debt free. Working with the police, courts, and the California Veterinary Medical Board, he had a new name and a new professional identity. Goodbye Alexander Lennox-Johansson, hello Adam Lennox. Changing his licensure had been every bit as tiresome and even more necessary, since he was now supporting himself. He'd have left the state, but licensure wasn't that portable, and under his circumstances all but impossible to transfer. With all of that came a new job as an associate vet in a practice in Davis near his alma mater, the UC Davis Vet School, a new rental, a new cell phone. His new boss was delighted that he even came with an experienced intern.

The one thing he felt bad about—not only bad, horrible—was abandoning his practice and all the people associated with it. Only the state licensing board knew the truth, and he did so with its grudging permission, having planned his escape from his old life over long months, referring sick animals to other clinics and making sure that all boarded pets were picked up the previous week. He'd leave no patients in the lurch. Clients would show up to a state marshal and an empty clinic on Monday morning, and his employees would find fat cash severance payments on his desk, and that would be that.

"I think that's the last of them," Adam said as he shut the door behind Abulafia, the chocolate Lab.

"And we've got my car stuffed with boxes," Steven said.

"And mine," added the ever-hopeful Joey. Adam had to admit he was pretty cute in a corn-fed farm boy sort of way.

Amanda glanced around nervously. "Then can we please get out of here? I'm getting more creeped out by the second."

"You and me both," Adam said. "I've got one last thing to do."

He jogged back to the house and deposited his old phone and key ring on the kitchen counter. They were the hated symbols of his old life, signs of his subjugation, and if he could have found a way to make his escape without the Range Rover, he would've. He was still half-tempted to light fire to it somewhere so Jordan could deal with the repercussions. It would be so unlike him, and a well-deserved "fuck you" as a parting gift.

On his way out of the door, his gaze fell on the material artifacts of his life with Jordan, all the art, the furniture, the treasures, the mementos. None of it was his. None of it was him. There was absolutely nothing of him in the room, in the entire house. Other than his animals, which had been limited to the back room, and a few of his books, there'd been nothing of his. Jordan had even picked out his clothes. Suddenly he couldn't stand to spend another second there. He all but bolted from the house. He didn't even shut the door.

"Dude, the door..." Joey said.

Adam shook his head. "Leave it. The sooner we're out of here, the sooner we can stuff ourselves on pizza and beer. I think I need to be drunk this afternoon."

Chapter Three

Early autumn

Deanne Lawson looked up from her computer monitor when the treatment room door opened and her patient rolled in. "Well hello there, Owen. I'm glad to see you."

"Hi," Owen said. He was bright pink, and he knew it. Gingers... There was no hiding a massive blush, that's for sure. "I'm sorry."

"For what?" Deanne stood up and began to set out the equipment she'd need for his treatment and exercises.

"I know I've missed some of my therapy," Owen mumbled, eyes downcast. He looked at the floor, anywhere but his physical therapist, really.

"Some? By my count, you've missed more than a third of your appointments since you were released from the rehab facility," Deanne put her clipboard down and pulled up a chair so she didn't loom over him. "You're in your chair today. Legs weak again?"

Owen sighed. "Yeah, some days I can walk, some days I can't. Today's a can't."

Deanne turned the monitor on her desk around so they could both see it and then opened a tab on Owen's file. "The lacerations to the left side of your face and trunk were either sutured closed or healed on their own. Likewise, the bruising of the muscle in your chest from where the airbags hit you went away on its own. There's not much to be done about it in any case.

"But your left leg was pieced back together, and you have a brand-new stainless-steel pin in your left hip, along with a letter for the TSA, I'd imagine. You should probably have it laminated, at least based on what other patients have told me." Deanne looked up from the screen. "So, let's see, mangled left leg, broken right leg and left arm. As of right now, your left leg is in a fiberglass cast, your right leg and left arm are in braces which you can do without for short intervals."

"I know all this, so why are you telling me it again?" Owen snapped.

"Because I need to know what you want out of PT," Deanne said, refusing to take the bait.

"What do you mean, what do I want out of PT? I want to walk normally. I want to return to work. I want my body back. That's kind of a stupid question."

Deanne snorted. "Not really, because your actions are giving me the exact opposite answer. What they're telling me is that you want your left leg to be shorter than your right leg for the rest of your life, and that you're willing to risk your right leg never bearing as much weight as it used to. That means never fighting another fire, desk jockey or not. That means no more weight lifting or most other sports. Light bicycling could work so long as you have a lift in your left shoe to equalize your legs, or special shoes."

Owen closed his eyes, resting his head in his hands. He felt like there was a weight pressing down on him all the time, all over him, no matter what he was doing. Sometimes just getting out of bed took all the energy he had. Sometimes the blankets weighed too much and all he could do was lay there, his body wrapped in his down comforter, his mind seemingly swathed in fog. He *knew* he needed the PT. Had to have it. He'd never be able to return to work without it. Hell, he'd never be able to walk normally again without it. He didn't need Deanne telling him that.

But damnation, some days, too many days, he couldn't even brush his teeth. He'd never felt this way, this...dead behind the eyes. He didn't have a name for it, but it scared the hell out of him. Was this what depression was like? He saw those commercials on TV, at least when he could stand to watch it. Most days even that was too much. Sometimes he wished he'd died in the accident that killed his driver, because this? This wasn't a life. It was a living death. His body was broken, his mind had switched off.

He felt a hand on his shoulder. "I'm sending a note to your doctor. I think you need to be checked for depression. Because you know what? Nowhere on that list I read off did I say you lost your soul."

"I'm a ginger," Owen rasped. "I don't have a soul." He tried to smile but it felt strange.

"Was that a joke? That's a good sign, you know. Your sense of humor's still in there somewhere."

Owen had meant to say, *I'm not depressed.* "Yeah. That...that might be a good idea. The depression thing. What're we doing today?"

"I'll be helping you with some gentle stretching, followed by some supported walking exercises to build up your strength."

"But we did those weeks ago!"

Deanne looked pointedly at his wheelchair. "And what have you done since?"

"It's...just discouraging, that's all. To keep doing the same thing over and over."

"But that's just it, Owen. You've haven't been doing them over and over. So, we're doing them again, and if you do them at home, then we'll move on to something that'll build on your new strength next time. In a way, PT's like building an onion. We're adding one layer at a time."

Owen managed a tremulous smile. "I have to walk before I can run?"

"Something like that, yes," Deanne said. "In a way, you really are learning how to walk again. Your body suffered a major trauma, Owen. The old balance, the old muscle memories, especially on your left side, just aren't there anymore. We also need to keep the healing tissues supple so they don't scar up. With any luck and"—she gave him a very pointed look—"some hard work on your part, it'll come back faster this time. After all, you've healed some in the interim."

"Fingers crossed," Owen said, but they could both tell his heart wasn't in it. Owen knew, however, that his body had damn well better be.

"I'm prescribing some light traction with the stretchy bands to help keep your left leg in particular from tightening up, but I want to you to use them on your right leg too. Arms and shoulders, as long as you're at it. We'll go over it all today. None of it's going to feel particularly good," Deanne cautioned him. "Do you remember what I said about discomfort versus pain?"

Owen rubbed a hand over his scruffy face. "Discomfort means I'm challenging my body, but pain means I'm hurting it and I need to knock that shit off immediately?"

"Pretty much, yes. Are you ready to get started?"

He shrugged. "No, but that doesn't mean anything."

For the rest of the hour, Deanne put him through his paces, first stretching him and then reminding how to stretch correctly at home, twice a day at first and then three times daily. Then they worked on the assisted walking course. It bore no resemblance to the obstacle course at the fire station, but it made Owen sweat far more. That above all else told him just how much conditioning he'd lost since his accident, a sobering reminder of the cost of his moping.

Deanne handed him a water bottle.

"I'm not—"

"Shove it," she said. "Drink it all and another after that. Then I'll show you how I want you to do the resistance work with the bands at home. You may be a stubborn macho ass, but I'll get you back on schedule even if it kills us both. You do want to go back to work, don't you?"

Owen groaned and took the bottle. She'd already loosened the lid. At least he didn't have to worry about being roofied at the high-end PT clinic the department and his private disability insurance sprang for. It was funny how the wallets opened up when the injuries were oh so actionable. The only thing Deanne might slip into his water would be an anti-inflammatory.

More stretching, and then she showed him how to use the bands, and then it was a brand-new world of pain. Two different workouts in an hour just seemed cruel and he said as much.

"Oh, boo hoo. If you'd do this regularly you wouldn't feel like a train'd hit you, so you have only yourself to blame," Deanne said. Owen noticed that the usual smile and good humor with which she delivered her sermonettes had disappeared. "From here on out, it's going to be boot camp. Not only that, I have something else I want you try since traditional physical therapy apparently isn't to your liking." She shoved a brochure in his face. "It's from the Capitol City Rowing Club. Ever heard of it?"

"It rings a bell, but I know there's a couple of college crews in the area, CalPac, UC Davis, Sac State," Owen answered, looking at the pictures on the cover. Sure, the rowers looked fit, but all of them were handicapped in some way. The boats themselves didn't look quite right.

"The Adaptive Rowing program at CCRC is the practicum of a PT student at Sac State I work with sometimes, Nick Bedford. He used to coach at CalPac College. He knows a lot about rowing and has the making of an excellent physical therapist. The goal of the program is to restore functional strength to the body while lending support where it's needed. You read the details in the brochure. I strongly urge you to check this out," Deanne said, "and in the meantime, I'll see you in two days. When you come back, I expect you to have done your exercises. Keep in mind, since this is work-related, I have to report back to your supervisors sooner or later."

"Right," Owen sighed as Deanne helped him to his chair. Maybe he wouldn't need it on his next appointment, but that day, he was certainly grateful for it, along with the orderlies who helped him to his SUV and the handicapped placard that let him park close to the door.

*

Owen made it home but slept for the rest of the day. It felt like honest sleep. Exhausted sleep, not the kind of sleep that resulted from...depression. He hated to admit it, but Deanne was probably right. But really, he chuckled to himself, what did he have to be depressed about? A work situation he hadn't even begun to sort out, including a decision about whether to sue the city and the fire department? A catastrophic, life-changing accident? The fact that he couldn't remember his last steady boyfriend? That was him, always the hookup, never the boyfriend. He thought maybe that depressed him more than anything else.

Deanne must've been truly worried about him, because late the next afternoon his doctor called him with the referral to "behavioral medicine," which he thought was a generous euphemism for crazypants. He sighed. He still couldn't come right out and say it.

He tried it in the bathroom mirror.

"You're crazy."

Owen made a face. That didn't feel quite right.

"You're crackers."

He shook his head slowly.

"You, sir, are a few fries short of a Happy Meal." He wrinkled his nose. "Jeez, who even eats those anymore?"

Owen continued to look at his reflection, hazel eyes to hazel eyes. It had been a long time since he subjected himself to such scrutiny, and truth be told, he was making himself squirm. He knew he hadn't let himself go per se, but nonetheless, gone to seed he had, and it didn't seem like it had taken him all that long either.

"You're depressed," he said softly.

He stared at himself a moment longer.

"Damn," he muttered. "You look like crap."

It was true.

He pulled off his T-shirt and dropped the sweats that now hung off his hips. A month and more spent indoors had robbed him of whatever color he'd had, which wasn't much to begin with. It wasn't like he'd ever been tanned. No ginger ever tanned. Mostly their freckles got darker and the pink skin in between just stayed pink, probably working on becoming cancerous. Now he was just pink all over, save for his left leg, which was pink with a maze of darker scars.

His muscle tone felt shot despite the temporary boost from the PT. Sure, it'd come back in a hurry, especially if he stuck with the exercises and then went right back to weight training. But for now, he felt like the proverbial ninety-eight-pound weakling. Two sets of ten reps on a rubber band shouldn't exhaust him. They did. And damnation, those leg exercises were going to kill him.

He poked himself in the side. Some of the flab was just more of that lack of muscle tone, but ugh. What was an injured gay to do? Owen sighed. He could eat better than he had been, that's for sure. Just because the grocery store delivered it didn't stand to reason they had to deliver crap. He was pretty sure there was a "produce" tab on the webpage, just as he was pretty sure he'd studiously ignored it. Clearly the "fun" with chips and candy was over, and if he were honest with himself, he hadn't really enjoyed a steady diet of junk food all that much. *Just because you can, doesn't mean you should, Owen.*

The hair situation was out of control, with orange tufts sticking up from behind his ears and his bangs making a run for his eyebrows. Then there was his beard. It looked like a pile of autumn leaves had drifted down from the trees and affixed itself to his face. He hated that.

He knew he shouldn't give himself a haircut, having learned that lesson the hard way in grammar school and then again one drunken evening in college. But the pile of leaves? That he could fix. He couldn't remember the last time he'd shaved but knew it hadn't been recently.

As he waited for the water to warm up, he turned his face this way and that. Still a bit sun-weathered, still a few gray hairs at the temple, but maybe… Yeah, why not? He was still young enough to pull off a goatee. Besides, if it grew tiresome or if the neighborhood children pointed or giggled, he could always shave it off.

He rubbed the shaving cream into his beard to soften it up, and then got out extra blades for his razor. He had a feeling he'd need them. He caught sight of his eyes and looked away. They were flat and lifeless. Ugh. After that, he kept his eyes on his beard. It was probably safer that way, anyway.

It wasn't until he was fresh and clean from his shower that Owen realized just how much he was stalling. He knew he needed to read that rowing brochure and couldn't put it off any longer.

Until he put on clean sweats and went to climb into bed and smelled just how stale the sheets were. Damn, he must really be depressed if he was willing to put up with funk of that magnitude. He laughed at himself as he stripped the bed. At this point, it was almost a game. What else could he do to stall? Kitchen, living room, bathroom? Counters, fixtures, vacuuming? Hell, it wasn't even stalling, it was functional strength training! He was proving he wasn't depressed by showing an interest in his environment for the first time since his accident.

An hour later, when the wild hare and his strength both abandoned him, he had to admit his small house certainly looked—and smelled—better for his efforts. Not that he'd ever harbored any delusions about entering his bungalow in any *House Beautiful* contests, but it was home and it was his.

And now Owen couldn't put it off any longer. He grabbed the brochure and climbed into bed. With his body's protests growing louder by the minute, he knew he'd not be getting out any time soon, not until or unless hunger drove him to it, and his appetite hadn't been worth much lately, along with his libido, or his will to live. But no, he wasn't depressed. That was for crazy people, he thought dryly as he pulled the covers up to his chin, and he wasn't crazy. He was just depressed.

So. Adaptive rowing at Capital City Rowing Club. He looked at the glossy brochure. He recognized some of the pictures as being local because of the Sacramento skyline in the background, but some of them had to be stock photos if the program was as new as Deanne had said, like the pics of racing shells modified with pontoons. Still, it was pretty cool to see athletes working hard in one- and two-person boats, for athletes they were, even if they couldn't use their legs or swing their trunks. They were doing what they could with what they had.

The brochure included links to USRowing's adaptive rowing page. Before he knew what he was doing, Owen was up and in front of his computer, waiting for it to boot up, and as soon as it had, he watched the videos over and over, riveted in place by the images of the 2008 Paralympic Games, when adaptive rowing made its debut. He didn't know if his left leg could sustain the kind of power that rowing generated, but he could see why Deanne had dangled adaptive rowing in front of him. Even just using his arms and back, rowing would whip the rest of him into shape whether he wanted it or not. He hoped the coach would go easy on him at first. Deanne had said he was studying to be a physical therapist...

After an hour, he retreated to his bed, more dispirited than ever. How could he do something like that, flying across the surface of the water, when he couldn't even stay out of bed and it took everything he had just to complete his strengthening exercises in the privacy of his own home? Jeez, he couldn't even face going out to the grocery store, and that might even help build strength in his leg. No, he had his food delivered. A few minutes of his time online and it magically appeared on his doorstep a day later. How did that help anything other than his newfound feelings of stranger-danger?

He stared at the pictures in the brochure. So many happy people. He knew objectively they must've had their own problems. After all, some of the disabled rowers probably weren't born that way. In fact, there were links to projects designed to help wounded veterans stay as active and useful as possible. Compared to them, he was lucky. His surgeons had pieced his leg back together instead of making the most of what wasn't blown off by an IED. He pushed the thought away. He didn't need logic when he was wallowing in self-pity. But other people had gotten used to limitations, and the point was, he could too.

He kept staring. One of those rowers...he knew him. It was Brad. It had to be. He sighed.

Brad. It's not like he'd expected Brad to keep in touch or anything. That'd been the whole point of their hookup. No-strings, burning hot fun, and damn, was that ever hot. Unprofessional for them both, and it could probably get him fired if it ever came out, but—Christ. It still got him hard. These days, it was the only thing that sparked life down there. He wasn't carrying a torch for the big guy. He wasn't expecting flowers. They hadn't even exchanged phone numbers; the only way he'd been able to track Brad down to nag him into calling his on-again/off-again boyfriend was because of Brad's business with the city in restoring the Bayard House.

But Brad. They'd had their fun, those two, but once again, there was Owen, always the hookup, never the boyfriend. More and more, Owen felt like that was his fate. He didn't blame Brad for that. In fact, there was no one at all to blame, save for possibly himself for gratifying the short-term urge at the apparent cost of a long-term relationship. Then again, there were no guarantees in life, no promise that if he'd held off on the gratification either one of them wouldn't have been hit by a bus the next day.

Or by a fire truck that was where it shouldn't have been.

And there he was, alone in his bungalow nursing his injuries and apparently depressed, alone. All it really meant was that he lacked real human contact in his life. That was why he was going to do it, why he was going to sign up for adaptive rowing, even if he knew he'd feel vulnerable and exposed the entire time, and why five days later he still hadn't done it.

He didn't raise the subject at his next PT appointment and Deanne didn't either. It took him days of reading and rereading the brochure and turning on his computer and getting distracted by news and analysis websites—okay, porn—and all he could do was stare at the coach's e-mail.

Chapter Four

Adam sat at his desk at the clinic early—very early—one morning, reading journals since it was too early for the paper. Unlike some in his field, he had no problems spending the night at the clinic to be closer to sick patients. Sure, he had animal-health technicians, but he always put his name down on the duty roster too. They'd end up calling him if one of the sick ones crashed, anyway. Maybe if he had a boyfriend he'd feel differently about it, but as it was, he could just as easily sleep on a cot as he could in his house, even if T'Pau let him have it when he came home.

He had settled in nicely, both in his new town and as the associate veterinarian in a practice whose senior partner approached retirement age. The arrangement suited them both, at least for now. Dr. Endicott could play at being a veterinarian with her favorite clients while dumping the rest on him, and in a reasonably short amount of time, he could step into the ownership of a mature practice whose clients already knew and trusted him and whose prior owner felt comfortable leaving the practice in his hands. It also gave him time to reestablish credit so that when the time came, a bank would loan him the money to buy the practice.

He didn't count his first morning in Davis as far as settling in went. He slept until noon, partly due to all the beer he'd consumed the night before, partly because he was finally free. Thinking about it even all these weeks later, all he could do was shake his head. He was free of his abusive boyfriend, and he slept. It certainly wasn't because he could let his guard down. It'd be a while before he could do that. He was just exhausted, and he slept. He was certain his therapist or the detective handling his case would chew him a new one, and with all justification. At the very least, he needed some kind of security system, because despite the new name and everything else, he hadn't moved very far. He needed to keep his guard up. He jotted a quick note: *Call security companies at lunch.*

It wasn't simply starting over professionally, he realized. Adam felt like he'd hit rewind on his entire life, in some strange way going all the way back until just before he'd met Jordan. They'd met in college, he the tall, awkward geek there on a patchwork of scholarships, Jordan the dark, brooding rich kid. Adam had never felt like he fit in, not even on the rowing team where he was a natural, his skills earning him a place he never believed he'd deserved, but when Jordan had spotted him, suddenly he had a place, the place Jordan created for them both. Adam hadn't noticed the bars, not at first and not for years after.

In a way, he'd been given a chance to start over, recreating the life Jordan had stolen from him starting from their first date. In a trashy kind of way, it was fun. He'd gone to a few parties with Steven, sticking out more for his life experience than for his height amongst all the undergraduates. He felt a little pervy being a good ten years older than most of the other attendees at these parties of Steven's, although a surprising number of guys seemed to find that a bonus feature. But even if undergrads had been his thing, he felt like he owed it to one undergraduate in particular to give him a chance. So yeah, he hooked up with Joey a time or two. Or five.

Okay, maybe six times at the most. Thank goodness for young men with daddy issues, he thought on more than one occasion, or he'd be stuck using his hand, and Joey was the sweetest guy ever.

Adam realized something very important from the time he spent with Joey, not all of it in the sack. Undergrads were cute enough, he thought as he turned off the clinic's alarms and went downstairs to get the paper from outside the back door, and my God, the endurance, but that said, he'd rather not get any on him. Or any more on him, as the case might be, he acknowledged with a wry chuckle. Joey really was a nice guy and would make someone a terrific husband, but after the last time waking up together, they'd both realized they were done with each other. At least he had. That didn't mean Adam didn't hope to lure Joey into working at the clinic if he decided on going into vet medicine. Even if Joey leaned toward large-animal medicine, he'd still have to do some small-animal work to earn his DVM, and why not do it where he knew (intimately) the associate vet?

Obviously, he couldn't go all the way back to the time before Jordan. He already had a degree and a profession, a sense of self that was missing from the man he had been all those years ago. He knew who he was in a way he didn't back then, but only in some ways. He couldn't help but wonder whether he would've knuckled under so easily if his self-identity had been stronger. He tucked that one away for his therapist. In the meantime, he had things to do. It was time to feed the beasties.

He fed the boarders first. Their owners generally provided food since the clinic's charge for doing so was astronomical. But hey, they had to pad their bill somehow, and they sure weren't going to charge people any more than they had to for medicine, that was certain. The boarders were the easy ones, them and animals residing at the clinic itself, animals too crotchety for the vets or the animal health technicians to take home, or castoffs whose owners couldn't or wouldn't take care them of anymore. He reminded himself several times a day not to judge.

After the healthy animals came the sick ones. They were why he didn't shower first. He inevitably got something on him he didn't care to wear for the rest of the day. They couldn't help it, and it came with the territory. He was almost more worried when they didn't fight back or sling their medicine back at him or fight the IVs.

Adam flipped the switch on the coffee maker in the clinic's kitchen and then jogged upstairs to take his shower. The other early-shift people would arrive in an hour or so, which gave him just a bit more peace and quiet with his thoughts, the clinic residents, and the morning paper. People wondered why he liked the early mornings at the clinic, and mornings like this one were why. No terribly sick patients, time alone, and a small parade of animals behind him—some residents, some boarders— with no agendas more complicated than breakfast and attention, not necessarily in that order.

Adam flipped idly through the paper while he ate his breakfast when he spotted it: an ad for the Capital City Rowing Club. He didn't know how long he stared at it before it registered. Rowing. He'd gotten out of crew when he graduated, of course. Even if he'd known about masters rowing, he was in vet school and wouldn't have had the time, and Jordan always seemed to resent it, maybe because it had a hold on him Jordan didn't. But now that he was starting life over...

He wondered if being on the water as the sun rose still promised a day full of magic. Even if things went straight to hell, for those few golden moments, the day was always perfect. He sat frozen at his desk, caught in the memory of eight oars catching the water simultaneously, eight backs bending as one, pulling on those oars with but one purpose: to move the boat under the cox'n's guidance. Some of the best times of his life.

Could it be that easy? Could he truly just set foot in a boathouse and find that magic again, especially when he'd never really felt like he'd fit in? But the sunrise on the water...

Before he knew what he was doing, his skin all a-tingle at the thought of being on the water again, he tore the ad from the paper and practically ran from the kitchen to his office. Once there, he lifted Jasper, one of the clinic cats who had adopted him as soon as he'd started working there, off the monitor—all that fur couldn't be good for the computer—and e-mailed the coach his name, his stats, and the basics of his collegiate rowing career, as well as an explanation for the differences in his name, then and now.

Even new clients noticed Dr. Lennox seemed rather chipper that day.

*

Nick Bedford let himself into the apartment he shared with the love of his life and was greeted by the smell of pasta sauce. He inhaled deeply, savoring the smells of love and home. There was a faint overlay of something burned, but wisely, he made no mention. He only smiled, his heart filling even fuller with love. He'd had no idea when they'd moved in together months before, but his highly competent boyfriend—now partner—had no idea how to cook. None. Morgan Estrada could burn water. Nick simply appreciated those nights he tried.

"Lucy, I'm home!" he called.

"That'd be funnier if I'd actually grown up watching that show," Morgan called from the kitchen.

Nick set his backpack down by his desk in the living room. "I know I'm older than you, but I didn't exactly see *I Love Lucy* during the first run, and besides, you're the hot-blooded Latin, remember?"

He came up behind Morgan to embrace him from behind. He loved that they lined up so well, as apparently did Morgan, because his partner ground back against him. Nick groaned.

"Save that for later, babe," Morgan said. "Dinner's almost ready. Set the table?"

Nick adjusted himself and did as he was asked. That was their deal. Whoever didn't cook set the table and cleaned up, at least when they managed to eat dinner together. Since they were both graduate students, it didn't happen as often as they liked. They insisted on once a week at a minimum, but rarely achieved more than three times.

"So, what did we learn at school today?" Morgan said as he dished a helping of pasta onto Nick's plate.

Nick sighed, doing the same with the salad. "I think I'm in trouble again."

Morgan set the pasta claw down and cocked his head to one side. "How you manage this is beyond me. What'd you do this time?"

"That's the thing, I'm not actually sure. You know I don't have the best political acumen, but I'm getting a lot of side-eye action from the faculty. I know I was lucky—damn lucky—that so much of my MS in kinesiology transferred to my work in physical therapy. I guess that's ticked a lot of people off?"

"That sounds like a question, but I can't think why you'd be asking me," Morgan said.

"I guess I'm just thinking out loud. But it certainly seems to have ruffled some feathers." Nick frowned, lost in thought for a moment.

Morgan nudged Nick's foot under the table. "What'd you do this time?"

"I love how you assume I've done something wrong," Nick said sourly as he played with his food.

"You don't go looking for it, but trouble just seems to find you." Morgan regarded him with studied curiosity.

Nick looked up at him with a sly smile. "I think that's going to be your new nickname: 'Trouble.' Because as I recall, you were pretty definite about making your wants known."

"Yeah, but you went looking for it and me," Morgan said. He slowly ran one foot up his partner's leg, all the while looking as innocent as a kitten, an innocence they both knew was a load of crap.

"I thought that was dessert," Nick said.

"I didn't want you to forget."

"I see." Nick picked a cherry out of the fruit salad that was dessert and plucked the stem off. Then, making sure he had Morgan's full attention, he popped the stem in his mouth and tied a knot in it with his tongue.

Morgan stared, dumbfounded. "You..."

"Dessert, remember? Anyway, trouble. It's not like I'm in official trouble or anything or I'm about to be kicked out, but all of a sudden I'm getting a lot of glares from some of the faculty." Nick sighed. "And it's not like I want to piss any of them off."

Morgan nodded slowly. "Not when you were lucky they let you count so much of your MS."

"Or that I'm doing some internship work already, like my practicum."

"What could be wrong with that?" Morgan demanded, all thoughts of footsy or amazingly dexterous tongues forgotten.

Nick scratched his chin. Morgan wanted him to grow a little scruff and it itched. "I'm not actually sure. I don't know if it's that my rowing contacts allowed me to score not only a fat monetary grant but thousands of dollars of donated equipment, or that I did it without asking." He shrugged. "I figured it was my practicum, and if my advisors thought it was fine, I could go for it. It's not like I don't have support in the community for it with Capital City Rowing letting me use their docks and having space in their boathouses, and it's not like I'm rubbing anyone's face in it."

"But you don't have to, do you?" Morgan guessed shrewdly. "I bet your professors do it for you. You just keep your head down and do your job, same as always."

"And trouble finds me anyway," Nick said. "It's not like I can't deal with it. I'm hoping once I've got the adaptive rowing program up and running and show that I'm right in what a difference it can make in terms of physical recovery and mental outlook, the fuss'll die down."

"There'll be another one. You done?"

Nick nodded. "Yep."

They cleared the table and then Nick cleaned up. Fair

was fair, and Morgan cooked so he washed the dishes and put the leftovers into serving-sized portions in the fridge or freezer, wherever they stood the best chance of survival. With two busy athletes and grad students, premade, premeasured meals were a must.

After dinner, as they often did, they went their separate ways to study, Nick to his desk, and more often than not, Morgan to the sofa, there to sprawl provocatively, maybe even seductively. Nick wondered if he did it on purpose, but that was why he sat with his back to the room.

Reading, reading, reading, that was all Nick did, or so it seemed. When he couldn't face any more of it, he checked his coaching e-mail for Capital City Rowing before making plans for the morning's practice. One of the hardest things he'd learned about master's rowing was that he really didn't have the sort of power over grown-ups he'd had over collegiate rowers. If they didn't feel like coming to practice, he could guilt-trip them and explain that lackadaisical attendance was why they kept getting handed their asses at regattas, but that was about it. Fortunately, most of his rowers were the competitive sort.

Then he found the e-mail from a new rower, one Adam Lennox. He loved new acquisitions. They always shook things up, jarring people out of their complacence and their sense of their place in the order of things. The shift in dynamics was good for the team. Also, Nick enjoyed watching that sort of thing.

Nick read the e-mail. Then he read it again. Wow. Sure, he hadn't rowed for a while, but it was like falling off a bike. You never really forgot how. He opened a browser window and started a search but came up completely blank.

Then he reread the guy's e-mail again. Huh. He

changed his name somewhere along the way. Interesting.

He searched under the old name.

Nick wasn't aware how long he was reading online.

"You're drooling. New recruit?" Morgan said behind him.

Nick jumped. Blushing, he scrambled to hide the screen. "It could've been porn."

"We both know it's not." Morgan reached over Nick's shoulder and pulled up the browser window in question to reveal a webpage from a university's athletics department. Morgan whistled.

"He's six foot five," Nick said. He knew he sounded like a gearhead talking about car engines, but in a way, he guessed it wasn't that different.

Morgan laughed. "Don't ever change, Nick. Promise me that."

"What does that mean?" Nick said, eyeing his beloved Morgan suspiciously.

"That you've got a very fixed focus and that somehow, all that rower flesh never manages to turn your head."

Nick pulled Morgan onto his lap. "Just once."

"See that it stays that way," Morgan said. He didn't— couldn't—say any more after that because Nick was doing that thing to his neck he liked so much.

Then Nick stood up and, lifting his younger, taller lover by the thighs, he carried Morgan to their room.

Later, when they held each other before drifting off to sleep, Morgan asked, "Any regrets?"

Nick didn't reply right away. They had this conversation from time to time. He still wasn't sure what they were really talking about. He rested his head on the top of Morgan's, his cheek pillowed by Morgan's black curls, breathing deeply of his scent. "What kind of regrets?"

"You got out of coaching for me. I've seen how you look at those CalPac boats as they go by," Morgan said softly, his voice heavy with impending sleep.

"I got out of coaching for us, you and me together. There'd always be a cloud over my coaching career, and we both know it. Even once you graduated and were no longer one of my rowers, I'd always be *that* coach, the one who preyed on one of his rowers and never mind that we have a solid, monogamous, and continuing relationship. I'd still have some rules committee or other breathing down my beck. How we met is our past, and for our future, I'm doing something else with my life."

"You're doing it again..." Morgan mumbled.

"Doing what?" Nick asked, but Morgan was asleep.

What he didn't tell the sleeping man he hoped one day to marry was that after Drew's assault and recovery earlier in the year, coaching no longer held the same meaning for him. Other people could coach overfed and overprivileged collegiate rowers. He, Nicholas Bedford, wanted to help people get back into the shape where they could do that sort of thing again or even just walk around the block. Bodies in motion fascinated him, any kind of motion, and not just rock-hard bodies, as he'd realized when he'd helped Drew recover. In fact, for Nick, that recovery was more important than athletic performance, so he'd more or less started grad school over, from kinesiology to physical therapy. Oh well, student loans were fashionable now, right?

At least Morgan's parents were covering the costs of their son's master's degree and teaching credentials, and since the Estradas were loaded, he and Morgan wouldn't have that much more debt weighing them down.

With a sigh of contentment, Nick finally relaxed against Morgan and fell asleep. Mornings arrived early in the Bedford-Estrada household, and they both needed all the sleep they could scrounge.

Chapter Five

Owen pushed his way into his bungalow with a bag of groceries on the seat of his fancy new walker. His leg still bothered him, and now prone to random power failures, he never knew when he'd have to sit down. That had proved to be inconvenient on more than one occasion. That evening, however, the walker made a handy shuttle to ferry grocery sacks from the back of his SUV to his kitchen. Between the bags on the seat and the ones swinging awkwardly from the handles, he only needed one trip. He felt smug about that.

He did his PT, but now he added therapy and happy pills. He "got" to go meet with a therapist or counselor or something and emote once a week. He was a man. He didn't have feelings. Right? He'd been listening a lot to Kenny Loggins's "I'm Alright" from *Caddyshack*, which he felt was an underappreciated movie, along with all of Rodney Dangerfield's oeuvre. Next week, he was going to print out the lyrics and hand them to his shrink. He was all right, dammit. Why wouldn't anyone listen to him?

In fact, he'd just returned from another bout with his therapist, a well-meaning older woman who wouldn't quit rooting around at the edges of his emotions. Actually, that was what they'd talked about that evening, his alleged lack of feeling. They'd talked about it the previous week, too, because for some reason she found his thesis that men don't have emotions enormously offensive.

He stowed his walker in a corner. That was progress, as she'd pointed out. No more chair, although he still had it, just in case. Deanne had refused to take it back, which he interpreted as a slap, like she expected him to relapse or something, and never mind her impatient explanation that since his insurance had paid for it, he owned it. Never mind how much he hated it or what a symbol it was. Deanne didn't seem to get that.

He sighed, flopping down onto his sofa, one arm over his eyes. All he'd done for the last ninety minutes was sit in a dimly lit room and talk, so why was he so damn tired? Maybe it was the meds. He'd been going to his PT most of time. Okay, more of the time. He should be back in shape, or getting there, but his body, his fucking broken body, wouldn't cooperate. He wasn't that old, and when he came down to it, he didn't think he was that injured anymore. So why wasn't he back up and at 'em? Why wouldn't his body just cooperate and do what he wanted it to do?

What he needed it to do.

He couldn't even go to the library, therapy, and the grocery store without needing a nap afterward, and it sucked sweaty donkey balls.

And speaking of balls, there'd been no interest in *that*, even if he'd had someone to do it with or for or to him. He felt like a eunuch, and it was one more way his body let him down. Maybe it was the damn meds.

He clicked on the television, but unlike most nights he didn't bother to accompany his viewing with a beer or four. As usual, it failed to deliver anything redeeming or entertaining. But when the phone rang, it did project the caller ID on the screen. Not that he recognized the number.

But he sure recognized the name.

"Brad? This is a surprise."

"Yeah, hi, Owen. I was just calling to check on you. Um...you know, after the accident."

"How'd you know about that?" Owen's mind jumped into unaccustomed motion, another reason to get out of the house and back to work. This was totally out of the blue and kind of weird.

"They called me, the nurses at the hospital. After the accident, I mean."

"That's...odd. I wonder why."

"You kept muttering my name or something. I...saved your number after the last time you called me earlier this year to nag me to call Drew."

Owen didn't say anything, but for some reason the thought made him blush. *I wonder what else I said about the big guy?* He looked down at his lap. *Well I'll be... You've picked a fine time to weigh in. Turncoat.*

Just why his cock could be regarded as a turncoat he wasn't too clear on, but the fact that now of all times for his body to show any interest in sex, any interest at all, for the first time since the accident, when he was talking to someone else's boyfriend or husband or whatever they were by now, was too much.

"So...how are you?"

Owen sighed, too tired to dance around the truth or play with words. "I'm okay."

"Just okay?"

"Okay is good."

"But is it good enough?"

He frowned. He knew Brad was more than he'd seemed, but what was this, the inquisition? "It's what I've got, buddy. It'll have to be."

There was an awkward silence before Brad asked, "So how's PT going?"

"Ugh, that's a painful subject," Owen groaned.

"I'm sorry, I didn't mean—"

"No, I mean it really hurts. I've got this bruiser of a physical therapist—"

"What's her name?"

Owen frowned. He hated being interrupted. "Deanne Lawson, why?"

"Hey, honey!" Brad yelled into the room on his end of the connection. "Guess who Owen's PT is? Deanne Lawson!"

Owen heard a different man groan. "Someone's got to rescue that man. Just not you."

"What's that mean?"

Brad sighed. "Drew's got a few issues where you're concerned," he said softly, "and never mind the fact that you badgering me to keep calling him is why him and me are a couple right now."

Owen couldn't help it. "Sounds like someone's insecure."

"Don't even start, please," Brad begged. "So, tell me about PT. It'll give me some ammo when Drew starts going in on how I couldn't possibly understand what it was like yada yada yada. Everyone's got a reason to feel sorry for himself, and I don't usually have time for it."

So, Owen did, the short version, because he knew he was developing a tendency to whine. His sister had commented on it, repeatedly and at length.

"You haven't been going as often as you should?"

"Guilty as charged." Owen tried to make it sound like a joke, but he knew Brad wasn't buying it.

"What the fuck are you thinking? How the hell do you plan to climb back onto a fire engine?"

"We don't really call them fire engines, you know," Owen pointed out. "Actually, a fire engine is any—"

"Nice diversion," Brad snapped. "Too bad I'm not that stupid."

"You're really angry." Owen just couldn't figure out why.

Brad sighed. "Look, hot daddy firefighter, you're too young to be crippled permanently. Is that what you want?"

"Whoa, calm down. Why's this even your business?"

"Look, I know we barely know each other—"

"Just biblically," Owen snorted.

"Yeah, other than that," Brad said acidly. "Listen, I've got a good thing going here, and I wouldn't, not without you. I owe you. I don't want to see you screw yourself up for life."

Neither he nor Brad said anything for long moments.

"I appreciate that, Brad, but there's a lot going on right now and sometimes...sometimes it's just hard to get out the door." Owen didn't feel like going into the depression and other issues, and really didn't feel like having a heart-to-heart with someone else's boyfriend right then, not when for all he knew that insecure boyfriend might be listening in. But still. The big guy had reached out. "There's this thing Deanne's mentioned, some adaptive rowing program I've been meaning to check out. Maybe I'll have better luck with that."

And just like that, the rampaging bull was quiet. "You know about that?"

"*You* know about that?" Owen laughed, mimicking him.

"Dude, I'm helping coach it. My old coach from CalPac developed the program. The program's full, I think, but if you want, you're in."

"But..."

"No buts. If you've been skipping PT, you're doing this. I'll talk to Nick, explain things. There won't be a problem," Brad said.

He sounded so confident, for a moment Owen believed him. He wanted to believe him. "Brad...sometimes I can barely walk without this stupid walker with its damn fold-down seat. How the hell am I going to row? I've seen what that demands."

"Dude," Brad laughed. "That's why it's called *adaptive* rowing. We *adapt* the boats to you. You said walker, your legs the issue?"

"One of them, yeah."

"Then we'd put you in a boat with an experienced and able-bodied rower, with the seats bolted down so you just use your torso and arms. See? Adaptive. The whole point is to work with the abilities the athlete has to achieve fitness and wholeness, not to obsess about what you can't do. Fitness and a different frame of mind. Sound like something you could use?"

Owen knew they both knew the answer to that. "When does it start?"

"Two weeks ago," Brad said cheerfully. "I'll pick you up at about eight thirty Saturday morning. It's going to be a quick drive-by after my own practice, just so you know. Gimme your address."

Owen dutifully complied. They got off the phone quickly after that, leaving Owen to wonder just what he was in for.

*

The next morning, however, brought second thoughts, and Owen spent the day second-guessing himself. What if he'd agreed to something due only to rusty hormones and not because this "adaptive" rowing really was the best bet for his recovery? This on top of his existential issues was just a bit more than he—a man recovering from a nearly fatal accident—thought he should have to deal with.

So, Owen did what he hadn't done for a while and called an old friend of his, and because it was the middle of the morning and he was hungry, he called him at work. Who knew, maybe he could cadge some lunch out of it.

"Sac PD, Detective Cabot," a gruff voice answered.

"Hi, Mike, how's it going?"

"Owen! This is a surprise." The tone of Mike's voice softened immediately. "I was wondering when you'd call."

"Um…you could've called, you know. I'm pretty sure my phone receives calls as well as makes them," Owen said, feeling alone and kind of pathetic for even calling Mike in the first place, because according to his therapist, it was the nature of a depressed person to isolate himself.

"I didn't want to bug you because I figured you'd be exhausted from all the well-wishers from work, plus friends and family," Mike said, a little awkwardly.

Yeah, it sounded lame to Owen's ears too.

"Turns out, not so much." The silence stretched out. "Listen…are you free for lunch or something? I need your vast wisdom and insight."

"I'll be by at eleven thirty," Mike said.

And an hour later, they were at an out-of-the-way restaurant nowhere near downtown.

"Why here?" Owen asked.

"Because none of the cops like this place," Mike said.

Owen knew Mike passed the fitness tests, but he didn't strike him as a hulking meathead cop. Mike was fairly slender at six feet tall or so, with blond hair and brown eyes so light they were almost golden. Sometimes Owen wondered why, with their history, they'd never clicked.

"Sounds safe enough," Owen said, "since I don't think anyone in the fire department's heard of it either."

They placed their orders and then Mike leaned across the table. "So, what's up, Owen?"

"Well, not to hammer home the obvious..." Owen gestured to his leg in its brace.

"Yeah, I read the papers, but what's going on? You wouldn't have called just to tell me about a cast."

"Perceptive as always, Detective," Owen sighed.

Mike inclined his head. "You wouldn't like me if I were stupid."

"Probably not." Owen thought for a moment. "I dunno, the usual? Single? Older than the dating pool? And yeah, injured? It's all just a lot, you know?"

"No, I don't, but I can imagine." Mike thought for a moment. "Look, Owen, you can't change the fact that you're north of forty. You don't look it, but you are. I happen to think you're attractive, and if you put yourself out there, I think a lot of guys would think so too. Based on your dating history, for lack of a better term, I think you'd admit that, yes?"

"But—"

"Let me finish. What you want is a relationship, not getting your rocks off, but somehow you got yourself hooked into the pick-up and from what you've told me in the past, I'm thinking you never really learned how to be in a relationship."

"No wonder you're a detective," Owen grumbled.

Mike shrugged. "I do my job, they pay me. What can I say? But when you meet the right man, I think you'll realize you know more than you think, but a bit of advice—don't rush into anything." He gave Owen a hard look. "That includes sex. Especially sex. That's your default and if that's not working for you, don't do it."

"Damn, bull's eye on the first shot." Owen sat back, thinking, because yeah, Mike saw right through him.

"So, what else is up?" Mike said. "Because I don't think you called just for a dating pep talk."

The arrival of their lunch gave Owen a chance to stall. "Well, now that you mention it…"

Owen told him about his lackluster record where PT was concerned.

"Are you stupid?" Mike shook his head. "I mean, seriously? You want to recover, right?"

"Yes." Owen glared at Mike. This was supportive?

"Then fucking act like it. After you got me sobered up, do you think I did it half-assed?" Mike demanded.

"No," Owen mumbled. He knew full well Mike hadn't, because he'd been there to hold his hand.

"Damn right. Ninety meetings in ninety days, and every time I missed a meeting, the ninety days started over."

Owen groaned and buried his head in his hands. "The thought of that alone is enough to kill me."

"I highly doubt your physical therapist wants you to do ninety sessions in ninety days. That's not enough recovery time, for starters." Mike rolled his eyes. "Something tells me regular attendance is all she's after."

"She's also after me to try something called 'adaptive rowing,' if you can believe that," Owen said.

"How can I believe it, if I don't know what it is?" Mike replied.

Owen explained it to him. "I mean, no matter how you dumb it down, it's still an Olympic sport."

"I don't know, I think you should give it a try, since you won't do your regular PT."

Owen didn't say anything, but with the mulish set to his face, he didn't have to. "I'll think about it."

"You're such a child sometimes," Mike laughed.

"I guess if that's the worst you can say about me..." Owen sighed. "So, what's going on with you? Still in homicide?"

"No, thank God. I'm working in domestic violence, now. It's not as gruesome, even if all too often I've seen it turn ugly and conclude with a killing. I'm the new liaison to the gay community. There's been an uptick in male-on-male or female-on-female domestic violence, and the department wants it stopped. So yes, I'm the ambassador to our people—don't smack each other around or the Sac PD will get you."

"But I thought I read somewhere that even if it's reported, too often they don't press charges."

"That's only too true, gay or straight. A lot of what I do is education. Everyone deserves to feel safe at home. Everyone deserves to feel safe in a relationship. It doesn't matter if you're rich or poor, a high school dropout or a doctor."

"It sounds like getting the abused partner to admit it's a problem is half the battle," Owen said.

Mike nodded. "And keeping him or her from going home is the other half. Somewhere in there is getting him or her into counseling, sometimes even getting them new identities, new jobs, basically hiding them from their abusive exes. It can be a real mess. It almost makes me wish I still drank."

"The hell it does. You worked too hard for your sobriety." That was the last thing he expected to hear from Mike, and even as a joke it scared him.

Mike looked at the table and fiddled with his napkin. "Yeah, I know. You worked too hard for my sobriety, too, you know. I'll never be able to thank you enough for dragging me to my first meeting and then all the dirty tricks you used to keep me going back. You know that, right?"

Owen shrugged, trying to pretend it was nothing, trying to pretend it was every day he saved someone's life.

"So that's why I'm going to do the same to get you to PT or adaptive rowing. Your choice, but you're going to one of them."

"Doesn't that count as police harassment?" Owen said.

"No, but it will if you don't go. I've got friends who owe me favors in all parts of the department," Mike said, "including parking enforcement. You want a ticket in your own driveway? Don't go to this rowing thing."

"But...someone's giving me a ride."

"Then you'd better have him call me, hadn't you?"

Chapter Six

One thing he hadn't realized about going back to crew, Adam thought as he stretched out after practice, was that people might actually want to talk to him. Just...talk. No scripted interaction, like at the clinic during an exam or at the store. Talking meant social interaction with nothing to guide him. If it went on too long, he started to panic. He *knew* it was Jordan's lies, that people didn't really think he was shit, but still...what if they did?

So, he stretched after practice. A lot. Not because he'd just worked out or to prevent future injuries; he'd already taken care of that. No, he stretched his long, lanky form to avoid social interaction. Sure, it felt good to stretch in the cool autumn morning, and sure, he wore fresh and dry technical-fiber workout clothes to help out with the adaptive-rowing program. Yes, someone had thoughtfully brought them coffee and bagels. All good things, but as people and chatter swirled around him, none of them changed the fact that he found it hard to mingle without his immediate past forming a barrier.

But in one thing, Adam felt very, very lucky. As it turned out, his memories weren't nearly rosy enough. He leaned against the wall of one of the smaller boathouses of the Capital City Rowing Club, the one holding the single-rower boats and their oars, the sculls themselves. Cup of coffee in hand, he watched the sun finish rising over the Port of Sacramento, the waters still in their golden moments before the mundane reality of day intruded. Out on the water, other crews bent their backs to moving their shells, the synchronized *thunk-thunk-thunk* of the oars in their oarlocks a strange music to his ears, lulling and calming him in a way that was almost meditative. No, not rosy enough.

Adam thought it would be at least somewhat more difficult to get Saturday mornings off, but as it happened, Dr. Endicott liked to work Saturday mornings. It allowed her to hold court with her favorite clients, and after a nap, he was fresh as the proverbial daisy to come in Saturday afternoons once the doors closed to check on their patients, plus more of the same on Sundays. It also gave him and Steven a chance to have a cackle, just the two of them.

Had it solely been a morning off for recreation, Dr. Endicott might well have balked, because as much as she liked playing the *grande dame*, she disliked scut work, but when Adam had hesitantly explained just why he'd wanted the entire morning, she'd all but fallen at his feet to give him the time. Adaptive rowing? Rehabilitating injured members of the community, first responders, and veterans? She'd seen the PR possibilities long before he had, and even before he'd left her office was already on the phone with the clinic's web designer to splash this far and wide, along with a revealing picture of the clinic's hunky associate vet, of course.

He didn't feel too much like a prostitute posing in his old collegiate racing uniform with its colors and insignia digitally altered but having his face in the paper scared him. However, Dr. Endicott promised it would only be the local and collegiate papers. Still, the thought made him sick with nerves. What if Jordan saw it? It wasn't as if the man couldn't drive from Sacramento to Davis and find a paper, or hello? look the local papers up online. Why was he the only one who understood that?

But even that dire thought rumbling at the back of his mind couldn't spoil the perfection of the light that morning. There was just too much to look at. The men's crew at CCRC spanned the entire age range of masters rowing, from guys just out of college who for some inexplicable reason hadn't gotten enough torment to the most senior of "veterans" who Adam was pretty sure would die out there in their singles doing what they loved the most. In between was a younger, although maybe not as young as some of them clearly thought, cadre of rowers who still wore the unisuits of their old schools, pulling the tops down to expose their chests, and God bless them for it, Adam thought.

Especially the one he'd spent a lot of time rowing behind. Brad. Brad the big fucking stud. Day-um. That was one fine piece of man flesh. Coach Bedford had put him behind Brad his first day in the boat and never mind that he was several inches taller. Adam thought for sure it was a mistake, you know, taller guy, longer reach, but Brad quickly showed him how wrong he was, because Brad had a beautiful stroke and Adam quickly realized that no, it wasn't exactly like falling off a bike. Sure, he hadn't forgotten the crude parts of the stroke, but the finer points were long gone, and Brad was their master. All thoughts of Brad's hotness quickly vanished as Adam strove to focus on Coach Bedford's carefully chosen corrections.

Speaking of Brad, the big guy sure went tearing out of there in a hurry that morning. Oh well, it wasn't his problem. Adam returned his attention to his coffee. It had gotten cold, and he had time for another cup before it was time for adaptive rowing. He was just about to go in search of more, but someone had other ideas. "Coach!"

"I keep telling you to call me Nick," Nick said.

"It just seems kind of rude." Adam squirmed slightly.

"Even when I tell you to?"

"Kind of, yeah." Eager to change the subject, Adam said, "So what're we doing today?"

"Funny you should mention that, because *we* aren't doing anything. *You* are going to wait until Brad Sundstrom comes back with a new rower for the adaptive program."

"You're sending me out in a double this week?" Adam's eyes went wide.

Nick smiled up at him. "I think you're ready."

"But it's only been a few weeks since I've been back in a boat," Adam pointed out.

Nick shrugged. "True enough, but you're a good rower and the adaptive boats are rock solid, thanks to those pontoons. You'll also have Coach Sundstrom in a launch."

"We'll have our own coach?"

"Partly because you'll be the last boat going out by an hour or so, but partly because this new guy is a special case for Brad, I think. Old friend or something," Nick explained. "Anyway, I just wanted to give you heads-up. No more launch lizard."

Adam grinned. "But it was so much fun hearing your muttered comments about the rowers."

"You weren't supposed to hear those." Nick turned bright red. Adam pretended it was from the sun. "So, you can just hang out until Brad gets back. Shouldn't be too much longer. I'm going to get the rest of the adaptive crew onto the water and out for their row."

So, Adam kept out of the way in the main boathouse, avoiding idle chit-chit by staying warmed-up on one of the ergs, the specialized rowing machines that came close to the rowing stroke. He closed his eyes, the better to feel where his body was on the erg and in space.

But when he opened his eyes, Brad Sundstrom was entering the boathouse behind a truly stunning man. They were talking and joking, and the jealousy that rose up almost overwhelmed him. Right then, Adam wasn't sure just which one he was jealous of, since yeah, he could admit he might've had a teeny tiny crush on Brad...who suddenly didn't seem like the big fucking stud anymore. He was Brad Sundstrom, assistant coach, and he had a partner who by all reports was a very nice if somewhat temperamental man, and it wasn't as though Adam had spoken more than a handful of words to him.

But the man in front. Suddenly Adam struggled to breathe. The new guy was tall—and yeah, that was a nice feature since he himself ducked going through standard doors—and a bit sun-weathered. He looked like he might be a few years older than Adam, perhaps in his early forties going by the few gray hairs in the red, and oh my God, a ginger. How yummy was that? His skin was pink and pale, and not just from his coloring.

Adam looked closer and saw the care lines around the newcomer's eyes and wondered what had happened to him to land him in the adaptive rowing program. He was in good shape, even his limping leg and even with the walker, and Adam hoped the new guy's shirts were reinforced at the shoulders because it looked like his deltoids and traps were going to pop right out of the delicious form-fitting workout shirt. Not that Adam would've objected, because right then he wouldn't have minded knowing how hairy that chest was, not in the least.

But then Adam noticed something else. According to the sensitivity trainer Coach Bedford had brought in, they weren't supposed to help. Injured and recovering people needed to do for themselves and learn that they *could* do for themselves as part of their recovery. But there was Brad, hovering over his charge—for that's what Brad was doing—like he'd been spun out of thin glass. Interesting. Sure, Brad laughed and joked with him, but there was a tightness around Brad's eyes that Adam couldn't figure out, and Adam had a lot of experience reading authority figures. Too much.

"Adam, there you are!" Brad called. "Come meet your new pair partner!"

Adam unfolded himself from the erg and made himself amble over to where Brad and the newcomer stood. He tried not to appear too eager, so no dashing over there and salivating like an overeager puppy.

"Adam Lennox, this is my friend Owen Douglas." Adam stuck out his hand, and Owen took it. "Owen, Adam."

"Hi." Adam knew if he weren't careful, he'd lose himself in those hazel eyes. He wasn't in any hurry to drop Owen's hand either.

Owen appeared just as enchanted. "Hi."

Brad snorted. "All right, you two. We've got a lot to catch up on. I told Owen about how things worked on the ride over, but talking's one thing, doing's another. Adam, on this first day, your job's to be my model and I'd say someone thinks you're a damn pretty one." He laughed as Adam and Owen dropped their hands, their faces flaming. "Let's go find the modified ergs and get out of everyone's way. We should have plenty of time to practice the stroke and get out on the water before the others get back."

Adam dutifully followed along behind Brad and Owen to the smaller boathouse that contained CCRC's doubles, the shells designed to carry two rowers, given over for the time being to the adaptive rowing program and its modified boats. Watching Owen's broad back, he knew who he was jealous of: Brad. He was going to have to watch his step or risk making a complete ass of himself in front of the man Coach Bedford was trusting him to help. Yep, he could definitely rock some jealousy because Brad had spent some one-on-one time in a car with Owen. But with neither paying much attention to him, he could look openly too.

Brad pulled down two of the modified ergs. "Adam, you'll be my Vanna," he said, pointing to one of the ergs. "Owen, just watch for a moment. Then I'll have you follow along."

Adam sat down, and Brad continued. "Owen, since your legs are the most injured part of you right now, Nick's got you in the arms and back program, meaning you'll be rowing in boats modified so you'll only use your arms and back. The seats in these rowing machines—called ergometers—and in the boats are bolted down so you can only use your arms and back. Vanna?"

Adam rolled his eyes but complied. He was still new enough at CCRC that he wasn't sure how far he could push things, but he had a feeling Brad pushed them plenty far.

"Pay attention to the sequence," Brad told Owen. "See how the handle is against his chest, up against his ribs, with his arms tucked back, before his back even begins to swing forward? A little slower there, Adam. Notice that the back motion is coming only from the pelvis and not actually from his spine?"

Owen nodded. "Yeah."

Adam glanced up. He had to have that low, growly voice aimed at him. "If you've been in any kind of accident, that's going to be particularly important."

"Gotcha," Owen said, locking eyes with Adam. Adam smiled at him.

"Hey, who's running this?" Brad said.

Adam went wide-eyed. "Why, you are, Coach Sundstrom."

Brad muttered something under his breath. "Anyway, it's a pivoting motion. I don't want to see you rounding your back or hunching or anything."

"You know I'll be in the boat with him," Adam reminded Brad.

"Yeah, but I keep going back and forth on whether to have you stroke or steer," Brad said, scratching his head.

Adam shrugged. "That's your call. Think it's time to put the big guy here on an erg?"

"What? Oh. Yeah. Have a seat, Owen."

Owen gingerly sat down and strapped himself into the ergometer's foot-stretchers. "So now what?"

"You grab the handle," Brad said.

Owen leaned forward from his hips. "Damn, my hamstrings are tight. I thought I'd been stretching them, but I guess not enough."

"Probably not enough, not if you've been off your legs for a while," Adam said. When it became clear Brad wasn't going to help him, Adam hooked his own handles on his erg's stay and then leaned over to grab the handles on Owen's machine.

"Damn, you're tall," Owen said as Adam leaned over. "Thanks. You a doctor?"

Adam shook his head. "Probably not the kind you're thinking. I'm a vet, but a mammal's a mammal when it comes to a disused tendon tightening up. You might ask your physical therapist for some new stretches now that your workout routine's changing."

Owen smiled. "Thanks, I will."

"Are you two done? Because I think we've got some ground left to cover before we get on the water," Brad said.

Brad watched while Adam and Owen practiced the shortened rowing stroke together, gradually bringing their strokes into synch more often than not. When Brad pronounced himself satisfied, he dragged them outside. "Okay, we're not going to achieve perfection in one day or even in a week or month. It doesn't work that way. The goal is something more subtle, and that's learning to relax and be at ease in your body while it heals."

Owen raked his eyes up and down Adam in a way that made Adam feel underage. "You look pretty at ease to me."

"But never easy," Adam said, gulping.

"Oh yeah?" Owen said. He leered a little. "Tell me about that."

"Not now, you two," Brad said. "Honestly, this is a family establishment. Don't make me hose you down."

"I have no idea what you're talking about, Brad," Owen said, a picture of innocence. "Adam?"

Adam shrugged and shook his head. "No idea whatsoever."

"Yeah, whatever," Brad snorted. "Adam, since you're as pure as the driven snow, maybe you can introduce Owen here to the dock box. I'll let you know if you fuck it up."

Adam's cheeks heated right up, he could feel it, and he also felt Owen's eyes on him as he led the way out of the boathouse. He stole a quick glance over his shoulder, and Owen was looking right at him. Damn. Adam yanked his gaze forward where it belonged. This was getting out of hand fast. His training partner or whatever Coach Bedford was calling the adaptive rower assigned to him seemed like the kind of guy he'd like to get to know, and as far as Adam was aware, there wasn't anything intrinsically wrong with two rowers like this hooking up, but this was heating up fast, maybe too fast. Shy around strangers and unscripted contact was one thing, yet something about Owen made him want to open up, maybe the fact that he was wounded too.

"What is that?" Owen said, pointing at an unlikely-looking contraption occupying a picnic table.

Brad held his hands up and shook his head. Adam sighed. "That's the dock box. We have one for the big oars that actually goes on the edge of the dock, but the one for sculling, which uses two smaller oars, has to be put on a table because the dock's too wide for both oars to be in the water. It's a way to get a feel for the rowing or sculling strokes without getting into a boat." He looked at Brad and smirked. "You there! Lackey! Fetch some sculling oars."

Brad's eyes narrowed dangerously, and for a moment, Adam thought he'd gone too far, but really, what did Brad expect? Adam smiled sweetly at him until Brad stomped off to get the oars.

"You're bad," Owen said.

Adam gave him that same sweet smile as he climbed up onto the dock box. "I can't imagine what you mean."

"I'll just bet," Owen said with a grunt.

"Do you need your walker? I'll keep this explanation short, but if you need to sit down, let me know."

Owen inhaled, and it looked to Adam like he was going to object, but he only said, "Thanks, my leg's starting to hurt. If it gets worse, I'll let you know." Then a wicked look stole over his face. "You could massage it for me."

"Oh, look! Here comes Brad with the oars."

Owen chuckled. "Coward."

Brad glowered at Adam as he handed him the oars. "Who's the Vanna here, anyway?"

"You are, since you put me in charge," Adam said. He took the oars and settled them in the oarlocks, explaining to Owen as he did so. "As I'm sure you've been told, the boats have pontoons, but making sure the oars are secure is a good habit to get into. Yours seems to be an injury, not a condition, and you won't always need these accommodations. So. Sculling. The most important thing to remember is left hand over right."

Adam sat with his legs flat, his torso just a few degrees past his hips. He held the oar handles loosely yet firmly, with his hands at the very end of the handles, his thumbs covering the rounded ends. Then he let his hands fly. "Small movements in the hands make for large movements in the oar blades."

"So I see," Owen said. "Does it matter which hand's on top?"

"Yes," Adam said. "Like I said, it's always the left."

"I'm not sure there's any particular reason it has to be left over right, but according to Nick, the hands can't be at the same level because in sculling the oar handles actually cross each other twice: once during the drive and once during the recovery. If the oars were at the same level, they'd collide. So, left over right. I guess it could be right over left, but it's not, and every single, double, and quad in creation is built left over right. That's the convention," Brad said. "You also want to keep your hands close together. Like, really close together. Scullers keep their fingernails super short, it's that close together, otherwise you'll be taking divots out of your right hand, so remember—left over right."

"You didn't tell me it was a blood sport," Owen said.

Brad shrugged. "It'll put hair on your chest."

"As you may recall, there's plenty of hair on my chest," Owen said.

"Oh, really?" Adam said, his interest slipping through. Damn, he was trying to keep it professional.

Brad actually blushed. "I...uh, had other things on my mind."

"Yeah, like Drew," Owen snorted.

"I cannot *wait* to hear this story," Adam said.

"Later," Owen and Brad both said.

"Your turn, Owen," Brad said.

Adam climbed down, but when Owen paused before the picnic table, he figured it out. "Here," he said softly, climbing onto the bench. "Take my hand." When Owen hesitated, Adam sighed. "Take it. You can get all macho later."

"I'm going to hold you to that," Owen said.

"Just take my hand, Romeo."

Adam provided a steadying hand to help Owen climb gingerly up onto the picnic table and then settle into the dock box. He jumped down and grabbed the oars, which had gone flying once he'd let go of them. "Got them?"

Owen closed his massive hands over Adam's, shooting him a challenging look. "I think so."

Adam felt his cheeks pink. Where Owen was concerned, that seemed to be their natural state. He coughed to cover his embarrassment, but at that point it was like throwing a doily over a hippo. "Remember, the biggest difference between this and the erg is that you *have* to control the oar handles. If you let the water do it, you'll jack the set of the boat. So, left over right, and minute adjustments to control the depth of the oars' blades in the water, but—"

"Oh? Do I get to see your butt while we row? This just keeps getting better and better." Owen grinned at him like a hungry wolf, and for once even Brad was at a loss for words.

"Just take some strokes and if you do what I think you're about to do, just remember," Adam said, "mammals are mammals. I know how you're put together. I can take you apart."

Brad burst out laughing. "He's got you there, dude. Just do as he says. I think I'm going to have him in bow seat, so he can steer the shell. If you give him too much flack, you're going to end up with his oar handles in your kidneys, and you'll be pissing blood for a few days."

With a sly smile for Adam, Owen did as he was told. For his part, Adam admired the view. Even recovering from what must've been a horrendous injury, Owen was still amazing to look at as his efforts pulled his stretchy workout clothes tight across his back.

"Remember the sequence," Brad cautioned.

"Right," Owen said.

Adam tried to focus on Owen's technique, but he kept straying to Owen's physique. He really was a lot to look at, but what was his deal? Why was he in the adaptive program? How did he and Brad know each other? There were stories there, that was for sure.

"Good enough," Brad pronounced. He helped Owen down while Adam took the oars out of the dock box.

"Brad, oars down to the dock with us or back to the oar locker?" Adam said.

"Back to the locker. I already took two pairs down. I'll meet you guys on the dock," Brad said.

Adam jogged the oars back to the locker on the outside of the singles house while Owen set off after Brad at a much slower pace. Adam easily caught up to him.

CCRC's members did what they could to make the dock and the ramp leading down to it nonslippery, but that only went so far. There was still water involved, and it still lessened the friction between feet and the dock's surface.

"Can you make that?" Adam said softly.

Owen looked down the ramp to the dock below and shrugged. "I'll do my best."

Adam walked slowly beside him. He did what he could to make it look casual, just one guy walking next to another down an incline to the dock, you know? Because even though they were supposed to let the adaptive rowers fend for themselves, Adam could see Owen's leg was bothering him, and besides which, the ramp down to the dock was steep. The river was tidal, and when the tide went out in the San Francisco and San Pablo bays, the river's water level dropped. Naturally, they were heading for a low tide.

"You don't have to do that, you know," Owen said.

"Do what?" Adam pretended he hadn't been caught red-handed.

Owen sighed. "Shadow me to make sure I don't fall. It looks awkward but I'll be all right. I'm just slow."

"You're not going down, not on my watch."

"That's what you think," Owen said, leering. Adam hadn't noticed the dimples before.

Then Owen's walker slipped, and Owen lost his grip on it, sending it skittering the rest of the way down the ramp to hit a surprised Brad in the legs.

"Shit!" Owen swore, his left leg starting to buckle.

But then there was Adam, sliding under his arm to grab him around the waist. "I've got you. You're safe." He felt Owen tense for a moment and then sag against him. "Can you walk?"

"I...yeah. I think so." Owen sounded a little shaken, like he realized he could be flat on his back on the dock right now, or even in the mud below.

Adam stooped a bit to accommodate Owen's somewhat shorter height, but it wasn't that far, and he wasn't that much taller. Besides, he really liked the feel of Owen under his arm, even if he had to tell himself a surprising number of times for so short a ramp that this was no time for such thoughts.

But apparently, he wasn't the only one, because Owen wasn't in any hurry to let go when they reached the bottom of the ramp.

Brad regarded them with naked amusement. "Uh, guys? The dock's pretty much flat here. You can let go of him now, Adam."

They both jerked their heads to look at him, like somehow, they'd forgotten he was there.

"My...uh, leg's still a bit iffy," Owen said.

Adam felt himself heat right up. Again. "I'm just helping him to the boat."

"You two actually believe that, don't you?" Brad cocked his head. "Whatever, just get in the boat."

Adam helped Owen to the boat. "This'll be a bit tricky. Because of the pontoons, we can't get the hull right up close to the dock like we usually do."

"I'll make do," Owen said tightly. Adam didn't think he'd been bullshitting Brad. His leg genuinely hurt.

"You'll be sitting in stern, or the stroke seat, which means you'll set the pace. Of course, if you get too carried away, I'll tell you," Adam said. "I'll be in the bow where I can steer. You'll notice that we're sitting backward, by the way."

"Yeah, how come?" Owen asked.

"We sit backward relative to the forward movement of the boat so our bodies can use the oars as levers to pry the boats past the water. It's the most efficient way to harness our quads and lats," Adam explained.

"Or not," Owen grunted.

"Oh hey, I'm sorry. I didn't...think," Adam stammered. "I'm sorry. It's the way the boats are built, but dude. Your back... You're not going to have any trouble."

Owen sighed. "So how do I get down into this thing?"

"In your case, very carefully," Adam replied. He pointed. "See that rough patch?"

"The one that looks like sandpaper?"

"That's the one. The boat's reinforced there. It's the only place that's safe to step. Otherwise all this awesome studliness will crack the hull. So, go ahead and put your right foot there."

"Put my right foot in, huh?" Owen turned his head to stare into Adam's eyes. Adam's breath hitched at his one-sided smirk. "Wanna see what I can wave all about?"

"You're horrible," Adam murmured, his fingers seeking and finding a rib.

"I'm not ticklish, at least not there," Owen said.

Adam sighed. "Just get in the boat."

"Aye, aye, Cap'n."

Owen put his foot where indicated, but hesitantly, Adam thought, like he wasn't quite sure either the boat or his body would cooperate. Adam knew the boat was safe as houses, but he guessed Owen had reason to be wary. "I've got you, big guy. I'm not going to let you fall."

For just a moment, Owen's bravado slipped, and Adam saw fear, vulnerability, and gratitude in those devastating hazel eyes. He knew if he weren't careful, he'd lose his heart in them too. "You good?"

"Yeah...yeah, I think so."

"Good, now we'll lower down. When you get low enough, reach out and grab the gunwales, then swing your other leg in. I'll be holding you the entire way. It's going to feel like a stretch since we're not right at the dock, but don't worry. I've got long arms and legs, and I can hold you that far. It's all good."

Together they eased down until Owen was in the boat. Adam had to adjust his grip as his position changed, and he tried not to pay attention to the body underneath his arms. He tried not to feel the firm musculature beneath scant layers of workout clothes or the warmth radiating up from Owen's skin. He tried not to hear the suddenly ragged breathing in his ear. He tried not to realize that if he turned his head, he could feel those full, lush lips on his own. He tried to pretend that last little squeeze before he let go wasn't a hug.

He failed.

As he pulled away from Owen, he thought about what had happened since Owen had walked into the boathouse. They weren't supposed to do too much for their pair partners, and Adam figured that included hitting on them.

He was now reasonably certain Owen was gay, but damn, couldn't he keep his own hands to himself for the space of one lousy practice? It seemed like ever since he'd escaped Jordan's clutches, he was nothing but a horndog, after anything with a dick. *Good going, Dr. Lennox. Jump on the poor guy while you're teaching him to row.* Suddenly he was disgusted with himself.

Once Owen was seated in the boat, Adam climbed in, saying, "Go ahead and grab onto your oars. We didn't sweat it this morning, but usually it's a huge no-no to leave the oars flapping every which way while you get in."

"That was interesting," Brad said from his launch as he motored up to them.

"I got him into the boat, okay?"

"Yeah, so I saw."

"My leg's killing me, Brad. I needed help, and Adam provided it. I couldn't have gotten in without him, all right?" Owen said. He did sound weary...

Still, Adam couldn't believe he'd allowed himself to cross that line. "Are you ready, Owen? Left over right. If you hold your hands low, the oars will clear the dock. I'll walk us down..."

And with that they were off.

Chapter Seven

Later that afternoon, Owen reclined on his sofa, staring at the ceiling. He'd eaten, showered, napped. His leg still ached, but thanks to anti-inflammatories it was due more to overuse than his injury. He was stiff and sore from working injured muscles and uninjured muscles in unfamiliar ways. He groaned just thinking about the morning. All that work on land, and then they'd gotten on the water. Rowing. Really, rowing and erging. They seemed like two different things to him. Similar ideas, but not quite the same.

When Brad dragged him out, he hadn't expected to like rowing, but much to his surprise, he had. A lot. He had no words to describe the feeling of the power that had coursed through his body the first time the blades of the oar grabbed the water. It might not have been the full stroke, but he hadn't felt so alive since he awoke in the hospital cocooned in pain. After he'd rested up a bit more, he'd e-mail Coach Bedford and sign up officially for the rest of this adaptive rowing session and the next one. He'd be back at work by then, maybe sooner if this sped up his recovery, like his PT thought it would.

He'd have to thank Coach Bedford, since the adaptive program was something of an experiment for the man, maybe write a letter once he'd recovered fully. That could help him, right? Maybe a more personal note for Brad.

Brad.

When Owen saw Brad at his door, he kind of took his breath away. Damn, the kid was still hot. He was touched that Brad cared enough to call, cared enough to force him to take care of himself, even though he didn't want to, so he pretended to be resentful. But he hurt to see Brad again, especially a Brad in his prime, healthy and happy and practically glowing with vitality and knowing it wasn't for him. He'd almost hated Brad in that moment.

Then they'd walked into the boathouse and Owen had seen that blond giant on the rowing machine, and all thoughts of whatshisname had fled his mind. Wow. Sure, the place had been crawling with hot guys, and if he'd been a few years younger, Owen would've taken that as reason alone to sign up for the sport. But him. Just...wow. Then the gods of rowing must've been smiling on him because that giant turned out to be his pair partner, the able-bodied rower assigned to help on land and in the boat, and his name was Adam.

When he met Adam, he wanted to fall to his knees and service that tall god then and there. Of course, he couldn't get on his knees—let alone back up again—without a block and tackle rig, and didn't that just make him feel old and used up and worthless? But the cool thing, the amazing thing, was that Adam seemed to find him just as hot. That someone as attractive as Adam, someone who could have anyone he wanted, would want someone like him—and when did he start wallowing in trite Harlequin plot devices, assuming they traded in worn-out firemen and strapping younger veterinarians? The thought blew him away. Maybe there was hope for this old warhorse, after all.

He just wished he could've seen Adam in action in the boat that morning. He bet it would've been a sight to behold. Awe-inspiring. He'd seen the other boats coming back to the dock while they'd been futzing around so he could get the hang of it—or start to. Sure, some of the guys had been good-looking, but meh. They weren't Adam, and he had nothing more to say on the matter.

Adam wasn't just a pretty face, plus whatever he was packing under those workout clothes. He must've handled their boat like a pro because Brad hadn't said anything about it, and yet somehow Adam had managed to keep up a steady stream of low-voiced corrections that had kept Brad from riding him too hard. Owen adjusted his semi. He'd had one all day. Okay, not *all* day, not get to the ER *now* all day, just when he thought about Adam and rowing. Mostly Adam.

Adam.

From the moment they started erging, the two of them had been involved in an extended flirtation. No, he corrected, something stronger than that. More of a slow-burning seduction, like they'd both known what the outcome would be, but they had plenty of time to get there and they didn't feel like bothering Brad or anyone else with the details.

Then they touched for the first time thanks to Owen's bum leg, and stars had exploded in his head. Something about the way Adam had said, "You're safe." He'd known instinctively that he truly was. He'd relaxed as soon as he'd heard Adam say those words, deeply, almost totally. Sure, he could've been seriously hurt by a fall, but then there was Adam before he'd barely done more than wobble. He hadn't even had time to get pumped up on adrenaline before his pair partner had swooped in to save him.

Then Adam had helped him down the ramp to their boat. It felt so nice under Adam's arm, so protected. So intimate. He never wanted that to end, and okay, sure, he hadn't really needed any more help after getting down the ramp on the dock, but he hadn't wanted to leave that shelter where his broken body didn't matter. He never wanted to leave that shelter.

That wasn't to say he hadn't been perving on his pair partner, although to be fair, Adam had been perving right back. Holeeee shit, Adam helping him into the boat? He'd had lovers who'd caressed him less intimately than Adam had. He hoped his hard-on hadn't been too obvious because it had been nearly instantaneous. Sure, it had been an accident, but the one time Adam had grazed his nipple? OMG. He hadn't groaned, had he? Oh, hell yeah, his cock was up and rarin' to go. They were both in full agreement on that score.

He and Adam had been sparking hot and heavy all morning, trading shots, and it seemed like they might've sealed the deal right after practicing, aching leg or not. He was interested and he knew Adam had seemed interested, and...nothing.

Adam had backed off, not that he'd turned cold or anything. He'd seemed into it but had only taken their high-stakes game so far and no further, where Owen had been ready to fuck him in the back of the boathouse.

He froze. That was it, wasn't it? He groaned and then buried his head in his hands. He'd done it again, just like he had with Brad and who knew how many hookups before, just like Mike had warned him not to do. Come on strong, take what he wanted, and then end up alone. Whir, blur, thank you, sir! This was exactly what he'd been whining about during those long, boring days of his recovery. This was why he was the hookup and never the boyfriend.

Then he realized something else. He wanted more than Adam's load. He wanted Adam, or at least a chance with him. The kindness and patience the more experienced rower showed him? He couldn't remember the last time a man that hot had simply been kind to him. Sure, they'd flirted and bantered, but Adam had been so good to him. What had he said he was, again? A vet? That explained it. Owen bet children liked him immediately too.

He knew he had.

Owen leaned back and closed his eyes. Okay, so he'd come on too strong and scared Adam off, but not permanently. He still caught his pair partner looking at him out from under his bangs. That didn't mean Owen was out of the game, it just meant he had to back off and be a gentleman about things. That was fine. In fact, it was better than fine. In the long run, that'd get him what he wanted. Adam for a boyfriend, hopefully. He'd had fuck buddies and that had gotten old. He wanted something more and he wanted it with Adam and if he didn't stop thinking about this *right now,* he was going to lose his mind so think about something else *right now.*

Ergs and rowing. Not the same. He'd already figured out the boats were full of little details to master that the ergs lacked, like balance and that damn left over right with his hands. But on the erg, it was just legs and back, back and legs. Even with that little exposure, he could easily see how he could just zone out, potentially for a long time. Sure, when he recovered, he'd have to figure out adding the legs in, but still, he'd basically be sitting on his ass without a care in the world while a rowing machine ate his body fat. He made a note to look into acquiring some for the stations in his battalion. Maybe Brad or someone from the rowing club would offer clinics to show his people how to use them, someone like Adam...

He smiled to himself.

*

Even as autumn debated turning chilly, Owen continued his regimen of physical therapy and rowing, albeit with a much-improved outlook. He felt well enough that it was time to face the last great hurdle: his job. Would he ever be able to return to it, and in what capacity? He already dreaded the possibility of a disability hearing. Between the city trying to prove him completely able, the union dithering about whether he was completely disabled, and his fellow firefighters turning on him for milking the system, it looked like a nightmare. He was still trying to decide whether to sue over the accident. Adaptive rowing was causing his lawyer fits, but his goal was a working body, not a fat bank account. He understood the idea behind liability and all that but didn't want to be comfortably well-off in a wheelchair. He'd rather be able to work, thank you very much.

And at work was exactly where Owen was that beautiful day. He felt strange putting on his uniform that morning, the first time in months he'd taken it out of the closet. It was worryingly baggy. All unawares, he'd lost a lot of muscle mass since the accident in what? Mid-August? Now it was late October and Halloween was right around the corner. He sighed. At least thanks to adaptive rowing and a few tentative forays into the weight room, his lats had a little bulk to them, so he didn't feel too much like a small boy wearing his daddy's uniform. And there was plenty of room for his brace under his uniform. Always look on the bright side, right?

This first day back at work the sky rewarded Owen with a special blue only found in Sacramento in autumn, a blue so pure it pierced the soul. And he...he was behind his desk, cleared for light duty and back at work. It was a test, really, and as he stared out of the window, he wondered if he truly wanted to pass. He still felt like an imposter in his job, hell, in his life.

He shook his head. What the hell was he thinking, of course he wanted to be there. This was his life's work, and he'd struggled damn hard to get here. Just because the sky was blue and there was no wind and it would be perfect to go out in the pair... Owen grinned. Brad would swing by in two hours to take him to the boathouse for the evening row, and with any luck there'd be a certain blond pair partner he'd get to see. Some evenings Adam couldn't make it, depending on his schedule at the clinic. Those days, Coach Bedford sent him out in one of the modified singles. Far from being scary or disorienting at night, Owen found it amazingly beautiful out on the river after the sun went down. Away from the city lights, the stars shone in profusion, and he'd had no idea meteors were as common as they apparently were. He made lots of wishes where a certain blond vet was concerned.

Owen caught himself with a big goofy grin. Again. He checked the clock. Again. He made himself get back to work, although with the size of the paper mound on his desk there wasn't a whole lot of point. He was sure most of it was of the FYI variety so he could see what the acting chief had done in his absence, but what was the point of a substitute if he had to go through and rubber-stamp everything? The man was clearly competent, or the department wouldn't have put him in there in the first place. In fact, Owen expected to see him with a command of his own in the near future, just as soon as someone was promoted or retired. Or was forced out due to injury after a disability hearing, he thought glumly.

Owen put in another few hours of work, and then it was time for the "welcome back from the dead" party. He thought the theme was morbid and more than a little inappropriate, but given the proximity to Halloween, it was inevitable. The A shift was almost over, so the guys from B shift were coming in a bit early. He wasn't sure if anyone from C shift would actually be in, and he wouldn't blame any of them in the least if they didn't. He'd done his time on shift in the wee hours of the night. Some of the humor on A shift was a little odd; he suspected a few of the secretaries were behind it. His new driver hadn't been here long enough to contribute to the institutional culture in any meaningful way, although a few of the B and C shifters could always be involved, and there were four other stations under his command, so really, fingering culprits was a waste of his time, pure and simple.

He paused before the door to his office, leaning his forehead on it. For some reason he was...nervous. Weird. Before the accident he never would've paused. He'd have strode boldly out there, secure in the knowledge that he belonged in this or any other fire station under his command. Now, the thought of being among everyone made him twitchy. They said beating death changed you, and maybe they were right. Maybe the unofficial theme of the party wasn't just morbid talk after all because he'd sure changed over the previous several months.

Oh well. He sucked it up, squared his shoulders, and walked out of his office, with a smile that in the past was genuine but now felt fake. His leg already bothered him, and he'd deliberately stayed off it all day, for all the good it had done him. He had forearm crutches in his office that he'd die before he'd use, along with his trusty walker with the fold-down seat. Huh. That was odd. He had no problem using either one as the circumstances demanded at CCRC's boathouse, but for some reason the thought of displaying that kind of weakness, that kind of vulnerability, at the fire station now scared the crap out of him. He knew he was pushing the envelope on being silly, but he felt like the accident was the universe's way of showing him he was an imposter in this job. *First out battalion chief? Not so fast, cowboy. You weren't on the job very long, so what makes you think you're just going to waltz back into it? You can't even walk without assistance, and you're about to smuggle a brace into that party by hiding it under your pants. What makes you think you can fight fires? The last time you tried that you were smashed to pieces. Maybe you should let a real man do the job.*

With that weighing him down, he made his way to the first engine bay. The engine had been backed out and someone—several someones—had gone all-out. His "welcome back from the dead" party was no mere potluck. It looked like they'd raided the entertainment budget, such as it was. He wondered who'd authorized that, since he obviously hadn't signed off on it, but then Owen spotted Prissy Morrain and that answered his question. Given the time of year, there were a few Halloween touches, but mercifully only a few.

Owen made his way into the party, smiling and laughing and playing his assigned role, refusing to let his sudden transformation into Captain Comedown ruin everyone else's fun. Standing on the bay's concrete floor would be murder on his leg, so he discreetly parked himself in a central location and let people come to him.

"Rumor has it you've been spotted around the Capital City boathouse," Prissy said as she took a seat next to Owen. Oddly enough, when two people with the bugles of command on their collars started talking, a circle opened around them. It looked like privacy, but Owen knew it was an illusion.

"I was shanghaied," Owen replied, "by a press gang of one."

She laughed. "Yes, Brad can come on rather strong, but he means well."

Owen almost choked as his mind rearranged her words. *Yeah, he can come rather strong too.* "That he does, and I'm grateful. The adaptive rowing program is a large part of why I'm back as soon as I am. My PT says it's made a real difference in my recovery, certainly in my outlook and attitude. Another week or three and she wants me to try it with my legs."

"Owen, that's wonderful news!" She clapped him on his arm.

"Thanks." He reddened a little.

Prissy held him at arms' length. "You," she pronounced, "have the look of a sculler. You know what I mean about the water, now."

"I do, indeed. There's nothing quite like it, even as inexperienced as I am," Owen replied.

"Just remember, there are two kinds of scullers: those who've rolled their boats and—"

"Those who will," Owen finished. "I know. I won't have those pontoons holding me up forever."

"We hope," she added softly. "Anyway, I've monopolized too much of your time as it is. Best wishes for a speedy recovery and all that."

He smiled and thanked her, even though from what he could read in her eyes she doubted he would. Huh. That came through loud and clear. Maybe an improved ability to read people came with the command bugles on his collar. Or maybe it was just that apparent.

Or maybe she was just a bitch, pleasant demeanor aside, and he couldn't read people for shit.

Since it was a welcome-back party, there was a get-well card, more of a get-well poster, since people from all five companies he commanded signed it, along with others he'd served with at other battalions over the years.

And cake. There was definitely cake, and Owen wasn't shy about hogging the biggest rosette for himself. He allowed himself to be jollied out of his fantods and have a good time. Time passed and surprisingly, there were no calls, itself something of a minor miracle, and before he knew it, it was almost time for Brad to pick him up for rowing therapy.

Owen stood off to one side making small talk with his new driver, a slip of a guy Owen couldn't imagine passing the physical exam. Maybe he was one of those tough, wiry men who could lift four times their body weight over their head. Maybe he'd check the man's file when he found the time, something of a laughable notion.

Then he heard two voices, loud voices, voices he knew too well, and neither sounded happy with the other.

One belonged to a brash firefighter, Prefontaine. He lived fast and would probably die young while singlehandedly saving an entire residence from a fire, even if it was a house full of hookers.

The other belonged to Brad.

Owen sighed. Two bull moose bent on rampaging in his firehouse.

"Hey, asshole! You're supposed to bring snacks when you visit another firehouse!" Pre bellowed.

"What?" Brad said, confused and offended by the verbal onslaught.

"Don't play dumb," Pre laughed. "You know the rules."

"I have no idea what you're talking about, but I really don't like that tone of voice," Brad rumbled.

"Are you missing a chromosome or something? Is that why they let you into the fire academy, for affirmative action? Everyone knows when you visit another station, you bring snacks. That doesn't change just because you're blowing the chief."

Aaand all noise in the room stopped. Owen knew his sexuality was bound to be an issue sooner or later, but not like this. He'd never imagined it'd be with one of his friends. Right then, Owen longed to beat Pre with one of his crutches. Or crawl under the nearest engine.

"Brad, don't worry about it, it's a firefighter thing," Owen said. "Pre, Brad's not a firefighter, and do you really think that's a good way to phrase things? Really? You'll be in my office at the beginning of A shift tomorrow to explain why."

"But Chief! I work B shift," Pre yelped.

Owen glared at him. "Then that will give you plenty of time to think about your disciplinary action after I'm done talking to you and before you start your shift." He looked around the room. Suddenly he couldn't wait to get out. "Let me just get my duffel bag, Brad. The party's over."

And just like that, the first call of the evening came in and he couldn't breathe. He motioned wildly for Brad. "Get me out of here."

Chapter Eight

Adam sat in his car and debated whether to crank it back on and head home. Yes, he had the late afternoon off so he could help out with adaptive rowing before he returned later that evening to help whoever was on duty tonight get the beasties settled in for the evening. He hoped it was Steven. They had some new interns, student volunteers from UC Davis, and Steven seemed adept at managing them. In his present frame of mind, Adam would probably bite their heads off. He wasn't angry per se, just…yeah.

The plan when Dr. Endicott hired him was that, as part of gradually handing control of the practice over to him as the associate veterinarian, new clients would be his. Their clinic had been inundated with new clients, all of whose pets needed to see Dr. Lennox *now*, or so their owners claimed. If that weren't enough to keep him busy and harried, Dr. Endicott appeared to be having if not second thoughts, then at least a hard time letting go. The latter he could handle, but the former was a real issue, since they were both contractually bound. He didn't want to have to rub her face in it, but if it came down to it, he'd have to, if only because his compensation was pegged to it.

So between sick pets, some of which were actually dying and needing close monitoring, and post-operative animals, which needed tending and cosseting, and the ever-present boarders and clinic hangers-on, which just needed affection to keep them out of trouble, he felt like work was consuming his life.

But that's not why he needed to chew through the shoulder strap on his seat belt to calm his nerves. Oh no. He could sum the reason for that up in two words: Owen Douglas. The effort of keeping his hands and other body parts off his pair partner was tearing him apart. He loved seeing the progress Owen made in the double, and by all reports Owen even acquitted himself well in a modified single on those times when Adam couldn't make it to practice. He loved it when patients turned around like that, except he was a vet and Owen wasn't his patient, even if he was pretty sure that was why Coach Bedford had matched the two of them in a boat. Well, mission accomplished! Could he please drag Owen behind the boathouse, now?

Should be easy, right? Ask the man out. Men did that all the time. Go out, do the date thing, fuck like monkeys. So, what was the problem? Adam didn't know, but he sure had one, and it was making him kuh-*ray*-zee.

Adam reached for the key in the ignition. He was going home. This was absurd.

He turned it far enough to activate the car's electrical system. The heater purred to life, blowing warm air on his feet, while the audio system started sucking music off his iPhone.

"Damnation." Adam banged his head back against the headrest.

He cranked the car off. "Just get out of the car. Go change in the locker room. Just...go."

He slammed himself back against the seat in frustration. "Gaaaah! Get a grip," he told himself, and before he thought better of it, he grabbed the bag with his rowing kit off the front seat and got out of his car.

He made it halfway to the gate leading to the boathouse before he stopped. What was he doing? Wasn't he just setting himself up for more torture? Innuendo-laden practices aside, what made him think there was anything to this but his own overheated hormones? Nailing some warm and willing undergrads didn't mean he was ready to get back into the game, not with a real man. But men like Owen didn't come along every day…

Adam threw his duffel bag to the ground and because he was still frustrated, his car keys too. Then he kicked his duffel, punting it most of the way back to his car. "Jeez."

He stomped back to his car. For good measure, he kicked the tire. His foot lit up with pain. He rested his arms on the roof of the car, head on his arms. He needed to rethink his entire approach to the evening, if not to life.

"Hey, Adam, you all right?" someone said, one of the women's cox'ns.

"Just trying to see if I locked my keys in the car."

His horn honked as the locks clicked several times.

"I think you just dropped them."

Adam looked up with what he hoped was a realistic smile. "Thanks, LaTonya. I'd have been out here for hours."

She handed him his keys. "You giants. You can reach the top shelf at the market without stretching but put something on the ground and it's lost forever."

"Pretty much," Adam said. He patted her on the head.

LaTonya grabbed his wrist. "Do that again and you lose the hand."

Adam smiled and put his hands atop his head. "If you can reach it."

They headed off to their respective locker rooms. Adam practiced the deep breathing his therapist recommended, trying to steady himself while putting on his workout gear, none of which ever quite fit right. Sure, he got that he was taller than normal, but not even the things bought from rowing-specific vendors were long enough. He thought the warm-ups designed for a sport that selected for tall people should, at least, fit properly, but apparently, he was in the minority on that score. By this point in his life he was used to his ankles and wrists showing, and it's not like he would've paid for bespoke workout wear if it had even been available.

Adam hung out around Coach Bedford, pretending to warm up on one of the fully functioning ergs just as he pretended to listen to his coach brief the rowers who were already there for the adaptive program and banter with other rowers, like his coach's partner. Morgan Estrada was busy with school so the times he and Adam were at practice at the same time were few and far between. He didn't know Morgan at all well, but he seemed nice enough. But then, most of the guys on the men's team fit that criterion, and a goodly number of them were gay too. Once word got around that the winningest coach in CalPac's rowing history had jumped ship to coach at CCRC and that he was gay too...well, they'd crawled out of the woodwork for a chance to work with Nick Bedford—work with or gawk at, according to Brad...

"Adam, slow down, you're rushing the slide, and you're slouching at the release like there's a prize for it," Coach Bedford's prize cox'n, Stuart Cochrane, said. "Oddly enough, there's not."

Adam liked Stuart, but for a guy over a foot shorter than he was, he could be a real asshole. Then, that was part of the cox'n's job.

"There's just something about you really tall, skinny guys," Stuart continued, "but when you collapse down on yourself at the finish like that, it's glaring."

"Stuart! Leave him alone!" Brad bellowed as he entered the boathouse.

Stuart's hands clenched, and Adam thought he heard Stuart's teeth grinding over the noise of the erg. Swearing under his breath, Stuart pulled off one of his shoes and threw it backward over his shoulder at Brad, narrowly missing him.

Brad cackled. "Missed me, missed me, now you've got to kiss me!"

"I'd rather swallow arsenic," Stuart hissed.

"I always knew you swallowed," Brad laughed, whacking Stuart on the back of the head with his shoe, but lightly because he was a friend. Sort of. "Here. You dropped this."

Adam stopped rowing. He eyed the chain connecting the erg's handle to the flywheel. Brad wasn't close enough, but he was pretty sure he could get it around Stuart's neck before anyone could stop him, because if the two of them didn't shut up, and shut up now if not sooner, he was going to end one or more of them. He leaned back as far as he could to get as much chain as possible...

Then he saw Owen behind Brad. He swung forward, pivoting from his hips and moving gracefully up the slide.

"Now that's what I'm talking about. That's what I want to see. Wait, where're you going? Don't just get off, you've got to reinforce—Brad, make him get back here!"

Brad rolled his eyes. "Not hardly, shrimp."

Stuart looked to where Adam had bounded over like a big rangy puppy, to where Owen was standing. "Oh."

Neither Adam nor Owen said much, but Adam felt immediately more at ease. Something subtle shifted, and tension he didn't know he'd been holding in flowed out of his shoulders and neck. Suddenly the deal with the devil he'd made to leave early in the afternoons but return after practice to take care of the animals seemed like a great idea.

"Hi," Adam said softly.

Owen smiled in return. "Hi yourself."

They stared at each other for long moments, drinking the other in, saying nothing. Adam thought it would be, maybe should be, uncomfortable, but no, it felt perfectly companionable, even if what he really wanted to do was rest his head on Owen's shoulder. It really had been a long afternoon. But Adam supposed that would only confuse Owen. He sighed. These days, he was pretty confused himself.

Then he noticed something, and he took a step back to get a good look at Owen. "Wow," he said, licking his lips.

"What?" Owen said. "You're embarrassing me."

"I knew you're a firefighter, but you never told me how hot you look in your uniform."

"Aww, jeez." Owen flushed and turned away as Brad hooted with laughter nearby, as good a reminder as any that they weren't alone.

Adam felt himself blushing, too, as Owen picked up his gym bag and all but bolted for the locker room. Suddenly he felt like a complete ass, so he avoided looking everywhere but the floor.

Owen returned a few minutes later, looking every bit as delectable in Adam's eyes, but more appropriately attired. He couldn't help it. He had to look, and talk. He forgot all about his embarrassment.

They made chitchat while they warmed up on the ergs. People seemed to have figured out that the pair partners were "together" even if they weren't together like that. Adam supposed the gossip mills had them in bed by now, if not shopping for china and silver during their spare time, but they knew the truth and that was fine. But he could already tell Owen seemed off. Huh. That made two of them.

"What's wrong?" he asked Owen.

Owen chuckled. "You mean besides you drooling on my uniform?"

"I'm sorry, I didn't think—"

"Don't worry, it's cute." Owen leaned over to bump Adam's shoulder.

"Yeah?" Adam looked at him from under his bangs. Owen shuddered. "You seem subdued this evening."

"Nothing." Owen sighed. "Everything."

"That sounds like a lot. Can you narrow it down?"

Owen looked at him. "Don't take this as a brush-off because it's the last thing I'd do to you, but I'm not sure I can reduce it to bullet points yet. Is that okay?"

"It's your angst," Adam said, trying to make light of it, even though yeah, it did kind of suck that Owen couldn't tell him. He felt the tension in his neck and shoulders returning through the rest of warm-ups and announcements, too, even though he told himself not to be a diva. But why the hell did being an adult have to suck? Wasn't growing up supposed to have taken care of all that?

Adam sighed and got on with it, putting it aside or at least trying to as he and Owen took their boat down to the dock. Only then did he notice that Owen's leg was in a brace of some kind. He felt like a real ass. Some friend he was, and one more thing to feel like crap about. On the other hand, Owen didn't seem to be in a talking mood. They launched in relative silence, without much more than the minimum talk needed for that. Lights on, oars out, and away they went.

Usually the water swallowed Adam's troubles, but on the river that evening, he felt just as irritable and out of sorts as he had in the parking lot. At least he now had an idea why, and his behavior in the boathouse, as embarrassing as it was, told him. He knew he was falling for Owen. He was pretty sure his reaction to Owen's unwillingness to talk was a good indication that he was a goner. He just didn't know what to do about it. Part of him, the rational part of him, knew he needed to back way off. It had only been a few months since he'd escaped an abusive relationship. Then there was the work stress. So, on top of that he needed to add a relationship? Really? Yeah, like a hole in the head. If he were going to do that, he thought darkly, he could've stayed with Jordan. He was great for giving Adam unneeded holes.

Owen must've picked up on his brooding, because after they completed the warm-up sequence and stripped off their now-unnecessary extra layers, he matched Adam's punishing stroke rate and power, two frustrated men alone with their thoughts.

"Rough day?" Owen said.

Adam breathed deep, considering his reply for a stroke. "Busy days..." He stopped talking to keep his breathing even while he rowed. "When I row, long nights after practice."

They rowed in silence for a few strokes.

"So why do you row..." Owen said, his words coming in short gasps "...if it's a burden?"

You, Adam wanted to say, *I row to see you,* even though he'd rediscovered rowing before a certain gorgeous, sardonic ginger had gimped into the boathouse. "Because it's rowing," he said, as if that explained it all, "and it's never a burden." *You're never a burden.* "What about you? You almost...bit my head off...in the boathouse."

Owen was silent for a moment. "I...did not."

"Okay...maybe not."

They rowed silently for a time, with only the sounds of the boat for company. "Everything's very...different after...the accident," Owen said at last, working to maintain even breathing, "and I still...can't make...sense of it."

"I'm sorry," Adam said.

"No...biggie."

Adam didn't believe Owen for a minute.

"So, how'd...you get...into vet med?" Owen asked, continuing their impromptu inquisition. Wasn't this the sort of thing people were supposed to cover on first dates and not while engaging in heavy aerobic exercise?

"The short answer," Adam puffed, "is...surgery and medicine...without the bullshit."

"What do you...mean?" Owen said.

"Surgery can be pretty...homophobic." Adam shuddered at some of the stories Jordan had told him.

"So, you went into...vet med instead?"

"Cats don't care...if you suck cock."

Owen started laughing. "Don't... Not when...rowing."

Adam grinned, pleased that he could take Owen's mind off his own day. "We might as well...weigh 'nuff. About time...to turn around."

Owen was silent as they turned their boat and caught their breath. Adam tipped his water bottle up to take a drink.

"What about dogs?"

Adam sputtered and coughed. "What?" He turned around to stare at Owen.

"You said cats don't care if you like the cock. I was just wondering about dogs." Owen blinked innocently, but Adam swore there was a glint in those hazel eyes, or maybe it was just the gibbous moon, orange and growing each night as Halloween approached.

They were alone out there on the river, the nearest boat far enough away that if Adam wanted to, he could lean back and capture Owen's lips with his own. Of his body's own volition, he tilted toward Owen. At times he loved being tall, and this was a bunch of them rolled into one. Owen looked surprised but moved to meet him.

Light blinded them as a launch roared up to them. "There you two are. Rowing obviously agrees with you, Owen, if you're getting this far just with arms and back," Nick said.

With a startled jerk they sat back, setting the boat to rocking. Adam wondered if Coach Bedford sounded amused or was he just feeling guilty? But Owen's low growl of frustration sure made him feel better. At least his balls wouldn't be the only blue ones...

"Anyway, guys, it's time to turn around," Nick said. "Sorry for the wake you're about to get, but you shot out ahead of everyone else, and now I've got crews up and down the river. If you can, try to catch up."

And with that, Coach Bedford was off, and sure enough, he kicked up a pretty good wake, despite the allegedly wakeless design of his launch.

"Uh… Adam?" Owen said after they'd rowed for a while.

Adam cringed. This was it. This was when Owen asked what the hell happened or worse, said he liked him, but not like that, or any of a number of other terrible little lies, because he'd seen that look in Owen's eyes. He'd seen Owen lean toward him. Damnation.

"Yeah?"

"Way 'nuff," Owen said after he'd caught his breath for a moment. "I know I haven't been rowing nearly as long as you or anything but based on everything you and Coach Bedford and Brad have told me, I really don't think your shoulders are supposed to be that tight. It's like you're plugging your ears with your deltoids or something. Also, you're stabbing your oars into the water so hard you're burying half that shaft. Even with the pontoons you're really jacking the set."

Adam flopped back onto Owen's legs and laughed helplessly. "When you're right, Owen, you're dead on."

Chapter Nine

Owen's head swam and not from oxygen deprivation. He wore a brace on his left leg, but he itched to try real rowing, the full rowing stroke, all the same. But for once, his leg wasn't the problem. No, the problem, as it was so often of late, was a certain giant with curly blond hair, and jeez, when Adam looked out from under his bangs at him, his knees turned into Jell-O. But then, he always wanted to be on his knees in front of Adam. He'd sink to his knees and wrap his arms around Adam's legs and hold him, resting his face against him, hoping that Adam felt the same way. Maybe Adam would reach down with one of those long, graceful arms to run a hand through his short, spiky hair, caressing him, relaxing him, tilting his head up. He'd look up into those blue eyes and see a hunger there, a need to match his own. He'd reach up and...

The boat lurched then, even with the pontoons helping to balance it.

"You all right up there?" Adam called from the stroke seat.

His face flaming in the darkness, Owen looked over his shoulder to check their course. "Yeah, keep rowing. We're going to be late enough as it is."

They rowed on in silence. Owen had no idea what Adam was thinking of, but if his actions at the turn around were any indication, then...

Owen wanted to stop the boat then and there and pursue the matter, because they had some unfinished business. The problem was, he couldn't think of any way to finish it once they got back, not with a dock and boathouse swarming with rowers. They'd get back to the dick...er, dock, and put the boat and the oars away, and go their separate ways, and who knows when they'd revisit the subject? Would they ever, or would Adam pretend it had never happened? Or would he regret his move and pretend he'd never tried to kiss the older, broken man?

But damn, when Adam fell against his legs? He'd longed to lean forward and finish what Adam had started. It would've been so easy too. All he needed to do was hold the oar handles between the tops of his legs and his belly, and then lean forward to kiss the man of his recent dreams. He'd almost forgotten they were only halfway back to the boathouse. But it was just as well they were only rowing with arms and back, because he would bet good money that rowing with a hard-on was uncomfortable...

"Owen!"

"What? This is your fault, you know!"

At least Adam had the decency to laugh, Owen thought, but it damn well better have been at them both.

They made it back to the dock without further mishap only to find it dark and deserted.

"What the...?" Adam began.

Owen looked around. "At least the boathouse lights are on."

"Think you can bring us in with the dock dark?"

"Yep," Owen said. "I don't have a choice. Take it slow."

They inched their way back to the dock, with Owen twisted around to see ahead of them, calling course corrections to Adam, who provided the power.

When they made it back to the dock, Owen climbed out and then held the boat steady for Adam. "I'll get the dock lights," he said.

Owen straightened and stretched his back as he walked up the ramp. It seemed like forever ago that Adam had practically carried him down to their boat, but in reality, it only been a few weeks.

The singles house door was cracked open, and since that was where the light panel was, Owen stepped inside and flicked the lights back on. A hand closed over his.

"Wha—!"

"Shhhh," Adam whispered in his ear.

The sensation of Adam's lips against his ear sent shivers racing across Owen's body.

"You like that?"

"Christ, yes," Owen said. His throat went dry and he swallowed to lubricate it.

Before he could do anything about Adam's tormenting proximity, Adam slowly licked his ear.

"You're killing me." Owen turned around and grabbed Adam's shirt, pulling him in for a rough kiss. Not that the lick wasn't driving him toward insanity, but it was time for Adam to put his tongue to a better use.

"Is that a problem?" Adam said, voice pitched lower than usual. It sent a shiver down Owen's spine, straight to his cock.

"No," he said, playing dumb. "Brad was my ride, that's all."

"Yeah? I can give you a ride."

Owen smiled, a wide lazy grin. Usually bad lines during sex were his job. He pulled Adam into him, chest to chest, groin to groin. "Will you, now? Somehow you struck me as the kind who liked to ride, not drive."

As he said that, Owen ran his hands down Adam's ass and brought his mouth up to Adam's neck and started sucking right at the base. Adam groaned and pushed Owen back into the wall as his hands fumbled with Owen's shirt. When Adam's hands finally reached bare skin and found that fine ginger pelt, he whimpered, he actually whimpered, and didn't that make Owen feel like a million bucks.

"Feel free to explore. It's all yours," Owen said, lifting his mouth from the territory he was marking.

He went back to Adam's neck, this time right below the jaw. He couldn't peg why he felt the need to mark Adam. They weren't dating—yet—although mating looked like a real possibility, but mark him he would. He didn't know what Adam's plans were, but at least it might scare other guys off for a few days.

"What're you doing?" Adam moaned.

Sounded like he'd struck pay dirt on his guy. Owen blinked. *His guy.* Was that how he thought of Adam? "Making you feel good, I hope."

"You're doing that, all right."

Then Adam's roving hands found their way north to his pecs. He'd always been a tit pig. He had some toys at home he'd love to show Adam, and...*sweet baby Darwin!* "Damn, Adam!" he gasped.

"Looks like I found your number." Adam sounded smug as he scratched fingernails over the pebbled nubs of Owen's nips. He dropped his head back, barely hearing

Adam chuckle. Then Adam licked his ear again, and wasn't that the hottest thing? It took Owen to heaven even as it returned part of his senses to him.

"I'm not going to be the only one coming in his pants," he murmured. He sucked on two fingers and then plunged them back into Adam's warm-up pants, seeking Adam's entrance with that hand even as he used the other to press Adam even closer to him. He circled Adam's—his guy's—hole slowly as Adam started bucking against him.

"God, yes," Adam breathed in his ear. "Hurry. I'm not going to last much longer."

"Me neither." Owen breached Adam, but with agonizing slowness, deliberately so. He wanted to drag it out for them both.

He could only grin when Adam started swearing. "You like that?"

"Fuck you," Adam whined, jamming himself back onto Owen's hand. Owen took pity on him, adding a second finger.

But Adam wasn't as far gone as Owen thought. He yanked their pants down enough to liberate their cocks and spat into his hand. Then he went to work. It wasn't the safest thing they could've done, but damn. They were almost there.

"Awww, Christ—!"

They both jumped, but Adam, bless him, shielded Owen while they tucked themselves in. There wasn't anything Owen could do about where his hand so obviously was, but he removed his fingers as subtly as he could, enough so it looked like copping a feel.

"We j-j-just finished," Adam stammered.

Brad snorted. "Looks to me like you were just getting started."

"Go get the oars and then take off. I'll deal with Brad," Owen whispered in Adam's ear with a light kiss. Adam gave him a shy smile and then hurried down to the dock to retrieve the oars.

"Well, you left, and Adam offered to give me a ride," Owen said, realizing too late how that sounded. Rather than double down, he stood his ground, pretending he hadn't just thrown a slow one right over the plate for Brad. There was no way to pretend he wasn't bright red, however, but then, he'd been blushing furiously since Brad had caught him with his hand in the cookie jar.

"Looks to me like it was the other way around, you sly dog," Brad said, grinning. He reached over and pulled a piece of paper off the boathouse door. "Here's the note I left. In it I explained that I had to run home real quick because I was running late. Drew's disappeared into real estate hell again, and there was a chance he'd be home for dinner. I at least wanted to be there for a moment to beg for more time."

Owen raised one eyebrow. "Was he?"

"Does a note on the voice mail count?" Brad grunted.

"I'd say no."

"Me too. Wish I'd checked my phone. It'd have saved me a trip home." Brad looked at him slyly. "'Course, if I had, you and Adam wouldn't have—"

"Oh, shut up," Owen said.

"Apparently voice mail's not that reliable anyway, because I left you one too." Brad's eyes were merry.

"Let's get the boat put away and get out of here. It's been a long day."

"Just as soon as you wash your hands," Brad said loftily. "You looked deep into your—and Adam's—business, and those boats are expensive. It wouldn't do to get them dirty."

"Dirty? That water's filthy," Owen protested.

"Still, we have standards here at CCRC. We don't fuck in the boathouse, or on the boats."

"We'll see about that," Owen muttered under his breath as he rubbed a dollop of hand sanitizer in.

*

"Anyway," Brad said once everything was battened down and locked up for the evening, "you seemed…distracted out there tonight."

Owen shrugged. "Everything's changed, and I don't know how to describe it."

"I think it's called sex."

Owen squashed the surge of irritation, even anger, he felt for his younger friend. Brad was only trying to help. It wouldn't help to bash his head in with one of his crutches. Also, Brad was driving.

"Not that. That's under control."

"Yeah, that much was clear."

"Fuck you." The one thing he didn't feel like discussing was Adam with a trick, which when it came down to it was all Brad was. He crossed his arms over his chest in the universal code for *I don't want to talk about it; I want you to dig for it, no matter how big and butch I am.*

Brad scratched his head. "There's something you don't understand. You've done something no one else at CCRC has done, and that's gotten the Ice Princess to open up."

Not like I want him to. "What're you talking about?" he growled.

"There's no way you'd know this, but before you showed up, he was reserved and not even all that friendly," Brad said. "He still calls Nick 'Coach Bedford' and almost never mingles with the other guys. No one really knows what to make of him. You, on the other hand... You didn't see his face, but when you walked into the boathouse behind me that first day, he lit up like Times Square on New Year's Eve."

"He did not." Owen was grateful the car was dark. The thought was a sweet one, but people just didn't react like that for him.

"He did. And every practice you two have both been at ever since. Trust me, dude, even if that mating display I interrupted didn't clue you in, doesn't the fact that you two disappear into each other whenever you see one another tell you anything?"

"Maybe." Owen slouched in the seat. It didn't feel great on his back, but it seemed warranted under the circumstances.

"Okay, I get it, subject closed. Work, recovery, whatever you've got going on with Adam, you've got a lot on your plate right now."

Owen sighed. "That's just it, I don't know what's going on with Adam, and work? That's a mystery all its own."

Owen had never been so grateful to pull up in front of his house. He liked Brad, and truly appreciated that Brad had dragged him into adaptive rowing, but maybe it was time to drive himself to practices.

*

Brad watched Owen until he let himself into his house and closed the door behind him. That was plain good manners, what his mother would've expected of him, but his mind was already miles away. More was bothering

Owen than just being caught red-handed in the boathouse with Adam. Owen had said it himself, even if not in so many words, and it was more than just that night. It was in all the little clues people thought he was too stupid to pick up. Hard luck for them all he caught most of them, and what he couldn't figure out, he ran by his partner. Between Drew and him, they figured most things out.

In this case, however, Brad heard what Owen didn't say loud and clear because he saw it in Drew, even this long after his partner's bashing. Both men had had their lives fucked over by serious trauma, and if it still had the power to bother Drew a year later, what was it doing to Owen after only a couple of months?

Brad didn't have the answers. He didn't need to. He had Drew. Now how was he going to convince his partner to help out Owen, a man of whom Drew was unaccountably jealous...?

*

Drew came home from a late meeting with all the agents plus the broker to the delicious smells of a dinner he didn't have to prepare. Sure, it was just doctored leftovers from the weekend, but that didn't matter. What mattered was that his delectable partner had gotten his message, wasn't upset that their plans had changed, and was still feeding him, and—holy shit!—was dressed only in sweatpants that barely clung to his waist. Everything else, including that massive hairy chest, was bare. Not coincidentally, the heat had been turned up.

Brad drowsed on the sofa, his own sleeping beauty. Drew carefully set his briefcase down in the hallway and toed his shoes off so he didn't wake him. He wanted to wake his man in his own special way. He padded up to the sofa and knelt beside Brad. He still gave thanks each and every day this wonderful, amazing man was his, and that Brad had the foresight and persistence to keep trying even when he, in the depths of his own pain and confusion, had pushed Brad away. If his big lug hadn't refused to give up, they wouldn't have the wonderful life they were building together. Without Brad, Drew's dreams of life with a partner with whom he could share work in real estate and home renovation wouldn't be coming true.

Yeah, Brad probably wanted something. He usually did when he dressed that provocatively. The good thing was Brad didn't tease. He put out, and damn, did he ever. The last time Brad had dressed like this, Drew had felt it for three days. For a man who hadn't identified as gay when they'd first met, Brad had sure gotten with the program. The best part was that Drew didn't have to share him with anyone.

Drew kissed Brad's eyelids with light, fluttering kisses that conveyed all the love and tenderness he felt but couldn't always convey, all the feelings that sometimes were lost in the dust and details and pettiness of daily living. "Brad," he whispered. "Dearheart, I'm home."

Brad squirmed a bit, but then his eyes opened and he smiled. "Hi, hon. What time is it?"

Drew smiled back. "Too late. I'm sorry. The meeting ran long."

"They always do." Brad pushed himself up. Drew stifled his disappointment. He'd planned to make it up to Brad, starting by removing those sweatpants. "I've got dinner waiting."

"I could smell. Thank you. You didn't have to do that."

"I wanted to."

"At least you got my message."

"After I raced home from practice," Brad said.

Drew's face fell. "I'm sorry. I left you a voice mail—"

Any further protest was halted by a kiss. Drew returned it with enthusiasm. "Someone's hungry for more than dinner," Brad said.

"Someone's partner's stretched out on the sofa in his 'come fuck me' sweats. What do you expect?"

Brad smirked. "That someone's gonna get fucked. Duh. The one question is, before or after dinner?"

Drew had to think about that one. Which appetite was going to be satisfied first? Brad answered the question for him with his smirk and the hand slowly rubbing his belly, dropping lower and lower until he was palming a growing erection through his sweats, and...jeez, the little shit wasn't wearing anything under the sweats, not even a jock. "Dude, did you just whimper?"

"You know it." Drew pushed Brad back onto the sofa and then climbed onto him, grinding his ass onto Brad's now-sizeable hard-on. "I've been thinking about this all day. Wanting it. Wanting you."

Brad pulled Drew's tailored dress shirt out of his pants and then went to work on the buttons.

"Careful with those," Drew cautioned. He loved Brad to distraction, but the last time his Sasquatch got horned up while he was dressed for work, the price exacted from his bespoke suit and shirt had been a high one. But the sex had been hot. Really hot.

"One time," Brad muttered. Then he ran his hands over Drew's chest, using the extra friction generated by the undershirt, just like he knew Drew liked. He thrust up against Drew at the same time.

"Jeez, I've dreamed about this all day," Drew whispered.

Brad unbuckled Drew's pants, and Drew obliged by lifting his hips, waiting while Brad pulled his own sweats down, and yes, indeed, he was bare-ass naked under them. He was also hard enough to etch brass, and just the thought of where that was going to be in a few minutes made Drew salivate. He kicked his pants away.

"Turn around."

"What?"

"You heard me. Turn around," Brad repeated.

Drew complied. He was already breathing hard at the thought. He might've been Pavlov's dog for the conditioned responses, but that night, he was Brad's bitch and they both knew it. "Please. Hurry."

"Why do you think I raced home after practice?" Brad lazily traced his fingers around Drew's warm hole. It twitched.

"Brad."

"And what did I find? An empty house."

"I'm sorry. I told—Fuck!"

Without warning, Brad speared him with his tongue, hard, fast, and deep. Over and over and over. "I think some punishment's in order, don't you?"

"Uh-huh."

Brad smacked one butt cheek. Hard, but not too hard, just enough to pink it nicely. When he resumed rimming, he grabbed Drew's cock in a loose grip and jacked it slowly. "Brad..."

"Uh-huh. You don't get to feel too much. You were baaaad..." But then Brad couldn't say more. He ran his tongue around the outside of Drew's begging hole, just enough to tease, not enough to satisfy. Then he stabbed his tongue in again and again, teasing him with the fucking to come.

"I was really bad, but if you fuck me, I'll make it up to you, I promise," Drew panted.

"Yeah, you will." Brad grabbed some lube from between the sofa cushions and then slicked Drew up. This only made Drew hotter as Brad's fingers worked his entrance, gently stretching him and moving up into him to play with his prostate.

"If you want to be involved in my next ejaculation, you should stop," Drew said as Brad turned him back around.

Brad looked up into his eyes as he slicked his own cock. Drew saw fire there, to be sure, and hunger, but also the love they'd made between them. They'd gone latex-free a few months before, and they stared into each other's eyes as Brad guided him down onto his cock. "Easy, babe."

Drew breathed deeply as he willed himself to relax and open to take his partner in, the only husband he'd ever need for the rest of his life. Let other men cruise the clubs and smart phone apps and wherever else people picked up company for the hour or evening. He had his Brad and that was all he'd ever need.

They both sighed as Drew settled into place all the way down on Brad. Brad held him close, stretching up to kiss him tenderly before he started thrusting, gently at first, but with increasing strength.

Brad shuddered and Drew knew his man was close. So was he. "Almost there."

"Me too." Brad took Drew's cock in one of his slick, calloused hands, angling it toward his mouth. He knew what Brad was doing and that was it. That was enough to push him over the edge.

He cried out wordlessly and shot onto Brad's face and into his open mouth.

"Oh yeah, Drew. Please, give it to me," Brad moaned as he shuddered and jerked his own release into Drew. He licked what he could of Drew's cum off his face.

They held onto each other as they came down. Brad rested his face against Drew, heedless of his costly shirt, and equally heedless, Drew held him close, resting his head on Brad's.

Brad looked up at him. "You ready to eat? Because I am *starved*."

"We could maybe get cleaned up first?"

"If by cleaned up you mean you find your underwear and I pull my sweats up, yeah," Brad said.

Later, after they'd eaten and cleaned up, they cuddled up like spoons in bed and each shared his day's experiences.

"I'll bet it made for an interesting end to practice," Drew said. He tried to chuckle, but it came out as a forced gurgle. Truth be told, on some level, he felt threatened that his cuddly muscle bear was still in contact with the man he'd hooked up with while the two of them were maybe not quite broken up.

"That it did," Brad said.

When he was silent for a while, Drew nudged him gently. "Out with it."

"Okay." Brad took a deep breath. "I have a huge favor to ask."

"And what would this favor be?" Suddenly Drew had an idea why those sweats might've made an appearance that evening, although if that had been the case, why hadn't Brad said anything then...

"Owen needs both our friendships, not just mine."

"Me?" Drew was shocked. This was *not* what he thought Brad would say. "Why me?"

"Because you've had your life seriously derailed by trauma, just like he has. I can be as understanding as possible, but unless I've been there, I just can't help him," Brad explained. "You have, and I hope you will."

"It's not the same thing," Drew said quickly. "I was bashed. He was in some kind of work-related injury. Surely they have therapists—"

Brad rolled over and switched on the light. "Didn't you tell me that you wished there'd been some kind of support group for putting your life back together after you'd been released from the hospital and rehab?"

Damn. Why couldn't Brad be as dumb as his father had thought? "But...the man you..."

"Yeah, the man who blew me," Brad said bluntly. "I thought we'd gotten past this. I've told you a hundred times. You know what he said when we'd finished?"

"Maybe I need to hear it again," Drew said in a small, vulnerable voice.

Brad took his face in his hands, his large yet oh-so-tender hands. "'What's his name?'" he said softly. "He asked me the name of the man I'd been thinking of the entire time. Because I was obviously not thinking about him. You know what he said every time we spoke after that, including every call about the Bayard House?"

Drew shook his head like a little boy who needed to be reassured.

"He told me to call you. He's why I didn't give up on you, on us, you stubborn ass," Brad said fondly. "Owen's why we're here, right now, cozied up in bed. Owen could tell I was totally in love with you even then. Without Owen, you might even say that *we* wouldn't be here right now." When Brad put it like that, Drew felt a little stupid, but when Brad put his hand on Drew's chin, Drew allowed it to be tipped up. "So, what do you say you be the big man I know you are and extend a hand to someone who needs it."

"It really doesn't thrill me you're even hanging around this hookup of yours, and now you want me to help him?" Drew sighed.

"There's something you need to understand. I'm basically a stick figure for Owen. I might as well not even exist, he's so into Adam."

"I'll believe it when I see it," Drew grumped.

"I'm glad you said that." Brad grinned. "Don't schedule any open houses on Saturday morning, nothing before noon. Come to practice, and you'll see. I'll make brunch after, and besides, we haven't seen much of Nick or Morgan lately. Maybe free food will get their attention." He got a crafty look on his face. "It might be fun to get everyone in on it."

"On what?" Drew said warily.

"Adam and Owen. Seriously, if we all lived in condos, these two could heat them all. We'd save a bundle this winter."

Drew laughed in spite of himself. "That bad?"

"You have no idea. These two are so gone on each other. They just haven't figured it out yet, although I'd like to think that having their hands in each other's pants would involve a significant realization on both their parts." When Drew didn't respond right away, Brad continued, "C'mon, I used big words. Don't let them go to waste."

Drew laughed again. "All right. I'll come to practice. I'll check out these Owen and Adam people. If I see even one indication that Owen's still jonesing for you, you will be so far beyond screwed that the light from screwed will never reach you."

Brad grinned. "Aw, thanks, Drew. You won't regret it, you'll see."

Chapter Ten

Adam held the steering wheel in a death grip, his knuckles white, his face still bright red. He'd never been more mortified in his life. Seriously, Brad catching them like that had to be the most embarrassing thing ever. The only saving grace was they hadn't come yet. And Owen. He tried to think of the word for what Owen had done when he'd stayed to deal with Brad and basically told him to run away. Sure, he'd gone down to get the oars, but by the time he'd come back up to return the oars to the oar locker, Owen had drawn Brad away. Gallant. That was it. Owen had gallantly faced the heat from Brad the interloper, allowing Adam to flee.

He knew he'd been in serious lust with Owen from the moment he'd first seen him, but now? Now this evening prodded him to acknowledge something more, something deeper, something he wasn't ready to name. He wasn't even sure he was ready to discuss it with his therapist. It scared him. It was too precious, yet too tinged with terror. He didn't want Owen sullied with those memories.

Adam drove the rest of the way to the clinic trying not to think about it, which meant it was all he thought about, no matter how loud he played the radio or how often he flicked from song to song. Not even oldies like Blondie or the Eurythmics could pull him away from thoughts of Owen. It was, he thought ruefully as he pulled into the clinic's parking lot and let himself in, probably a sign.

"That better be you, Dr. Lennox!" Steven called from the back room.

"As opposed to...?" Adam called back.

Steven raced into the reception area. "Did you lock the door?"

Adam reached behind him and flipped the deadbolt.

"Great, could you set the alarm too?"

"What's going on, Steven?" Adam asked as he keyed the code into the alarm's panel. Dr. Endicott thought only the clinic's doctors should have the code to the alarm system, which Adam thought short-sighted, or at least inconvenient, since it meant only the two of them could see to the animals early or late. Practically speaking, it meant him. Personally speaking, he thought it was a stupid policy, since some of the animal health technicians had been practicing longer than he'd been out of vet school. Oh well, when he was in charge...

"Weird things lately," Steven replied. "Someone tried the locks tonight, front and back. It wasn't even that late."

Adam checked his watch. "It's still not. What do you mean, 'weird things lately' and why is this the first time I'm hearing about this?"

"Like I said, someone tried the locks like they wanted in, but not badly enough to break in or anything."

"And?" Adam prompted, growing cold. It couldn't be. Could it? He was in that program. Wasn't he?

Steven made a frustrated noise. "Nothing that really needs repeating, just little things. Like, it'd be a quiet afternoon and I'd call Candy, the receptionist, back to help me. We'd hear the front door chime, but when she got back to the desk, there was no one there, only all your business cards were upside down."

Shit.

"We called the police," Steven continued. He wrapped his arms around himself. "They said it was probably just addicts looking for drugs, but they'd send someone out 'when they had the time.'"

Adam took several deep breaths. He had to steady himself. He was in charge here, he had to be the strong one here, because for all Steven's apparent maturity, he was still fairly young and an undergrad. This was one part of veterinary medicine his volunteer work had clearly not prepared him for, but the reality was that animal drugs were essentially the same as human drugs, frequently every bit as pure and therefore a target.

"In Davis? What else could they possibly have to do? It's too early to bust people for violating the noise ordinances." Still, Adam felt like someone had dumped ice water on his head, because he knew perfectly well it hadn't been an "addict."

"Ticket bicyclists for failure to stop properly," Steven said bitterly.

"Still angry, huh?"

Steven's eyes glittered in the lights of the lobby. "You have no idea. It's going to take me forever to pay that off."

"Let's get to work. How many of the new volunteers do we have tonight?" Adam said.

"None," Steven replied. "After the bit with the locks, I sent them home. After we see to the animals, we're both going home."

"I'll give you a ride, but I'll have to let Dr. Endicott know what's going on."

"Yeah, I guess, but I'm not going to start spending the night here," Steven declared, "senior intern or not."

"I don't think you need to worry. Those are duties that are more likely to fall elsewhere, like on the associate vet and certain senior animal health technicians." Adam was amazed his voice wasn't shaking.

With that on their minds, they got on with their rounds, since neither really wanted to be there under the circumstances. Part of him wondered if he should tell Steven about his suspicions, but he was rattled enough, and Adam didn't want to spook him further when he couldn't say for sure it had been Jordan.

About halfway through, Steven stopped and stared at him. "Dude."

"What?" Adam replied, admittedly a bit on the irritable side. It had been a confusing, at times embarrassing, and latterly frightening evening, and this many hours after practice he was starting to stink.

"You didn't tell me vampires were a problem down at the boathouse. I had no idea."

Adam looked up from the chart he'd been studying. "What?"

"You have a hickey the size of an egg on your neck," Steven said with a Cheshire grin.

"Oh Lord, Owen," Adam muttered.

"So that's his name? Owen?" Steve was still grinning. "Is this the guy you've been smitten with since you started that special program at the rowing club? That was an awesome beefcake shot, by the way. I know at least four people who've got it pinned to their bedroom walls, including Joey. He'll be crushed that you're seeing someone, by the way."

"Smitten?" Adam wished he were anywhere but there. And the boathouse. Anywhere but there or the boathouse. "Is that what you're calling it? And Joey will live."

"Oh yeah. You're totally smitten with this guy," Steven said happily.

Adam was tired and scared. His day was catching up to him and he just wanted to be home. He rested his head against the cage of the animal he was checking. The small tabby inside snaked out a paw and pulled some of his hair into the cage and started grooming him. "Damn, I must really stink if sick cats are bathing me."

"They know if someone needs a hug." Steven made a note on another chart after feeding a dog in a lower cage. "All done here."

Adam shook a single pill out of a bottle and opened the tabby's cage. With deft hands, he opened the cat's mouth and sent the antibiotic down its gullet toward its stomach. "One thing I'll say for sick kitties. They're easy to pill. All right, let's get out of here. Complicated conversations are best had somewhere comfortable and well stocked with tea. Let's go back to my place. You can crash on my couch."

*

Twenty minutes later, Adam emerged from the shower clean and somewhat refreshed. He threw on some sweats and hurried down to the kitchen to find Steven rummaging through his fridge.

"Scoot," Adam said. When Steven showed no signs of budging, he simply picked him up and deposited him out of the way. "I know where things are, and I can cook something a lot faster. Now git."

"Fine, but can I at least have some coffee or beer or something?" Steven said petulantly.

Adam made a face at him. "Poor widdle short person. Did the big bad giant hurt your widdle feewings?"

"Jeez, you're an asshole."

"I know. I'm sorry. It comes out when I'm tired and hungry. Which do you want, beer or coffee?"

"Beer, I guess."

Adam dug out a beer while he pulled stir-fry ingredients from the fridge. "On these long nights, I have stuff thawing." He popped a dish in the microwave while he heated up the stove. "We're having quick and dirty."

Then he thought of what he and Owen had almost done and turned bright red, which naturally Steven saw.

"Somehow I think we're back to the hickey, so you're forgiven for the short joke," Steven said.

"All right, I'm too tired to be evasive." Adam started throwing things in a large wok on the stove and moving them quickly around with a bamboo paddle. "Yes, the only thing that prevented me and Owen from making complete whores of ourselves was that we were interrupted. Owen gave me a chance to fasten up and then provided cover so I could get the hell out of there."

"He took the heat for you? That's chivalrous. Or something."

Adam nodded. "Or what passes for it anymore. And you're right. I've had a serious boner for him since the minute he walked into the boathouse, but tonight made me think it might be more, so in a way, I'm kind of glad we didn't get to finish. Does that make any sense?"

Steven shrugged, fiddling with the label on his beer. "I guess. It's your story."

"Look, I've had enough hookups since I left Jordan. This felt...different, like it could lead somewhere else, and not just because he's older than I am."

"So, what's your hang-up, and before you protest, save us both the time and don't pretend otherwise. If you didn't have a hang-up, you'd either be at his house right now or be on the phone making a date," Steven pointed out.

"Yeah, probably. It's just..." Adam grunted in frustration. "What do I have to offer someone?"

"What?" Steven laughed.

Adam hunched his shoulders, like he was trying to collapse in on himself. "I'm a basket case. I don't even know if I remember how to love," he said softly as he dished up their dinner. He set two plates at the kitchen breakfast bar along with a beer and then sat down next to his friend. "I just got out of an abusive relationship, and—"

"Okay, stop right there," Steven said around a mouthful of stir-fry. "Damn, for quick and dirty, this is really good. Anyway, how long has it been since you left? A couple of months, right?"

Adam nodded, his own mouth full.

"But there's something else you've got to keep in mind. How long has it been since you actually felt anything—anything positive—for Jordan? How long has it been since it was a vital, loving relationship in your mind? How long have you been trying to leave?" When Adam didn't reply right away, Steven kept pressing. "Months? Or years?"

Adam finally said, "Years. But I don't know if I'm ready."

Steven didn't say anything. There wasn't much to say.

Adam kept thinking. "I'm just not sure. I mean, do I want a real relationship this soon?"

"Is that what this would be?" Steven shrugged as if to say *how would I know?* "You could always just fuck him. You want him, he wants you. So long as you're on the same page, there's no problem."

Adam shook his head slowly, lost in his own thoughts. "No. No, I don't think so. I think he's worth more than that. If I just wanted ass, Joey'd be over here in five minutes, lubed and ready to go. I think Owen's worth trying for more. But am I?"

"Wow," Steven said, setting down his fork. "Jordan really did a number on you."

Adam sniffed. They both pretended it was from the spices in dinner. "You have no idea."

"Then you have to tell him about Jordan."

They ate in silence after that, Adam thinking and Steven letting him think. Adam had seen a lot of hot guys since he finally worked up the gumption to leave Jordan, but not one of them had moved him. Something about Owen sang to him. He couldn't put his finger on what. It wasn't his looks, although he admitted they didn't hurt. Physically, the older man hit a lot of his buttons, but there was more than that, more to Owen, or so he thought. He seemed like the kind of guy who wrung the most he could out of life, who didn't let an accident stop him. Owen struck him as someone who might have some healing to do, just like he did, and that appealed to him too.

But really? Right now? If the universe was presenting him with his perfect man, it lacked all sense of proportion. He was starting over professionally and not sure if he could commit to a relationship, not the way he wanted to. Low man on the totem pole? Check. Refugee from an abusive relationship? Check. Not sure if he can trust his instincts and emotions due to same? Check. But seriously jonesing for the guy? Check check check.

"I guess I do." Adam took a swig of his own beer.

*

Work was work. Owen was glad to have it, he was glad not to have it snatched out from under him due to medical retirement, but that was all he could say for it. It was there, and he was glad when he wasn't. He assumed this was what people meant by the phrase "having a life," but he'd have to do something more than row and rattle around his house—that and physical therapy.

"You won't have to do this too much longer, you know," Deanne told him.

"Yeah?"

"Sure," she said cheerfully. "You've shown real improvement. Once you started with the adaptive rowing, you certainly got with the program. You're going to have some issues with your left leg that may or may not have anything to do with your lackluster early interest in therapy, but this is what we call a success in this business. More than, really. I'm not sure I'd put you on the front lines fighting fires, but you can surely handle more than your desk job. All of that's up to the fire department, of course. For daily living, and that includes rowing, you're in the clear."

Owen refused to think about that, because that meant a disability hearing and those were almost always an ordeal on a number of levels, with the firefighter being the rope in a tug-of-war between the union and the department. He'd better call Pearl Kim, his lawyer, and let her know. "That's...good news."

"You don't sound convinced," Deanne said.

Owen gave her a big fake smile. "It's just that you've been a part of my life for so long."

"You'll manage, I'm sure." She rolled her eyes. "I'd like to see you monthly for the next four months, but that's just to make sure everything stays as it should. Other than that, you're done."

"Thanks, Deanne. I appreciate it," Owen said, shaking her hand.

"So, what's next?" she asked.

He checked his watch and grinned. "I've got practice. Now that I'm cleared, I'm hoping the coach will let me out of the adaptive boats."

"Oh, one other thing," Deanne handed him a referral and a brochure. "This is a referral to a pedorthist. You're going to need some kind of correction in your left shoe, maybe a custom orthotic, maybe just a riser for your heel."

"The fun never ends," Owen said. "Thanks. I'll get this taken care of. I've already got an off-the-shelf thingy for my heel, and it helps a bit."

"So just think what something more or less made for you and your needs will actually do. Take care of yourself, Owen, and call me if you experience any problems."

And just like that, Owen was essentially done with PT. It had been a huge chunk of his autumn—that and adaptive rowing. He checked his watch again. Speaking of, if he didn't hurry, he wouldn't have time to talk to Nick beforehand, and he really wanted to get out of the adaptive boats. He couldn't wait to tell Adam either.

Adam. Owen sighed as he drove through the deepening twilight toward the boathouse. Nothing was ever simple. They'd gone from hands down each other's pants to...what, Owen couldn't quite tell, but it didn't seem quite as friendly as they had been, that much was certain. Then again, Adam wasn't unfriendly or hostile, just different. They still rowed together as much as possible, but there was a new tension that Owen honestly hadn't expected but probably should've. Maybe if he'd been better at relationships? He didn't know, but this sucked, and not in the fun spanky way. He really thought they'd be all up in each other's business by now.

He didn't even get a chance to talk to Adam either. Not like he'd wanted to. Sure, he was on regular equipment now that he was cleared to use his legs. Regular equipment, all right...the ergs. He had to learn to use his legs in the boat, something he'd never done in rowing. New sequence, new stroke, the whole thing. That meant no rowing at all, let alone having a captive audience to clear the air with. Did they need to clear the air? Is that what you did after you got caught with your hands down someone's pants?

And that was when it hit him. He could be such a doofus sometimes. He looked around the boathouse. There was no one around and he'd had about as much fun on the erg as he was going to, so that was enough of that.

He pulled his phone out and made a call. "Mike? You still on duty?"

"Owen! Hey, buddy. For another ten minutes or so, why?"

"Because I, uh..."

"The big bad fireman needs to talk?" Mike sounded amused.

Too bad Owen didn't feel amused. Why were all his friends assholes and what did that say about him? "Something like that, yes."

"I'll meet you at the Fox and Goose in a half hour," Mike said before disconnecting the call.

Suddenly Owen had something to do besides hate the erg.

Chapter Eleven

The Fox and Goose Pub was a Midtown institution, as beloved by rowers as cops, firemen, and everyone who liked traditional English pub fare and microbrews and live bands. The dim lighting and music made it perfect for people to trade secrets or bemoan their love lives—or lack thereof—or just pass the time after hours.

Owen beat Mike there, and it was a good thing, too, because he scored one of the last available tables. As it was, it was small, but it was in a dark corner that made Owen feel instantly at ease. He ordered two waters, plus a pale ale for him and a ginger ale for Mike.

He rose to greet Mike with a hug when he arrived a few minutes later. "Thanks for meeting me."

"No sweat," Mike said. He sniffed. "Except for you. What've you been doing?"

"Rowing." Owen grinned.

Mike snorted. "I never would've thought you'd be so taken with it, not the way you bitched about it."

"Well, there's this rower…"

"Aha! The truth comes out!" Mike cackled. "So, tell me about this rower."

Owen knew he was grinning like a lovestruck fool, but that was okay. Maybe it was good for the skin or something. "For starters he's a couple inches taller than I am, which is just fantastic in and of itself, with this amazing blond hair I want to run my hands through, and a chest I want to cuddle up against and never let go of."

"Uh-huh. Have you told him any of this?" Mike said. He regarded his ginger ale warily.

"It's okay, it's nonalcoholic, and no." Owen waited until Mike had a mouth full of soda. "But we did get caught at the boathouse with our hands in each other's pants. Actually, he was jacking us off while I fingered him. So, I figure he knows."

Mike snorted, spewing ginger ale across the table. Owen calmly wiped his face with his napkin while his friend recovered. "You bastard. You did that on purpose."

"Of course, I did. My finger didn't find its way up his ass on accident... Ow! That hurt."

"Next time it won't be your shin, it'll be your kneecap, and on your injured leg," Mike said.

Owen sulked. "Bully."

"Pervert. Now tell me the story."

Owen complied, with a slight interlude for their orders. "So, believe it or not, I'm actually grateful we were interrupted. I don't want whatever I can get going with this guy—his name's Adam Lennox, by the way, and he's a vet—to follow my usual MO. No more mayfly relationships. I want the real deal. There's just one problem—"

"You don't know how to do that, do you?" Mike said.

"Among other potential issues, no," Owen replied.

Mike sat back in his chair. "So, Mr. Love 'Em and Leave 'Em wants to settle down."

"More like Love 'Em and Gets Left," Owen muttered. "I'm tired of being the afternoon's delight. I want to be the boyfriend. I really like this guy. He's special. If we'd done the deed in the boathouse, sure it would've felt good, but what if that set the tone for us? Word on the street is that this guy's shy, but for some reason, he opens up around me. That makes me feel... I don't know, special or something. Like I want to be worth that."

"Wow," was all Mike could say. "So, what do you want to do?"

"I want to woo him," Owen said quietly, almost too quietly to be heard over the clatter of the band warming up.

Mike leaned forward. "So woo away. I don't understand the problem."

"The problem"—Owen leaned forward himself so he didn't have to shout—"aside from the fact that I don't know how, is..."

Their dinners arrived and after a quick thanks for their server, Owen continued. "The thing is, I've probably got ten years on this guy and I seem to be having this midlife crisis. What do I have to offer but angst, plus premature membership in the AARP and investment in Depends?"

"Don't forget Centrum Silver," Mike pointed out.

Owen said, "Unnecessary!"

Mike reached across the table and flicked one of Owen's ears. "What is there, less than a decade between you?"

"That hurt, man," Owen grumbled, rubbing his ear. "When I was in college, he was in junior high."

"So, how's that relevant?" Mike thought about it. "Let's back this up and start over. Don't make me flick your ear again either. He seems to feel something for you, and not just your admittedly well-endowed package. So, knock this junior-high nonsense off and let him reject you."

"Thanks! That's a little brutal," Owen said. Seriously, why'd he call Mike, again? He could've come up with this abuse on his own.

"But isn't that what you're doing? Coming up with reasons he'll reject you and beating him to the punch? Awfully nice of you to spare him the effort. The problem is, you're also sparing yourself the possibility of getting what you want. Maybe you should let him make that choice. The things that seem like reasons to you just might be nonissues to him."

Owen grinned sheepishly. "You fucker."

"I wish. This dry spell is killing me."

"I don't get why you're single. I mean, if I had a thing for smug self-righteous bastards, you'd be right up my alley," Owen said dryly.

"Ha ha," Mike said. "Mostly I just can't put myself out there. Work makes wanting to pair up with anyone a rocky proposition at best." He was silent for a time. Owen thought he had something more to say, but all he added was, "People can be real bastards to those they supposedly love, you know?"

Owen didn't, but he nodded like he did. Mostly what he saw in the line of duty was people who were grateful to be alive, and that tended to smooth over, however temporarily, any differences there might be. The sniping usually didn't start until the embers were cold, and by that time, Owen and his firefighters were gone.

They moved onto other, lighter topics and made their goodbyes, and when Owen left, he walked with a definite bounce in his step. Mike may have had a touch of the asshole about him, but he was Owen's asshole, and he knew he could count on him.

For his part, Mike sat in his car for a long time after his friend left, the weight of what he hadn't told Owen pressing down on his conscience. For Detective Mike Cabot of the Sacramento PD knew all about the man his friend wanted to woo. More to the point, Mike knew all about Jordan Sanders, the man Adam Lennox had gone to such lengths to escape from. For now, all he could do was hope that Adam was forthright with Owen and told him the truth about his past, because Jordan Sanders was one fucked-up son of a bitch and Mike never wanted Owen anywhere near him.

*

Thanksgiving crept ever closer along with the end of the rowing season, and Adam's puzzlement grew. Things seemed back to normal at the boathouse, or at least as normal as could be for a club full of gay men. For such a self-effacing person, Coach Bedford had quite a cult of personality. Or maybe that was Morgan's doing. Adam couldn't be sure, but he'd noticed that his coach's partner was not only a lot more outgoing but also relentless where Nick Bedford was concerned. He'd heard rumors that Morgan Estrada had poached every gay, bi, and questioning man off the CalPac teams this year, but no one was talking. A lot of the guys did seem kind of young...

"I can't figure it out," Adam told Steven. They were in the back room of the clinic behind the exam rooms, where Adam strove manfully to brush the teeth of one of the clinic cats who had other ideas about appropriate uses for chicken-flavored toothpaste and rubber-tipped brushes.

Adam wiped his eyes. "Owen's got his old swagger back, or some of it. You know, as much as you can swagger with a slight limp."

"Yeah?" Steven said. He was occupied with grooming one of the boarders, a friendly Chihuahua with a rhinestone collar who had certain expectations of her stay at the spa.

"Yep. There's no weirdness on his part or anything. He still lights up when I walk in, and I swear he doesn't do it for anyone else. Believe me, I've been checking. I've even seen him completely ignore guys flirting with him, and there are some seriously hot guys, younger and older, at CCRC. They've practically hurled themselves in his path, but he steps right over them to come talk to me. So why doesn't he call?"

Steven finally looked up from the manicure he was giving the Chihuahua. "Don't be such a dope. Why don't you call him?"

The way Adam said "Oh" indicated that he'd never even thought about it.

"Because I'm pretty sure your phone makes outgoing calls," Steven said, switching claws and colors, "and if it doesn't, the ones here do, and I promise I won't tell." He held the paw out for Adam's approval. "What do you think, the pink or the red? I can't decide, and Bathsheba here doesn't seem to care."

*

It took Adam a week to summon the nerve to ask Owen for his number. "You are being ridiculous," he told himself in his car one morning before practice, the second to last before rowing ended for the season. There wasn't much reason to take a break, in Adam's opinion, but the rowing "season" was a bequest from the East Coast. It made sense there. *If you have to chip through ice to put the shell in the water, then yeah, it's probably time to cross-train, but on the West Coast? If it's foggy or especially rainy, hit the ergs—otherwise why lose the time on the water?* "You're stalling," he accused, "and not only that, you're talking to yourself too."

Adam trudged into the boathouse in the predawn mist. The sun wouldn't be up for an hour or two yet, he thought sourly, so why the hell was he? Then he spotted Owen, whose face lit up, and he knew it was just for him. Sure, he felt a little conceited thinking that, but he knew it was true.

"Hey, you," Owen said as soon as Adam settled next to him on an erg to warm up. For a minute Adam thought he was about to be kissed good morning. He even parted his lips in anticipation, but all Owen did was hold up a large coffee. "Here, I brought you something."

"Oh, thanks," Adam said.

"It seemed so cold and dismal when I got up, I thought some hot chocolate might be nice." Owen smiled as he took a sip of his own, a neat trick while he erged.

That was when Adam noticed the dimples. He almost lost his grip on the cup. "Clumsy. I'd better set this down. I can't do two things at once in the morning, and it looks like breathing counts today."

They laughed, and Adam went back to kicking himself for not asking for Owen's phone number while a few people looked over at them to see what the fuss was about.

Coach Bedford posted lineups, and much to Adam's frustration, he and Owen were in different boats. Not a surprise, really, given their different skill levels. He could compete with the best of them if he had the time to put into the extra practices, while Owen...well, he hadn't been at this very long. He'd loved rowing with Owen while the shell had sported pontoons to keep it stable, but that was the thing with rowers. Put the nicest, kindest person in workout gear and he'd be screaming, "Set the fucking boat!" even before it was away from the dock. It was probably for the best that they not row together in the big boats for a while. A year or three.

But it also meant he couldn't ask Owen for his number. Oh well, it wasn't like he'd be able to write it down. So instead he made himself nervous for the entire practice, earning him several admonitions from the coach's launch and even a few snickered comments from Brad ahead of him. Now that he knew Brad better, he wasn't afraid to tell him to fuck off. The first time he did, Brad whispered back, "Better fucking off than fucking in the boathouse."

Adam didn't say anything. He didn't have to. All he did was throw the timing of the next stroke, just a little bit, only a fraction of a second, and Brad was the proud recipient of an oar handle in his back. "What were you saying?"

"Asshole."

And so practice went.

It wasn't until all the shells were put away and dried, the oars were back in the locker, and the rest of the equipment stowed that Adam managed to snatch a few minutes with Owen in the parking lot.

"Hi," Adam said, freighting the greeting with a wealth of emotion and words he couldn't quite say.

"Hi yourself," Owen said, smiling back. There were those dimples again, and damn, Adam just wanted to lick them.

"So I wondered…" Adam had to stop to swallow the lump in his throat. Why the hell was this so hard? He had a friendly audience. Real friendly. Or maybe that was the problem. He knew they could fuck, but he wanted something else, something more, and he was pretty sure Owen did too. So, the stakes were different, higher.

He honestly thought this sort of thing would be easier this far into adulthood, but then, why should it be? He'd met Jordan when he was fairly young, so when would he have developed those skills? He shivered. "Um…"

"What is it?" Owen asked, confused. It was right there on his face.

"CouldIhaveyourphonenumber?"

"What?" Owen laughed.

Aww, jeez, Owen was laughing at him.

"Never mind," Adam mumbled, more embarrassed than he could ever remember being in his life. What a stupid idea. Of course, Owen wouldn't want to go out with him, he was just a big clumsy fool…

He turned and ran toward his car, but only made it a few steps before a hand clamped onto his arm like a vise. "Wait, Adam! Don't go. Please."

"You move pretty fast for a guy with a limp," Adam said, refusing to look Owen in the face.

"I can when I have reason to. So, tell me, what did you say?"

"I wanted your phone number," Adam mumbled.

Owen tipped Adam's chin up. "Do you still want it?"

"What do you think? Would I be standing here making an ass of myself if I didn't?" Adam said, exasperated with the situation, but mostly with himself for being such a prat.

Owen smiled at him again and reached out his hand. "Your phone?"

Adam handed it over. Owen placed a call and said, "Now we both have each other's number" when it went to voice mail.

"You called yourself?" Adam laughed.

Owen nodded. "My number's now in your call list, and your number's in my missed-call log."

"Clever."

"I'm not just another pretty face."

Adam looked at the ground and said softly, "I think you are."

Owen took Adam's hand and kissed his palm. There was nothing obscene about it, but neither was it a chaste nineteenth-century suitor's kiss, and it burned whenever Adam thought about it for the rest of the day. Then Owen placed the phone back in his hand and closed his fingers over it.

"Call me," Owen said, and with a last sly, enigmatic look, walked toward his SUV.

*

Owen entered the last numbers and his younger sister Avril's face appeared on his iPad. "So, tell me, big brother, how's it going so far?"

"Hello to you too," he replied. She'd never had any patience, but now that she'd passed thirty-five and had three kids, she'd started losing ground.

"Yeah, hi, cut to the chase," Avril said. "Oldest is doing her homework, Middle should be doing his but could find an excuse to complain to me any time, and Youngest is in the bath. We're on borrowed time here."

"All right, all right," he laughed. "It's going okay, I guess. I put the weirdness behind me and just got back to being his friend."

"Someday, you're going to have to tell me what that 'weirdness' was."

"No, I'm really not. There are some things you don't need to know, trust me."

"But Owwwwen, we used to share everything," Avril whined, struggling to keep a straight face.

"Yes, and that stopped when I hit puberty. Like I said, I deliberately put anything uncomfortable behind me to help him do the same and that worked. Then I got on with the wooing."

Avril made a rude noise. "Such a ridiculous term. What else?"

"I've got his phone number and he's got mine. That was almost a week ago. I'm told he's shy, so if I don't hear by tomorrow, I'm calling him. I don't want to scare him off or anything, but this has been going on long enough. Oh, and the kissing his hand idea?"

"Yeah?" Avril said eagerly.

"Left him totally flummoxed. When I left him in the parking lot after practice, he was staring at his hand like it was burning. That's good, right?"

Avril shrugged. "I guess. At least he wasn't wiping it on his pants, right?"

"I s'pose," Owen said, suddenly feeling defeated by the entire prospect. His old MO seemed so much more reliable. Find 'em, fuck 'em, and farewell! "So, any more advice from the salon? Because any time I try to be smooth and polished on my own, I just end up looking like a fool."

"You realize of course that'd probably be far more endearing to him than anything my clients and I cook up, right?" The look of purest pity on her face made him feel pathetic, like the loser at love he knew he was. He rested his head on his arms. "None of that, now. We all have to go through it. You're just coming to it late, probably because when we were kids you couldn't be yourself. For what it's worth, Oldest tells me the little gaybies and baby dykes are learning it right along with the rest of them now, so that's something isn't it?"

"Bully for them," he sighed. "Any other suggestions?"

"Just be yourself, Owen. Follow your conscience. For all your tomcatting ways, you've got a good moral compass. Treat him with respect and go with what feels right at the time." She gave him a piercing look. "That's not necessarily—put the damn dog down this instant!—what feels good."

Owen chuckled. "Sounds like our borrowed time's up."

"Whatever else you might be dealing with, big brother, you don't have three kids driving you nuts. Just remember that. Call me about Thanksgiving. We expect you, and besides, you need a haircut."

"Will do, Avril, and thanks." He frowned. He didn't think he was that shaggy, yet.

Then the screen went dark. Owen wondered what his youngest nephew had done to the dog. He loved his sister's kids, but he was also glad he wasn't in charge of them full-time. Uncle Owen days were lots of fun for all of them, but they exhausted him.

Owen felt antsy. It was too early to go to bed, and he knew there was no way he'd be able to sit still for television. Brownies. They were the answer. He'd bake some and take them to the station he was visiting in the morning, set things off on a positive tone.

Cookbook, mixing bowl, dry ingredients, yep. Owen rummaged through the fridge, reasonably certain the eggs weren't too old. The weather had at least been cool when he'd bought them, so that was something. Yes, it was a bachelor's kitchen, but he liked to think the gay balanced it out to an extent. Uh-oh...cocoa powder. What were albino brownies called again? Blondies? Stupid name. *Please let there be cocoa powder...*

Just as he found some, his phone went off. He pulled it from his pocket and... "Damn," he breathed. "Hi, Adam."

"Um...hi, Owen. How'd you know it was me?"

Owen knew he was nervous, but Adam sounded like he was about to have a heart attack. "My cell phone has caller ID. So does yours, for that matter. I...uh, also programmed your name and number into mine, so your name pops up on the screen."

"Oh, yeah."

Owen would've bet that Adam was blushing furiously on the other end of the call.

"So...uh, how's it going? Work okay? Sleeping in with all that extra time now that we're off the water for a while?" Owen said, trying to fill the dead air and kill the butterflies in his stomach. The truth was now that he didn't see Adam several mornings each week, his life seemed emptier. Backing off and letting Adam take things at his own speed suddenly seemed like a dumbass idea if ever there was one.

Adam didn't say anything for a little while, but Owen knew he was still there. He could hear him breathing. Plus, the phone hadn't disconnected.

"Adam?"

"Can I see you?" Adam blurted out.

Owen smiled. Thank goodness for Adam blurting things out. It was already looking like they'd never get anywhere without it.

"Name a time and place," Owen said. "I'll be the one with the green carnation in my lapel. In fact, I was about to make brownies and it's not all that late. Would you like to come over tonight?"

Adam rewarded him with another one of his silences. It occurred to Owen that Adam might even be less experienced with this than he was. He'd just assumed his tall blond god had been on the receiving end of male attention ever since he was legal, but maybe not. Maybe his perfection meant he'd been unapproachable. Or maybe he'd come out late and hadn't dated.

"Hey, you still with me, buddy?" Owen asked.

"Yeah."

Adam's silences flummoxed Owen. Nervous, sure, but don't leave a dude hanging. "Well, if brownies don't appeal, how about coffee sometime?"

"Oh yeah, coffee'd be great!" Adam said.

"Tomorrow night after work?" Owen all but held his breath.

There was a pause on Adam's end. "I think that'll work... Yeah. That should be fine. But...do you mind coming to Davis? It's complicated and I'll explain, but I can't hang out in Sacramento."

"Okay, sure. Tomorrow night. Six p.m.?"

"Better make it seven," Adam said. "I'm almost never out before that. I'll text you a good place once I ask around. I haven't lived here long and don't get out a lot."

"Sounds like a plan, and Adam?"

"Yeah?"

"I'm really looking forward to it."

"Me too."

They disconnected, and Owen leaned against his kitchen counter, all bemused.

Then he shook it off and got to work on the brownies. Even if he couldn't have company, he still had an inspection tomorrow and a tradition to uphold.

Chapter Twelve

Even the next morning, Adam still couldn't believe what a fool he was. He leaned his head against the tile of his shower. "I should've come over, Owen. For you and brownies, I should've come over."

The thought scared the tar out of him. His reality was that he'd had only the one serious relationship, and just look how seriously fucked up it had turned out to be. No matter how much people like his therapist might say things like "It's just coffee, you don't have to date him" or "You don't have to have a relationship with him, you can just be friends," Adam felt like the two of them were already well on their way to being friends, far enough along to know he wanted more, far more, with Owen. He wanted it all with Owen. He wanted a second chance at love with the hunky fireman with hair the color of fire. He wanted to wrap his arms around Owen and never let him go.

"So, wait," Steven said later that day when Adam told him about the call. "He invited you over to his house to make brownies with him?"

"Yes."

"Do you like brownies?"

Adam nodded.

"And you didn't go?"

Adam shook his head.

Steven sighed. "You're kind of hopeless, aren't you?"

Adam folded his arms across his chest. "What would you have done, tough guy?"

"If a hot guy I'd been boning over for months invited me to his house to bake with him, I'd have packed an overnight bag and hit the road before we'd finished the call. Duh."

"Okay, then yes, I'm officially hopeless. I even knew that myself last night," Adam said. "I'm just so scared of screwing this up." He brightened. "But he invited me on a date."

"Yeah?" Steven sounded interested for the first time since Adam had started telling him about the previous evening's call.

"Yes. Where's a good place to meet for coffee?" Adam asked.

"That's coffee. That's not a date." Steven sighed again. "Besides, this time of the quarter? There isn't a good place to meet. Midterms are in a week. All the coffee houses will be full of desperate undergraduates. Your best bet is a restaurant students are too poor to afford. Or better yet, just make him dinner at your place."

"You don't think that's too forward?"

"Dude, you were jacking him off in the boathouse. I'd say the genie's out of the bottle, wouldn't you?" Steven said with a crude laugh.

Adam pulled out his phone and started texting. "You're a brat, you know that?"

*

Owen didn't recognize the address Adam texted him, but he wasn't that familiar with Davis. However, the navigator in his 4Runner bypassed the business district entirely and routed him into a residential neighborhood, and that raised his suspicions. It was either a hiccough in Davis's notoriously draconian zoning laws or…

A private residence. Yep. Owen parked his SUV in front of a modest house on a quiet street. It looked like an established neighborhood. Lots of trees. Not too many cars parked on the street. Not many people about, but then, it was the middle of November, so there wouldn't be kids out playing like there would in warmer months.

Smiling hesitantly, Owen rang the doorbell, and immediately a chorus of barking dogs greeted him, growing louder as they raced for the door.

"Who's there?" came Adam's voice over the intercom.

"I'm told this is the best coffee shop in town," Owen said into the intercom's microphone.

"I'll be right there," Adam said, laughing.

Well, that cleared that up, Owen thought as he waited.

In next to no time the door opened and there was Adam, looking edible in scrubs that barely contained his shoulders, and around him danced what looked like a pack of wild dogs, but in reality was only three, a chocolate Lab and two Boston terriers.

Owen could only imagine what wonders lay concealed behind those scrubs. Actually, he had an idea and hoped to find out firsthand in the very near future, at least if the dogs settled down long enough. "Looks like we both came here right from work."

Adam's jaw hung loosely as he took in Owen in his uniform. "You've seen this before."

Adam swallowed audibly. "Yeah, but it's still..."

"So, I can add you to the list of men with a uniform fetish?"

"I didn't think I had one, but apparently, I do, at least when you're wearing it. Damn."

"You should see me in my turnouts," Owen said with a wink. "Can I come in?"

"Oh! I'm sorry." Adam whistled sharply and the dogs settled, more or less. Hampered by his brace, Owen squatted somewhat painfully, extended his hand, and allowed Adam's pack to sniff to their satisfaction. "The Lab is Abulafia, the Boston terriers are Darwin and Huxley. The most recent addition to my menagerie, a lilac-point Siamese, will make her entrance in good time."

"Lots of animals." Owen looked up at Adam.

"Occupational hazard," Adam said with a shrug, "but this? This is nothing. I've had more in the past." A shadow passed over his face momentarily. Then he whimpered. "Did you say turnouts? I'll be drooling over the thought of that later."

Owen noted the change of subject. "You can drool all you want right now. I just don't think your neighbors need to see what I've got planned."

Owen shut the door behind him and dropped his gym bag. He didn't plan on wearing his uniform all night, and if there happened to be a toothbrush, razor, and fresh underwear in there, what of it?

The dogs as one moved to investigate, only to be beaten to the punch by an elegant feline. "Adam, your cat..."

"Yes?" Adam sounded amused.

"It's purple, Adam."

"What color did you think a lilac-point Siamese would be?"

Owen opened his mouth and then shut it, because in all honesty he had no idea. "She's gorgeous."

"T'Pau can be a bitch, so watch your hands if you don't want to be clawed."

As long as Owen was already down... "Oh, you're a pretty one, aren't you?"

T'Pau answered with a bloodcurdling meow that sounded as if she understood him. She craned her neck so he could more readily scratch her chin.

When Owen hauled himself up, she gave him the stink eye and another one of those raise-the-dead howls. "Sorry, my dear, but I'm not here to date you."

"No, he's not, so run along," Adam said, still staring at Owen and licking his chops like a dog in a butcher's shop. "You've got plans for me, you say?"

It would take a stronger man than Owen to resist being looked at like that. He'd never been able to resist being lusted after, not when he wanted the man in return... Not when he hoped for more with the man in question.

"Yeah," Owen said. When Adam slipped the deadbolt behind him, Owen grabbed him and held him up against the door. He used his greater strength and larger physical size to pin Adam, despite Adam's greater height and potential leverage.

Owen grabbed Adam's hands and, lacing their fingers together, held them up by their shoulders, and then launched an assault on his lips. After all those weeks of driving each other crazy at practice, after all the heated glances and weighted looks, after almost but not quite in the boathouse, Owen finally had Adam where he wanted him, or close enough, and he intended to make it something they'd both remember.

Beneath him, Adam shuddered as Owen ground against him. "That's right, you and me, and we've got all night. Let it out because there's no one to hear you scream."

But then Adam went completely slack, almost limp. Suddenly Owen was holding Adam up only by their hands. "Adam? Are you okay?"

"I...no," he sobbed.

"What's wrong?"

"I need to sit down."

More alarmed with each moment, Owen wrapped an arm around Adam's waist and looped the other one up over his shoulder, much like Adam had done for him that day on the boat ramp. He lowered Adam gently to the sofa and then spun around to sit next to him, still holding him. "Adam...can I get you something?"

Adam looked peaked; the only color high in his cheeks. He buried his face in Owen's shoulder. "Aw, jeez, a second chance?"

"None of that," Owen said, stroking his cheek. "Did I do something to upset you?"

"I... Have you ever wanted something more than you've ever wanted something in your entire life, but been afraid to reach out and take it?"

Owen thought about it. "I can't say that I have, no."

Adam looked up. "Then you're lucky, Owen. Very lucky." He sighed. "I'll go into more detail later, but my last relationship was a nightmare. Saying it ended badly is an understatement. It ended with me making an escape plan and sneaking away with the help of the few friends I had left. That's why we're here and not out in public, at least part of why. If we become serious, you may be facing a lifetime of eating in."

Owen wasn't stupid, and as a first responder he'd had enough training to recognize signs of domestic violence, at least once Adam started mentioning them. He suddenly felt like the biggest monster in the world. He slid off the sofa onto his knees before the man he'd just terrified by taking charge. "Adam, I am so sorry I scared you. I had no idea—"

"How could you have?" Adam said. "It's not like I go around with a sign on my neck. Kind of defeats the purpose of hiding, doesn't it?"

Owen wiped a tear out of the corner of his eye. Damn, they were a pair, two head cases. "You're...already, you're the last person on earth I'd ever want to harm or scare or...anything. I'll never do that again."

And then Adam was crying softly too. "But Owen, that's the worst part of this. When you did that? Before I freaked, I almost creamed my scrubs."

Owen started to laugh, but then he choked it off. "Wait...am I allowed to laugh? I don't really know what to do...or say."

"That makes two of us," Adam said, sniffling.

"Can...can I hold you?"

Adam nodded and Owen climbed up on the sofa next to him. He still felt the biggest jerk around but was calming down. This wasn't about him, it was about Adam, and his job here was to comfort his guy.

A little awkwardly he put his arm around Adam's shoulders. Adam seemed grateful for the comfort and snuggled into Owen's side, resting his head on Owen's broad shoulder.

Suddenly they had company. T'Pau, that crazy purple cat, jumped up on the back of the sofa and announced herself. "Mrrrrow!" She butted her head into Owen's, purring furiously.

"What's that mean?" Owen said, reaching a hand back to pet her.

"She's yours," Adam snorted. "Seriously, check your gym bag before you leave." He sniffled again. "Can...can I put my head in your lap?"

"Yes, of course." Owen raised his arms and Adam settled in, curling up like a little lost boy, only a lot taller. Owen abandoned the cat, much to her consternation, and put his arms around Adam as best he could. It didn't take long before he started to brush Adam's bangs off his forehead, an unconscious gesture of comfort that he didn't stop once he became aware of it. "This all right?"

Adam smiled up at him. "I think the cat's irked, but I'm happier."

Owen rolled his eyes and twisted one arm back to scratch T'Pau behind the ears, which seemed to mollify her.

"How about this?" Owen leaned down and kissed Adam's forehead.

"That's nice, but I think you missed your target." Adam squirmed and rolled over so he lay on his back looking up at Owen.

"I did? Maybe I should try again."

"Yes, I think you should."

Owen kissed the tip of Adam's nose. "How 'bout that?"

"Hmmm, closer, but no."

Owen pretended to frown. "Oh. I'd better keep trying." He peppered Adam's face with kisses before landing one on his lips.

"Finally," Adam muttered.

Owen smiled and kissed his guy again. Adam sat up and returned the favor, pulling Owen closer, all signs of his earlier trauma gone.

"I've been waiting all day for this," Owen admitted.

Adam licked his lips. "Me, too, so don't make me wait any longer, or I may do something neither of us would regret."

"Like what you did in the boathouse? Because if me dawdling gets us a repeat of that, I can spend a few minutes removing the brass from my uniform—"

A throaty growl was all the warning Owen had before he found himself on his back under Adam, but he rather liked it there. "Oooh, someone likes it on top."

"You know something? I think you're right," Adam said. He made himself comfortable right atop Owen's groin and then grabbed his hands and held them over Owen's head, repeating, unconsciously or not, Owen's own actions of earlier in the evening.

"I think I like this side of you," Owen said, his hazel eyes darkening. It was, he realized, a way around the problem he'd created earlier, but they'd need to test it. Just for fun, he fought back.

"Oh, no you don't," Adam growled, grinding down and holding him fast. Adam kissed him again, hard and punishing, and all Owen could do was moan.

"Please," Owen breathed.

"Please, what?"

"Please, don't...stop."

"For you...any—"

Then something intruded on Owen's awareness. "Adam, stop!"

"What?" Adam blinked as Owen struggled to sit up.

"I smell smoke!"

They looked at each other and then Adam jumped up. "Oh, shit! Dinner!"

Adam ran to the kitchen, Owen hard on his heels.

Smoke seeped out from around the oven, and when Adam opened the oven door, it poured into the room, flickers of orange showing.

"Close it!" Owen barked.

"What?"

Swearing, Owen moved around him to slam the door shut. Searching the controls, he turned the oven off.

"That was our dinner!" Adam objected.

"It was a fire," Owen said. "I'm sorry, but it had gone beyond smoking to actually burning. The best way to handle that is to shut the door to starve the fire of oxygen and turn the oven off. Do you have a fire extinguisher?"

"Um, no," Adam said, suddenly sheepish.

"Get one," Owen said. He took a few breaths. "I'm sorry, I didn't mean to get all Fire Battalion Chief on you, but it's important."

"It's also kind of hot seeing you all alpha like that."

Owen rolled his eyes. "We'll take care of you after dinner, Dr. Horndog. So how much is ruined? Do I need to order a pizza?"

"Since there was that much smoke and actual flames, I think the lasagna's a complete goner, but I should probably check," Adam said.

"If you point me in the right direction, I'll set the table..."

Chapter Thirteen

With all respect to his grandfather, who'd lived through the attack at Pearl Harbor, dinner was an event that would live in dating infamy, even though they'd laugh about it later. Who the hell ignites a lasagna he'd planned to serve a fireman for crying out loud? Even just knowing Owen a few months, Adam figured he wouldn't live it down any time soon. Oh well, humor was healthy or something.

"So where do we go from here?" Owen asked.

"Truth be told, I don't really want you to go," Adam said softly. What he really wanted was to drag Owen off to bed for a night of cuddling and maybe other things. Seemed like every time they got close to those other things *something* got in their way, and he was about ready to kill *it*, whatever it was.

"So, it'd be okay for me to admit that I've got a fresh uniform out in my SUV?"

"Since I noticed your duffel bag as soon as you dropped it in the front hall, yeah sure, admit away." Adam didn't say anything for a moment. "Since we're being so honest and all, can I fess up too?"

"Um...sure?"

Adam smiled at him, a devilish little smile. "I was hoping you'd spend the night but didn't want you to think I was a first-date slut."

Owen tried not to laugh. "Somehow I think we're beyond that, either the first date part or the slut part, I'm just not sure which one."

Adam flicked a bit of bread crust at him. "Bad!"

"Mean!" Owen cried, holding one hand over the spot on his cheek Adam had managed to hit.

Adam got up and pulled Owen's hand off. He kissed Owen's cheek; admittedly he missed the "wounded" spot rather often in favor of an oh-so-kissable mouth, but Owen didn't seem to mind. "There. All better."

"Maybe," Owen said, "but I think it needs more kisses to make it 'all better.' It's still very tender."

Adam stood and held out a hand. "I can only properly tend your wounds upstairs in the bedroom."

Owen smiled and rose. "I'll grab my bag."

"Might as well get your uniform, because I'm not letting you out before we have to get up for work." Adam waited at the door for Owen, mostly out of politeness but also to enjoy the view as Owen headed down the walk to his SUV.

But as soon as Owen returned, Adam locked the door and activated the alarm system. "See, Mr. Fireman? Smoke and carbon monoxide detectors, as well."

"Very commendable," Owen said. "You know, the fire department likes to give special commendations to eager and aware citizens like yourself."

"Yeah?"

"Definitely," Owen breathed, moving in close to Adam. He dropped his stuff on the ground, fresh uniform and all. He gently pulled Adam down for a kiss while he wrapped a leg behind to hold them that much closer together.

The full-body contact made everything hotter, despite their clothes, despite the knowledge of things he needed to tell Owen before they grew too much more serious, and serious was where he, at least, wanted to go. He could only pray Owen felt somewhere close to the same way, because sometimes you just knew.

"Upstairs," Adam said when they came up for air.

"What about the animals?" Owen said.

That Owen cared about his beasties... Adam fell for him a little more. "I ran the dogs before you arrived, and T'Pau will no doubt follow us upstairs in due time."

"They'll be watching us?"

The look on Owen's face made Adam laugh. "We'll shut the bedroom door, but T'Pau can open doors, both knobs and the lever-style handles. If I lock the bedroom door, she'll—"

"Make that god-awful noise, yes. She's in charge, isn't she?" Owen said, smiling.

"Completely."

Nodding, Owen scooped her up when he picked up his bag and uniform. But instead of resting in his arms, she scrambled up to his shoulders and draped herself across them. "That's different."

Adam looked at him speculatively. "She doesn't do that much."

"Is that so?" Owen leaned his head over toward T'Pau's and was rewarded with a lick and a purr.

Adam led the way upstairs, listening with amusement as T'Pau talked to Owen the entire way, and more remarkably, Owen talked back. He didn't suppose there were too many men who went with the flow like that where his animals were concerned. Jordan never had, but then in so many ways Owen had already proven he was utterly unlike Jordan.

They got ready for bed, as much a sleepover as a seduction. He noted that Owen left T'Pau on his shoulders as long as possible, going so far as to stand in front of the bathroom vanity in his underwear and uniform shirt while he brushed his teeth so he didn't disturb her. It might not show up in porn, but it was sure winning his heart, Adam thought.

Only when Owen had to did he evict T'Pau, and then he set her gently on the bed. "Sorry, my dear, but the shirt comes off, which means you have to."

"Mrrrow!"

"Don't get snippy with me, missy. You had a free ride upstairs. Take that tone with me and next time you walk."

If a cat could huff, she did and turned her back.

"I think I've just been told," Owen said.

Adam nodded. "You've been told." Then he got an eyeful of the man he'd hoped would be more than a friend. "Wow."

Owen pinked right up. "Undershirts don't really fit all that well, not even with tall sizes."

"Au contraire, I'd say they fit you very well." They weren't at the boathouse. Adam didn't even have to pretend not to look. "You don't look vacuum-packed, but close enough," he said, running his hands over Owen's chest. "Damn, you're hot."

Owen took Adam's hands in his own. "As much as you're making me shake, we should talk first, I think."

"A red-blooded American man opting for talking over sex? If I couldn't see your cock growing, I'd wonder if you weren't into me or something," Adam teased.

"Not into you?" Owen said, a hint of challenge in his voice. "Not into you? Huh." He walked up to Adam and put his hands on Adam's shoulders. "I'll show you how into you I am."

Then he fell backward, pulling Adam down on top of him, and grinning like a fool. "I'm here, in your house, in your bed, and I've just offended your cat, because I'm pretty sure we just bounced her off the bed. That's how into you I am. Here," he said, grabbing a hand, "feel."

Adam had to laugh. He did that a lot with Owen. "Yeah...you're into me all right. Maybe not the way I was hoping by now, but that's some powerful evidence right now."

"Damn straight," Owen said.

"Christ, I hope not."

They grinned at each other, and then Owen kissed him. Damn, Adam felt lucky right then. He had a hot man in his bed who was playful and liked his animals, and who didn't seem to mind charred food. He should probably chain Owen to the bedpost or something.

Instead Adam rolled over so he lay next to Owen with one hand resting on his chest. "You wanted to talk?"

Owen nodded. "I think it'd be wise, if only to clear the air about the boathouse incident." He took a deep breath. "Don't take this the wrong way, but I'm kind of glad we were interrupted. Not because I didn't want to, because I *really* did and I still do, but..."

"But what?" Adam said, starting to worry.

"I need to tell you about my past relationships, if I can even dignify them with the term." Owen stared at the ceiling. "I'm not very good at relationships, but I want to be."

"I'm not either," Adam said softly, "and I've got a lot of doubts about why you'd even be interested in me."

Owen turned his head to stare at Adam, cupping his chin in his hand. "Are you kidding me? Oh my God, you're the most amazing man I've met in a long time. You're tall, and gorgeous, and graceful. I'm ten years older than you are and kind of broken down and I've got a past, and after all that, I seem to be a bit of a head case these days. I don't get why you'd be interested in me when you could have anyone you want eating out of your hands. Hell, if that turned your crank, I'll eat out of your hand right now." He sighed. "The reason I'm glad we were interrupted is because it was too much like all the rest of my relationships." At Adam's confused look, he said sadly, "My relationships usually end with both of us zipping up and going our separate ways. I've been kind of a slut. I don't want that with you. Or for you." He swallowed nervously. "I want more than that with you. You're not a quick fuck to me. I want... I hope we can have a real relationship."

Adam grabbed him and held him tightly, like Owen would vanish if he ever let him go. "I'm damaged goods too."

"You?" Owen said. "I don't—"

"Me!" Adam said fiercely, suddenly angry. "Stop holding me up as some idealized image or something. That'll end us just as fast as treating me like a blow and go, maybe faster.

"You told me about your dating past, and no, the idea of the Golden Arches over you doesn't excite me, but I've got a story to tell, and when it's done you may realize I'm too much trouble after all or decide that you don't want to get involved with me. I'll understand if you don't."

Owen kissed him gently. "I'll listen."

"I met Jordan when we were undergraduates," Adam said quietly. "I didn't recognize it at the time, but what I took for passion and love on his part were actually jealousy and control. I just thought it meant he loved me, and that his obsessive need to know where I was meant he was concerned about me.

"He never liked crew, and I thought it was because he thought it was dangerous. No. He just resented anything that took my attention away from him." He found he could talk about this if he took a step back and kept his emotions out of it, as if he were talking about someone else falling into that trap.

Owen closed his eyes for a moment, holding Adam's hand to his cheek. "How'd you get through vet school?"

"He was in business school at the same time, and by the time he was done with that and internships, I was far enough along that there was no point in him derailing me, although I think he wanted to." Adam shrugged. "But by then he'd scared off all my friends, so maybe he didn't have to worry either.

"So, when I was done, he set me up in practice."

Owen whistled. "That's a lot of money."

"He had it. He controlled it all, just another way of controlling me," Adam said. He shrugged. "It was a very elaborate, gilded cage, but he left the running of it to me, and that was his mistake."

"What did you do?" Owen asked.

"Used it as a base to begin the process of escape. It took a while, but I did it."

Owen pulled Adam into his arms, which was where Adam most wanted to be right then. He felt safe and protected and above all wanted. "Physical abuse?"

"By the end I had standing reservations at most of the ERs in town." With that, Adam's control faltered, and he started shaking.

Owen held him tighter, burying his face in Adam's hair. "I am so sorry you had to experience that," he said, his voice cracking.

Adam tried to shrug it off, tried to say something strong, but all that came out was a racking sob. There in Owen's arms, he finally felt like he could let go.

Owen held him; he didn't know how long. By the end, he was pretty sure Owen was teary too. "Sorry to be such a downer."

"Don't say that," Owen said, kissing Adam's forehead. "Don't ever say that. I'm honored you could trust me with all that."

"Yeah, but I've kind of killed the mood."

Owen shook his head, his lips still on Adam's skin, his arms still around Adam's chest. Adam felt secure and cherished for the first time in… He couldn't think when he'd last felt like this. Maybe ever? "There'll be other days and nights."

Adam knew he was right, and his relief far outweighed his disappointment at yes, not having Owen in him, or he in Owen. Then, too, he had to admit that being held by a hardbody who genuinely cared had a lot to recommend it, especially one who passed muster with his beasties.

"I could fall asleep right here," Adam murmured.

"So could I," Owen replied, "although we really do need a few flea bags to make it complete."

"My animals do not"—Adam pretended to be offended—"have fleas."

But that didn't stop him from whistling for the dogs, who came bounding in and then jumped on the bed.

"I'm guessing you don't have pets of your own?" Adam said.

"Nope. Before my promotion I could be away from home for days at a time. It didn't seem fair," Owen said, "and I've missed them. Where's T'Pau? I need a cat."

Owen made what Adam supposed were summoning noises. They just made him giggle. "You realize no one's ever been able to get a cat to come when called, right? Least of all a Siamese?"

"You mean like this one?" Owen said smugly as T'Pau jumped up on the bed with a "Mrrow?" up near their heads.

Owen reached up to scratch her behind the ears as Adam muttered, "Turncoat."

"Which one of us?" Owen asked with a snicker.

"Both."

Owen pulled his hand back, only to be chastised by T'Pau when she reached out to swat him. "Ow!" But he was not to be dissuaded, and once again held Adam. "Sorry, T'Pau, but boyfriends come first."

"Am I? Your boyfriend I mean?"

Adam felt Owen freeze. "I'm sorry. That was probably too much, too soon. I didn't think. Was that what your ex did? Too possessive? Maybe I could call you my guy instead—"

Adam shut him down with a kiss. "I want to be your boyfriend or your guy or whatever we choose to call it. That you're even worried about smothering me or setting me off tells me everything I need to know."

"I don't want to do anything that makes you feel like I'm Jordan, but I'm not always going to realize it if I do. Will you tell me if I do something that triggers anything?" Owen said. He'd buried his face in Adam's hair again.

Adam nodded. "I'll do my best."

"Good," Owen said, kissing the back of Adam's neck, which made him shiver, but in the good way. "I've never wanted to be around anyone as much as I want to be around you. I could do anything with you and be happy. I could run errands with you or take out the trash with you or...or...anything and be happy because it'd be with you. Am I making sense?"

"Yes," Adam said. He yawned. "I don't know about you, but I get up early."

Owen chuckled. "I have to drive back to Sacramento."

Adam reached up to turn the light off and then rolled over to face Owen. "Goodnight, boyfriend."

Owen smiled in the darkness. "Goodnight, boyfriend."

Their goodnight kisses kept them awake a good while longer, however.

Chapter Fourteen

Sometime during the night, they'd switched positions and Owen was now the little spoon, but that was nice, too, Owen thought, especially what he felt digging into his butt. It really wouldn't take all that much to lose the underwear...

He wondered if Adam were awake, and he if weren't, if he might be amenable to waking up. Only one way to find out. He ground back against his boyfriend's crotch. Boyfriend. He sure liked the sound of that. He hoped Adam still felt the same way when the sun came up.

Owen reached down and freed himself from his briefs. He stroked himself lazily. It was a lot more fun with a cock pointed at his ass than doing it by himself, that was for sure, besides which, once he'd seen Adam that day no one else had done it for him. He was quickly moving from wanting it to needing it.

With his free hand, Owen reached back to see if he couldn't interest Adam. He fumbled with Adam's boxers, but quickly found what he was looking for. It helped that Adam's own cock wanted to be found. Free willy, indeed.

"What're you doing?" Adam mumbled into his neck.

Owen grinned in the darkness. "You know what I'm doing."

"It's the middle of the night."

"You know you want to." Owen knew he was winning because he felt Adam start to thrust back.

"Damn you," Adam muttered. Then he jerked Owen's underwear down and started thrusting between his legs. "That what you wanted?"

"It's a start," Owen said a little breathlessly. The rough slide of Adam's cock through his legs drove him wild; the way it poked between his legs, sliding down over his hole to nudge his sac made him want to howl. It made him want to beg. "Damn, you'd better be prepared to follow that up."

"You want that, do you?" Adam growled. He pulled his cock away and was that Owen whimpering like a bitch? The covers were thrown back, the light was switched on, and then Owen was pushed—none too gently—onto his belly. "This what you wanted? You're mine now, and I'm gonna make sure you know it."

Oh jeez, this just made Owen's head swim. It'd been a long time since he'd found anyone who liked to play like this, and here it was the not as shy and quiet as he seemed Adam. "Do it. Mark me."

"Oh, I will," Adam purred. "Hmmm, I love a ginger ass, so creamy and white."

"Yeah?" Owen wiggled for Adam's benefit. "Ow! Oh..." The sting of the bite was tempered with Adam's tongue as he probed Owen's opening.

"You like that?" Adam said.

"Yeah," Owen said, dazed by the surprises his seemingly quiet boyfriend held. This time, when the bite came to the other cheek, he was more prepared, and the sting was mitigated by Adam's finger seeking and finding his prostate. The combination of pleasure and pain was a heady one, and his own cock was soon hard and leaking.

But Adam wasn't done with him, not even close. "Roll over. Lose your T-shirt and underwear."

Owen scrambled to comply as Adam stripped off his own T-shirt and then kicked off his boxers. He looked up at his boyfriend, suddenly just a bit uncertain. Sex seemed to have awakened something in Adam that Owen didn't know existed, something he hadn't imagined, something that made him apprehensive.

But then Adam looked down at him and smiled, a warm and loving smile so at odds with the growling biter who was going to fuck the daylights out of him in a few minutes. Owen looked up at him, reassured, ready.

He pulled his legs up and Adam grinned. Adam dropped to his knees and pushed Owen's knees even further out of the way. "Now, where was I... Oh yes, here we go."

Adam caressed Owen's butt cheeks, pushing them gently outward. He bent down and flicked Owen's entrance again with his tongue, teasing the sensitive flesh. Owen threw his head back, right back where he was.

But Adam kept going, working his way up Owen's taint, licking experimentally at his sac. Owen let go of one leg and ran his hands through Adam's hair, affectionately yes, but also exerting slight downward pressure.

"Not a fan?" Adam guessed.

Owen shook his head. "Not really. Cock or ass, and I'm yours."

"I know someone loves getting rimmed," Adam said. He lowered his head and went to work. He started with a subtle tease, a warm lapping at Owen's hole that had him feeling relaxed and sensual in no time at all.

Adam looked up at him, a wicked gleam in his eyes. Then he smacked one of Owen's ass cheeks hard enough to sting. Owen gasped at the sudden intrusion of pain, but just as swiftly came a full-on assault with Adam's tongue. "Oh, damn," Owen gasped. "Yeah."

Within moments Owen was clawing at the sheets and canting his pelvis upward, trying to get closer to the source of the pleasure. "Adam…"

"Yeah?" he said, smirking. "Tell me what you need."

"You," Owen huffed. "I need you."

"Owen, you've got me. I'm not going anywhere."

Owen raised his head. "But all your working parts are out of reach. Fortunately, I have an idea."

"Oh?"

"This old dog's learned a few tricks. Now lay down on the bed belly up, please."

Adam complied, and when he was comfortable, Owen climbed on.

"Why didn't you just tell me you wanted to sit on my face?" Adam said.

Owen rolled his eyes. "Because that's not just what I'm doing. I'm also going to suck your brains out of your dick."

"That's a pretty tall claim there, Hose Boy. This is just a sixty-nine variant."

"'Just,' he says. If I don't deliver, I'll fuck you," Owen said. He felt Adam opening him, he felt himself relaxing. He knew Adam could go much deeper this way. He loved being rimmed. Truthfully, he could come just from this, plus some strokes on his cock, which he now stayed carefully away from. He wanted his first time with Adam to go on and on and on.

Owen lapped at Adam's cock for a few minutes, just playing and experimenting for the best angle of attack.

"I've still got my brains, Hose Boy," Adam growled.

"Can't have that." With that, Owen leaned forward just a bit and then swallowed Adam's cock down to the root. He had to hold his breath until he mastered his gag reflex, but the strangled noises coming from Adam made it all worth it. Breathing through his nose, he worked Adam's cock with the soft muscles of his throat.

"Owen..."

Owen reached back with one hand and found one of Adam's nipples and started circling it with his fingernail, not too much sensation, just enough to let Adam know it was there.

"Damn, you've gotta stop," Adam gasped.

Owen smirked around Adam's cock and simply sucked harder. But he pinched off the base. He wasn't stupid. He shook his ass in Adam's face.

Adam smacked his ass, hard, and as Owen opened his mouth to protest, he slid out from under him. "You won," he panted, "and if I didn't want to fuck you in the worst way, I'd love for you to suck my brains out my dick. Now hang on to the headboard."

Owen looked over his shoulder at Adam, and that look in his eyes was back. Adam's eyes were black with desire and hunger; Owen's earlier ministrations had done nothing to satisfy him, they'd only aroused him further.

Adam lunged for his nightstand and all but yanked the top drawer open. He threw condoms kand lube on the bed. He reached for the lube, but Owen beat him to it.

Owen held Adam's gaze as he popped the top and slowly dribbled lube into his hand. He reached around and worked it into his hole. He let his enjoyment show as he slowly worked his hole, now hypersensitive after Adam's marathon rimming.

He went back for more lube, and this time Adam tracked his every move. He placed his gel-covered fingertips inside his entrance, working them up inside himself. With his free hand, slick with lube, he started playing with one nipple. He looked at Adam from half-lidded eyes. Sure, everything he was doing felt amazing, but what Owen really sought was Adam's reaction.

Just as Owen reached for more lube, Adam growled, "You're trying to kill me."

"No, I'm just getting warmed up," Owen said.

Suddenly Adam was in his face. "You're plenty hot enough as it is. You know what I think?"

Owen shook his head.

"I think you're teasing me," Adam breathed. "Tormenting me."

"Would I do that?" Owen said. He reached out to play with Adam's nipples.

"Fuck yes!"

Owen leaned down to run his tongue over the sensitive nubs. At first Adam let him, seemingly trapped in the spell of sensation and attraction Owen wove about him, but then he shook his head. He grabbed Owen's hands and turned one toward him before roughly kissing one of his wrists. "You're destroying me," Adam said hoarsely. "Put the condom on me."

Owen ran his lube-slicked hand up and down Adam's cock a few times, coating it. Adam cried out, resting his head on Owen's shoulder. Owen kissed him on the lips before moving to the sensitive skin right below his jaw. He nipped and sucked as he gently rolled the condom down Adam's shaft.

Few of Owen's previous liaisons had stuck around long enough to find out, but despite the sometimes gruff exterior, there existed within the broad-shouldered firefighter a man with a taste for being dominated. Somehow Adam had picked up on it, and when he spun Owen around and pushed him onto the headboard, he filled Owen with racking shudders of pleasure. After all they'd done, a bit more play and Adam could have made him come.

"Adam…" Owen gasped.

Adam didn't say anything. He knelt behind his lover and without preamble, he speared him. Owen cried out.

"Too much?" Adam said.

"No, dammit. More!"

With a wicked grin, Adam gave Owen what he wanted.

Owen rested his head on his forearms, on his way to heaven as Adam drove him higher and higher. Adam braced his hands on either side of him as he settled into a rhythm of long, smooth strokes. Owen pushed out to meet each one, unable to get enough of the man filling him.

"Like that, huh?" Adam said. Owen could hear the challenge in his voice.

He nodded.

"Then you'll love this."

And with that, Adam took up a harder, fast cadence. He slammed in Owen, pushing him into the headboard with each stroke. He leaned down and bit the back of Owen's neck, not hard enough to draw blood, but hard enough to leave a mark that would linger. That, definitely. "You're mine, Owen. Mine."

"Uh-huh" was all Owen could say, because it was true. "Close."

Adam moved closer to Owen. He wrapped his arms around him, holding him tight. He reached down and started stroking Owen's leaking cock. Adam rubbed his face, bristly with almost a full day's growth of beard, over Owen's back. It scratched him, but somehow it only made the pleasure more intense and Owen arched into it.

"Yes," Owen breathed, "yes." He felt like he was coming apart, like Adam was the only thing holding him together. He shook with the force of it even as he felt it building higher and more powerful within him. His vision grew dim and all he saw was a blood-red heat rising all around him. All he felt was Adam holding him and a pleasure so intense it hurt centered at the root of his cock.

"Adam!" screamed Owen as his orgasm exploded forth, ripped from him by their lovemaking. He felt himself slipping away, unconsciousness creeping in as his orgasm dwindled and vanished.

*

"Owen," Adam breathed as he reached his own shuddering orgasm, quieter, but no less intense. "Jeez, Owen."

Adam rocked, slowing to a stop. Sheened with sweat, he rested on Owen's back, his head resting next to Owen's, his arms still surrounding Owen, his cock still inside. He felt Owen going limp, his legs buckling.

"Owen? Owen!" Adam called, but received no response. Despite his own strong climax, he forced his legs and arms to work and quickly slid off Owen's back. He gently lowered Owen to the bed, rolling him over on his back. Then Adam discarded the condom.

Adam checked for a pulse, and yes, Owen still breathed. He stroked Owen's cheek. "Owen. Wake up. You're scaring me."

*

Owen's eyes fluttered. When he saw Adam, he smiled. "Wow. I've never done that before."

"What, you've never scared the crap out of a fuck before?" Adam tried to sound light, but his voice shook.

"You are not," Owen said, the smile sliding from his face, "a 'fuck.' You're my boyfriend."

Adam rested his head on Owen's. "You scared me."

Owen put his arms around Adam. "I didn't mean to. It's not like I had any control over it."

"I know," Adam said softly. "I was still scared, though."

Owen kissed him. "Think of it as a testimony to your sexual prowess."

"I'm amazing, aren't I?"

"Don't go getting a swelled head, now."

"It's kind of hard to fuck you without one."

Owen shook his head. "That was really bad."

"But you just said I was really good. Which is it?" Adam said.

Owen pulled him down. "I want a cuddle."

"If I'd have known you were such a pushy bottom..." But that didn't stop Adam from putting his arms around Owen and snuggling up close to him.

"The term is power bottom, and I'm not even that much of a bottom," Owen said. He yawned.

"Sure, Owen." Adam didn't sound convinced.

"I'm not," Owen said softly. "Now if you don't mind, I'd like to get some sleep. Someone who really needs to be checked for lycanthropy woke me up in the middle of the night to satisfy his carnal lusts."

"You just keep living in the dream world of yours," Adam said as he reached over to turn off the lamp.

They settled down together, cuddling and holding each other as a light doze stole over them...and then the alarm went off.

*

Adam regarded Owen with amusement and something much stronger than fondness, something that frightened him a little, as his new boyfriend stood there, blinking and squinting in the bathroom's bright light. And scratching. There was definitely scratching of the manly variety going on. Adam realized if he didn't get busy with water and towels, he'd watch Owen scratch that yummy ginger fur all morning. Then he realized it wouldn't be that long because he'd start fucking him again. Hmmm, shower sex. That had possibilities.

Adam pointed Owen toward the shower. "Go turn the water on."

"I'm not really awake," Owen grumbled.

"And whose fault is that?"

"I don't know. Some horny werewolf jumped me in the middle of the night," Owen harrumphed. "I've got bites all over my back to prove it too."

"Yeah, and he gave you the best sex of your life. Admit it."

Owen got a big, goofy smile. "Hehe. Yeah."

"So, go turn the water on while I get fresh towels for us both."

The linen closet in the en suite bathroom was big enough to hold toiletries and not much more, so Adam kept the bath linens in a closet out in the bedroom, which was a good thing, because he got to the condom just before Darwin did. That would've been a mess.

He grabbed a stack of fluffy towels, the body-sheet size since they were both so tall. On a whim, he picked up the lube and more condoms. Just in case. When he opened the bathroom door, Owen was in the shower, and based on the mild grumbling, the water was getting into the bite marks.

Adam set the stack down on the toilet and knocked on the glass enclosure. "Is there room for one more?" He knew full well there was. One of the reasons he'd rented this house, besides the liberal pet policy, was the large shower in the master bedroom.

Owen, still bleary-eyed, smiled at him and opened the door. "Hey, you," he said, pulling him in for a hug. "I was just about to soap up. Can you soap my back?"

"That sounds like an invitation to trouble if ever there was one," Adam said. Somehow the sight of Owen in his shower the morning after scorching sex seemed right.

Owen made room for him and Adam stepped in the shower. Adam wetted his hair down, but he soon found a wet Owen in his personal space and also found that he liked it. A lot. "Good morning," Adam said.

"Good morning to you too," Owen said. He put his arms around Adam and held him for a moment, resting his head on Adam's shoulder.

Adam ran his hands gently up and down Owen's back, caressing and soothing and enjoying the broad muscles. "Boy, I really did bite a lot, didn't I?"

"Mmm hmmm," Owen murmured, content where he was, "and I'll get hard every time I think about it."

Adam reached down between them. "I hate to break it to you, but you're getting hard now."

"Am I? How 'bout that, but you know, if you're not going to do anything about it, you're just a tease. Wash my back?"

Adam chuckled. "Opportunist."

"There's a reason that cat of yours and I get along so well."

Adam did as he was asked, gently soaping Owen's back and as an added bonus, giving him a bit of a massage as well. He loved touching his boyfriend. "Turn around."

Owen did as instructed, and Adam washed his front for him. He knelt to wash Owen's legs and caught sight of the scars on the left leg and gasped. He couldn't help it. "Oh, Owen... I had no idea."

"How could you?" Owen said, as Adam hugged him tightly.

The thought that someone could be so damaged by random chance... Adam might've specialized in animals, but he was still a healer, and he hated the thought of what Owen must've been through, still might go through, depending on the circumstances. He knew Owen hadn't put the leg brace away permanently.

"No shower sex?" Owen asked.

"Not if you want to get to work anything close to on time." Adam laughed.

"We could skip breakfast." Owen held out his hand for the soap and started washing Adam.

"Tempting, but the alarm's already set for the bare minimum I need. Usually I shower at the clinic after I've done the dirty work," Adam replied. It was, he reflected, a fortuitous thing his boyfriend was a firefighter, because naked and in decent lighting he was even hotter than he'd thought, and with Owen running his hands all over Adam's body he might have to start something, after all.

"Then I'm glad you stuck around this morning. My feelings might've gotten a boo-boo if I'd woken up by myself."

"T'Pau would've kept you company." Adam handed Owen the shampoo. "Wash my hair?"

"Did someone say something about opportunism?" Owen said, but he took the bottle anyway and steered Adam over to the bench on the far wall of the shower. "It'll be easier if you sit down."

Adam tried not to moan, he really did, but as he sat there, Owen gave him what he could only describe as a shampoogasm. "Where..." he said, trying to remember how to speak. "Where'd you learn to do that?"

"What, the scalp massage? My sister's a hair stylist. Every time I visit, I get a high-end haircut for the price of listening to her advice about my life. When I come back from seeing her and her family on Thanksgiving? I'll have a new hairdo, I'm sure." Owen laughed.

Adam didn't say anything. He didn't know what he was doing for Thanksgiving, probably working, but then, he had nowhere else to go either.

"Time to rinse," Owen said. "Conditioner?"

Adam shook his head. "Just shampoo."

"Avril will be horrified."

Adam gave him the side-eye, trying not to feel bad about the upcoming holiday or the fact that being alone suddenly made him sad. "You're going to tell your sister?"

Owen kissed him on the cheek. "No, she'll figure it out when she meets you. We talk a lot and as soon as I tell her we're official, she'll invite you for Thanksgiving." He paused. "You know, I just assumed you'd want to come."

"I'd like to, but I'll probably be working at least part of the time. How far away does she live?" Adam felt a sudden need to hold Owen, so he grabbed him around the waist.

Owen scrubbed the shampoo through his own hair. "In the North Bay, Petaluma to be exact. You know, as long as I'm thinking about it, can you get some time off at Christmas? I'd love to take you to the coast. It's my favorite place on earth."

"I'll see. I get stuck with whatever Dr. Endicott doesn't want, but who knows," Adam said.

Owen beamed at him. "I promise I'll make it worth your while. Maybe spend a few days at the coast, head down into San Francisco, then finish up at my sister's house on Christmas Eve and drive home on Boxing Day?"

"Boxing Day?"

"Yeah, the day after Christmas when you traditionally box up presents for—"

Adam smiled. "I know what it is; I just want to know why you call it that."

"My family's from British Columbia, that's why," Owen said, laughing. "Anyway, does that sound like something I could tempt you with?"

"Time with you is all the temptation I need," Adam said before catching Owen's mouth in a kiss. He stepped Owen backward under the water to rinse his hair. "But now I'm afraid it's time to get out before we're both late for work."

"You're right," Owen sighed. "I hate being a grown-up, sometimes."

They dried off in companionable silence, and Adam marveled at just how easy it felt. They'd known each other for a few months, but this was their first night together. No awkwardness, however. Maybe this still counted as afterglow.

There was one hitch, however. While they'd showered, T'Pau had taken up residence in one of the sinks. Adam didn't think too much of it. She did it every morning, and it wasn't even the oddest thing she usually did while he got ready for work. But it certainly presented a problem when two men needed to shave at the same time.

But when Owen reached toward her, he knew he had to speak up. "I wouldn't if I were you. Just look at her eyes."

"But I need to shave."

Adam shrugged, lathering up his face. "It's up to you, I guess, but she's pointed on five of the six ends. I can always stitch your hand up if I have to."

"Some help you are. You could at least act concerned."

"I'm sorry, but she's a temperamental cat and she's not used to sharing. I won't take long."

"We'll see about that." Owen shrugged and turned the water on. "I adore you, you purple freak, but the two-paws needs the sink."

Adam looked on in horror as a wet purple cat shot out of the bathroom. "I can't believe you did that," he said as T'Pau cursed them both out from the safety of the top of a bookcase where she'd already begun the process of licking herself dry.

"I didn't see you doing anything," Owen said as he lathered up.

Adam shook his head. "She's never going to forgive you." No one ever listened when he warned him about T'Pau or her moods. He couldn't figure out why not. He was, after all, just her *owner*. It wasn't as if he'd reared her from the moment she'd been weaned or anything like that. Oh wait...

"We'll just see about that." Owen pulled a length of floss out of the package in his razor kit and went out to see the still-angry cat.

"Ha!" Adam scoffed. "Do you seriously expect to buy back the good graces of a cat as intelligent and sophisticated as T'Pau? Good luck with that."

Owen didn't reply. Instead he dangled the floss in front of T'Pau. At first, she played cold and aloof, but soon her feline nature got the better of her and she lunged. Unfortunately for her, she was on the top of a bookcase and she lost her balance. Owen scooped her up to keep her from falling and then set her gently on the ground. Trailing the floss behind him, he returned to the bathroom and ran the water for shaving.

"You're still bereft of cat," Adam pointed out smugly.

Owen shrugged, a smile playing at the corners of his mouth. "Just wait."

Sure enough, T'Pau, already bored with the floss that had stopped moving, soon started to pester Owen to amuse her. Sticking his tongue out at Adam, he picked T'Pau up and deposited her on his shoulders. "You were saying, dear?"

"That's not fair! My cat likes you better," Adam pouted.

"Don't feel bad. You still have three dogs to play with." Owen started shaving.

"Until you suborn them too," Adam muttered. T'Pau batted at the razor with a paw. He tapped her nose lightly. "No, T'Pau, that's not for four-paws."

Chapter Fifteen

He'd been right, Owen thought as he stared morosely out of his office window. If he moved just so, he still felt the evidence of Adam's enthusiasm even at the end of the day. For all that Adam's ex was an abusive bastard, he must've taught Adam a thing or three, because damn, Adam had mad skills, as the kids were saying these days.

What made it even better was that as they were kissing goodbye that foggy valley morning, T'Pau had tried to stow away in his duffel bag. He hadn't bothered to zip it up, but the only reason the purple freak had been caught was that the bag was heavier than it had been the night before. "Sneaky little miss," he'd said as he'd cuddled her before handing her off to Adam. "I'll be back, never fear. I will be back, won't I?"

"You'd better," Adam had said, pulling him back for one more kiss.

Picking lilac fur off his uniform gave him something to do with his day, and he found it far preferable to his actual duties. He didn't think he was still depressed, as he had been back when he was first dealing with his injury, but he certainly wasn't settling back into the firehouse, either, and every time a call came in? His heart raced and he broke out in a sweat. It was just as well he didn't usually go out on calls. He honestly couldn't say he could perform like he should. An engine running hot set off a panic attack, and why wouldn't it? One had almost killed him.

He stared out of the window some more, thinking, wishing he were with Adam. He'd rather be brushing cats and emptying litter pans at his boyfriend's clinic than drawing up duty schedules for firefighters and all those other administrative wastes of time. He knew they were a steady thing, but he also figured it was too soon to start texting hearts to him.

Then he thought, *says who*? Maybe not little <3s, but why not "I miss you"? Or he could even send flowers to the clinic with a note that read, *Tell your cat I had a great time last night*. He wouldn't even try to find any flowers that looked sexually suggestive. Maybe something pretty? Did guys do pretty? He so didn't want to mess this up. How many chances at something golden did men who were broken in body and spirit get with men like Adam?

He scrubbed his hands over his face, yanking his attention back to the matter at hand. A quick, cute text he could do, and he tapped one out. But anything else had to wait until he'd finished the next rotation's schedule. Not only did the men and women under his command deserve better than that, the people in their lives did too.

So, Owen bent to his task, shoving his own ruminations aside, at least until he was off duty. The paperwork wasn't going to fill itself out, after all. But he needed to find someone to talk to about...this, whatever this was, he thought as he stared out of the window as the rain started. Hmmm. Didn't Brad say something once about his partner struggling after he was assaulted? Maybe Drew could help him make sense of why none of the pieces of his life fit together anymore.

Schedules, Owen, schedules, he reminded himself, but he took breaks to check his texts. Adam was typically busy, but not so busy they weren't able to carry on an intermittent and horribly cute electronic conversation that was the bright spot of his day. At times it reminded him of the treacle of lovestruck teenagers, but then as Avril had pointed out, his generation hadn't gotten to do this as teens, so maybe he was entitled. He didn't dwell on the fact that Adam was younger than he was. At their age, it didn't really matter, and the messages were meant for no eyes but their own.

So passed his afternoon, with a break to e-mail Brad. Sure, professional help was good, but sometimes the personal touch worked better, and the job that Owen had fought so hard to win felt more and more like a prison. Something wasn't right, and he needed to deal with it. The dreary day, he reflected as he put on his overcoat, didn't help. Winter fog in the Sacramento Valley had its own Wikipedia entry, after all, and rain had moved in, even though the day had started out so winningly. He flexed his shoulders and yep, Adam's bite marks made themselves known. In a strange way, they comforted him.

"Have a good night, Chief!" one of the youngest firefighters called when Owen was halfway to his SUV.

Owen turned to acknowledge the woman, turning on his left leg...and went down, landing with his leg bent under him. It was a freak thing, but it hurt like a son of a bitch as his leg lit up like a neon sign.

*

"Sorry I'm late," Drew said as he rushed up. "Were you waiting long?"

Owen shook his head as he rose to greet Drew. "Not long at all, and if you give me something shiny to look it, I don't even notice the passage of time."

"Books on your iPhone?" Drew asked.

"Oh yeah," Owen said as they sat down. "Anyway, thanks for meeting me. I really appreciate it...under the circumstances."

Owen so did not want to have this conversation, but it was probably necessary if he and Brad were to remain friends. But Drew surprised him.

"It's okay." Drew looked mildly amused, maybe because Owen was blushing so hard he was practically emitting light. "I've actually been waiting for you to call. Brad said you might." He used his chin to point to Owen's leg brace, which ran from midthigh to midcalf. "That new? The last time I saw you it was nowhere in sight."

"Brand new." Owen made a face. "I fell at work two nights ago."

"And you raced right out to call me? Interesting."

"And you were watching me at practice? Interesting." Owen imitated him perfectly.

"Okay, I deserved that," Drew said, "and that's not how I wanted this lunch to go."

"How did you want it to go, then?"

"Look, I'm trying, okay? You're the guy who fucked my boyfriend, so don't push it."

Owen signaled the waiter. "Blew, and you'd let him think you'd dumped him, so from his and my perspective at the time, he was single." When the waiter walked up, Owen handed him a credit card, saying, "We haven't even gotten through ordering without fighting. Please charge me for whatever you need to."

"No, wait," Drew said. "Give me a chance."

Owen looked at him with burning eyes. "I could use your help, Drew, not verbal sparring, and not recrimination for something that you really should've worked out with Brad by now."

Drew sighed. "Brad made me come to practice one Saturday morning so that I could see you're not a threat to our relationship and never were."

Owen nodded. "True fact."

"You and that really tall guy—Adam?—were so into each other I don't think you knew anyone else was around, let alone that someone was there in 'civilian' clothes in the coach's launch spying on you."

"Probably not." Owen chuckled softly. "It's been that way since we first met."

"Love at first sight?" Drew said, smiling.

"I don't know about that, but definitely a deep and abiding interest."

Drew's smile deepened. "Brad also said you two made it really clear to everyone else not to get too close."

"We *what*? I don't think we ever said or did anything—"

"I'm just repeating what Brad told me." Drew shrugged. "For what it's worth, I don't think it was deliberate. It's just that you two saw each other and created your own little bubble. At least that's how it looked to me."

"Hmmm. Had no idea."

They ordered then, taking care of that task, at least.

"So," Drew said. "Coping after a major life trauma, I believe, is the subject of today's lunch?"

"Yeah, I was just... I thought I was getting my life back together, only to have it—"

"Knocked out from under you again in a rain-slicked parking lot at the fire department?"

"Something like that, yeah," Owen replied.

"Sucks, doesn't it?"

"And not in the fun way." Owen was silent for a moment. "So how did you deal with it?"

"With remarkably poor grace." Drew laughed. "I'd say I was horrible to be around, but I think I'd even managed to alienate Nick and Morgan by the end of my recovery, so for a while there may not have been any witnesses to the worst of it. Try not to let it get that far."

"Right, I'll make a point of not being an asshole," Owen said dryly. "It's just... Yeah."

Drew nodded. "Believe me, I understand. It takes time to get your life back to normal after a severe trauma—"

"Dude, I can't hear a fire truck without having a freak-out," Owen muttered.

"Aren't you a firefighter?"

"I'm in charge of five stations."

"Crap. I've still got days that are really weird, and my beating was almost a year ago. I still see a therapist, so if you're not..."

Owen nodded. "I am. I mean, seeing my scars can set me off. Sometimes all it takes is remembering what led up to it, since I can't remember the impact itself, thank God."

"And some days you don't know at all what sparks it, right?"

Owen nodded again. "How do you cope? How've you coped this long?"

"Sometimes, a lot of the time, I can talk myself out of it. I can keep it in perspective. Owen, we lived." Drew reached across the table to cover Owen's hand with his. "We had the shit kicked out of us and suffered a lot of damage, but we *lived*. My attackers didn't kill me. The fire engine that hit you didn't kill you. We can fake the rest.

Our doctors have pieced us back together and, sure, we're going to ache. I bet that leg of yours hurts like a fucker right now."

"You have no idea," Owen muttered, shaking his head.

"Actually, I do. I had to learn to walk again, so yes, I've been there. But we can walk. We can take painkillers if we have to. We're lucky enough to have insurance and we can use it to go to PT, and speaking of which, you need to get back there if you fell on city property. That's a worker's comp claim."

"That's what I did first thing yesterday morning," Owen said, grinning mordantly. "I'm not stupid and I'm not going to be a martyr. The city's going to pay for this and the city's going to pay for all of this. We firefighters may tend to die young, but if I die on the job it'll be fighting fires, not slipping in the parking lot."

"That's the spirit?" Drew said hesitantly. "Anyway, we're the lucky ones and it's important to remember that."

Owen found himself nodding in agreement. Drew was right. It could've been worse. "It seems like I was at my best after Nick Bedford's adaptive rowing program, and now that I'm not rowing anymore, I've started to slide back."

"You know, if you told him that, not only would it make his day, it'd probably help him with his project, especially if an exam could show any change physically," Drew pointed out. "Also, if rowing helped, why not look into using a rowing machine? I know they've got them at the CCRC boathouse, and you could always buy your own if you just had to have one without sharing."

"All good points." Actually, Owen felt kind of stupid. He had a key to the boathouse since he'd joined, and he knew some of the guys erged before and after work.

"Thank you," Drew said. "And you know what else? Some days I still can't cope, so I clear my calendar and stay home to hide under the covers and read cheesy gay romance novels. You learn to live with what you can live with and seek help for what you can't. But first—"

"You have to figure out what you can't live with."

Drew nodded. "Yes, and that's the hard part."

*

A blast of cold air caused Owen to look up from where he was helping Adam by entering statements into the computer to make some headway on keeping the clinic finances in the black. The woman who owned the clinic had some odd ideas about doing things herself, but from what Owen could see, the client volume argued against it. She might not have that many clients, but Adam was busier than a one-armed fan dancer. How he was supposed enter information about examinations, treatments, medications, etc. into a computer, send bills to clients, and then follow up for payment was beyond him. Frankly, Owen thought not collecting money when services were rendered was nuts. Maybe once Adam was in charge...

Some years it barely rained all winter; this year appeared to be one of the ones that made up for it, and Owen was glad he'd dressed warmly that morning in a soft brown sweater, even though T'Pau was shedding all over him at that very moment. She loved it when he wore cashmere, and he planned to stick around for a while since the roads back into Sacramento were already a parking lot, thanks to skiers heading up to Tahoe. The early rains meant they were already in skier heaven, clogging the runs up at Lake Tahoe before Turkey Day, but for everyone else, it just made life soggy. "Hey, what brings you in here?"

"Nice way to talk to a client, Hose Boy," Steven snapped. Owen spared him the barest of glances. He had some bug up his ass or something. Or maybe he was upset that Adam wasn't up his ass? Who knew? But meanwhile he was "busy" painting the nails of a Chihuahua who was apparently a regular visitor.

"Awwww, somebody's kwankypants. Did you miss your widdle nap?" Owen said in baby talk. For good measure, T'Pau hissed at him, or maybe at the dog.

Mike Cabot flashed his badge and then shucked his smart wool topcoat. "I'm here to see Dr. Lennox, but what're you doing here, you old dog?"

"Him? He lives here," Steven said irritably, focusing intently on the little dog's claws.

Owen rolled his eyes. "I had a PT appointment right before lunch and instead of going back to work, I bailed for the day and brought Adam lunch."

Then Steven looked up and his jaw fell slack. *Guess he's noticed Detective Hottie*, Owen thought with amusement. Adam wouldn't be getting any useful work out of him as long as Mike was still in the room, that much was clear.

"C'mon back, I'll take you up to Adam's office," Owen said. He hauled himself up using the desk.

"More PT?" Mike said.

"Mrrrrr," T'Pau rumbled.

Owen used his cane to point to his leg brace. "I fell at work. I managed to land on the leg my surgeons had to glue back together."

"Can you even take the stairs?" Mike said.

Owen grinned. "Carry me?"

Steven stood up abruptly, the Chihuahua tucked under his arm like a football. "Excuse me, sorry. Bathsheba needs to go out. Right now."

Owen and Mike, at least, saw the door Steven walked into.

"What's his problem?" Mike asked as Owen led him into the back of the clinic to the stairs up to the veterinarians' offices.

Owen took the stairs backward, holding firmly to the bannister. "You."

"Oh yeah?" Mike said, turning his head to catch a glimpse of the admittedly attractive younger man.

"Aren't you here in some kind of official capacity?" Owen said.

"Mrow!" T'Pau added helpfully.

Mike eyed them both. "Did...did that cat just talk to me?"

"If it sounded like it, I'd go with it. She's got sharp teeth, a bit of a temper, and she rides on my shoulders if given a choice." Owen reached up with his spare hand to scratch his passenger's ears and was soon rewarded with a rumbling purr, plus a head butt.

"She seems like a rather perilous pet," Mike said, eyeing her.

"T'Pau? She's a sweetheart, aren't you dear?" Owen indicated a chair opposite Adam's cluttered desk. He was pretty sure there was a computer under there somewhere but was also glad he didn't need to use it.

"Where'd you get her, anyway?" Mike asked.

"She's mine," Adam said, shutting the door to his office behind him. "Detective Cabot, thanks for coming all the way out here. I know this must be taking a lot of your time."

"As I said on the phone, I need to talk to you and it's the sort of thing I want to convey in person," Mike said.

"I'll be downstairs, Adam. I have the feeling this doesn't concern me."

Owen made it to the door before Adam said, "No, I think you'd better hear this, whatever it is, boyfriend."

"He calls you 'boyfriend'?" Mike said to Owen, smirking.

"You two know each other?" Adam said to Owen.

Owen shook his head, but at least he had his priorities straight. He knew which question to answer first. "Yeah, we met a few years back, Adam. I helped him out of a jam."

Mike snorted. "That's one way of putting it."

"And Mike, we call each other 'boyfriend' sometimes because we are," Owen said gently. He was about to say something moderately snarky, but then he remembered how Mike's one real relationship ended and swallowed the comment.

"Then he's right, Owen, you'll need to hear this too," Mike said.

Owen gimped back to the other chair in front of Adam's desk and sat down. "This doesn't sound good, Mike. What's going on?"

Mike looked at Owen. "How much has Adam told you?"

"I'm sorry, Owen, I've only told you the main points, but there's more I need to share with you," Adam said softly.

"Okay," Owen said as his imagination kicked into overdrive. What if Mike were here to arrest Adam? *What if what if what...* Owen stopped his mind from racing.

Mike exhaled. "I'll spare you the shouting match I got into with my captain about this case, but the short version is that the department has lost track of Jordan Sanders."

Adam sank back into his chair. "Damn. I thought you guys were supposed to be monitoring him for five years."

"We are—" Mike started to say.

"Or were," Adam snapped, his voice taking on an edge Owen had never heard before.

"Adam, why don't you give him a chance to explain," Owen said. "Maybe there's a good reason—"

"To lose the man who almost killed me? They told me they'd protect me. *You* told me they'd protect me. I took a big chance, Detective. Part of that was your department monitoring him through that 'special program' for first offenders." Adam laughed. "Five years, Detective. Five fucking years," he said bitterly. Owen had never seen his eyes that cold, that hard, that unforgiving. "I changed my name, I abandoned my practice, everything, based on that promise."

"I know," Mike said softly.

Name? His boyfriend had a different name? And police protection from the abusive ex? Owen almost spoke up but bit his tongue. This wasn't about him, even if Mike wanted him to stay.

"The last we were able to track him, he was in Southern California. All indicators were that he was leaving the country," Mike said.

Adam closed his eyes, trying to master his anger. "Jordan is richer than any of us will ever be. He's more than capable of buying tickets, setting up hotel reservations, or even making more permanent living arrangements, and then not getting on an airplane."

"For what it's worth, my captain's pissed. I think Jordan's testing to see what he can get away with. I've notified law enforcement throughout the state," Mike said.

"Wait, was Jordan even charged?" Owen said.

Adam shook his head. "Oh yes, he was charged. But since he's charming as hell and bought a team of lawyers, he was diverted into some program for first offenders. I'm sure if he shows back up, he'll talk it down to a slap on the wrist."

"So, what're we supposed to do now, Mike? Why're you here telling us this personally?" Owen said. Mike was great and a good friend, but right now Adam was in a lot of danger, or so it sounded.

"Because I don't believe the indicators. I think he's still in the area, so I'm going to do some work on my own time to try to catch him. For now, I want you to go about your daily life. I'll be working undercover in the area of the clinic, as well as your house, Adam. CCRC's boathouse, too, when you're back on the water," Mike said. "Since you know me, you may see signs of me. If you do, ignore me. Don't call attention to me; don't try to talk to me. In other words, don't blow my cover."

"What's going on, Mike?" Adam demanded.

"Any chance you'll just be quiet and let me do my job?" Mike said.

"At this point, not a chance in the world," Adam said. "I need to know exactly what's going on and why you're doing it."

Mike looked at Owen. "He knows, and he's the main reason I'm doing it."

Adam groaned and leaned back in his chair, covering his eyes. "Jeez, Owen, another hookup of yours? I know you said you'd had a lot of them, but suffering Christ, I had no idea you meant it this literally."

"Not now, Adam! We can go over that later, maybe when you're telling me what your real name is, but no, I have no idea what Mike's talking about," Owen snapped.

"I need you two to stop arguing. You have to stay unified. Jordan's not some kind of super villain, but he's cunning, resourceful, and obsessed," Mike said. "Right now, vigilance is your best defense, and you're not going to be very observant and aware if you're too busy sniping at each other. Owen, you saved my life. Twice."

Owen stared at his friend. "Awww, Mike, you can't be serious. The first was in the line of duty. The second is something anyone would do."

"No, it's not, which is why I was in that state in the first place," Mike said softly, "and why I took a leave of absence to finish this job. I'll be in touch, but in the meantime, try to go about your lives without looking over your shoulders every second. Not only will it wear you out, but it won't do any good."

"What should we look for?" Owen said.

"Ask your boyfriend," Mike said. "He knows Jordan better than any of us."

Adam thought about it. "Jordan likes two things: huge flamboyant gestures and small, subtle things that most people wouldn't notice."

"Like what?" Owen asked.

"Like...sneaking into a room and turning over one single thing that no one but me would notice," Adam said, shivering. "When we first started dating, he'd do things like that and leave little notes for me under the switched object. It was cute then. But now?" He shivered again, remembering what Steven told him about the business cards.

Mike and Owen looked at each other. "I'd suggest spending enough time at Adam's house to memorize all the little details," Mike said.

"Damn, that sounds rough," Owen said, smirking.

"That'd mean keeping your hands off me," Adam pointed out.

Owen frowned. "Maybe you should come to my house."

"You two work that out." Mike stood up. "I've got a job to do. Anything out of the ordinary, text me immediately."

"Should we keep you posted on where we'll be?" Adam said as he and Owen rose to show him out.

"If you're leaving town, yes," Mike said. "I'll notify my counterparts in other jurisdictions, even if I'm playing a little fast and loose with certain facts."

Adam motioned for Owen to sit back down. He appreciated it, even if things were suddenly brittle between them. His leg hurt again, and even though the painkillers were in his coat downstairs, he didn't feel like managing the stairs right then.

"Can I see you out, Detective?" Adam said, again in control of his temper.

"No, I'll find my way out," Mike said, "and again, I'm sorry, Adam."

Owen waited until the door was shut. "He just wants to ogle Steven without any witnesses."

"Oh really?" Adam said.

"I'm pretty sure. Steven was interested in him, that's for sure."

"How do you know?"

Owen snorted. "Call it a hunch."

Then it was just the two of them, without even other people to talk about, unless Adam's other identity counted. Owen was starting to think maybe it did. "Who are you? Really?"

Adam sighed. He looked far older than his years. "I was christened Alexander Johansson and went through most of my life with that name. I really am thirty-three years old, and I really am a vet. When I finally found the balls to leave Jordan with a lot of help from counselors and the cops, we decided that since Jordan has the resources to find me anywhere and whatever I call myself, and since I've got a profession to practice, the best bet was to hide in plain sight. So, my name was changed, but other than that, here I am."

"I don't understand why you didn't move across the country or something, get as far away as you could." Owen crossed his arms, trying to protect himself from this stranger, his boyfriend.

"Professional degrees aren't always that portable across state lines, and there are only thirty vet schools in the US. States tend to be pretty protective of their own vet med graduates. Given that in changing my name it no longer matched my transcripts or boards, it made sense to stick close to both the vet school I attended and the state capital with its Department of Professional Regulation."

It all added up, but nothing made sense, and Owen didn't know what to do or say. "It feels like my boyfriend's a stranger."

"Please don't say that," Adam begged, tears standing in his eyes. "Jordan can find me anywhere, so I'm hiding in plain sight. In his shadow if you will."

"You make him sound like a giant."

Adam shrugged. "He's...hard to define. Determined. Obsessed."

"Crazy?"

"You have no idea."

Owen looked at him sadly. "And he's got some kind of hold over you, even still."

"I'm trying to break it." When Owen didn't say anything, Adam continued, "Look, I found the strength to break away on my own. I made a new life before I met you. But...you make this life so much richer. I don't think I smiled that much before Brad brought you into the boathouse. After..."

"Brad mentioned something about that," Owen said softly. He hated this. He hated not knowing who Adam was, and he hated that Adam stood before him hurting and confused. Most of all, he hated standing there with his arms closed before his boyfriend, because he needed Adam too. He wiped his eyes and then opened his arms. "Please, Adam. No more surprises."

Adam rushed into his arms and buried his face in Owen's shoulder. "No more."

Steven knocked on the door and popped his head in. "I'm sorry to interrupt you two lovebirds, but you're really backed up, Dr. Lennox."

Adam looked up. "What happened to your eye, Steven?"

Owen snorted as Steven blushed furiously. "Um...nothing."

"Yeah, nothing that Detective Pump-A-Rump couldn't figure out," Owen said. "Isn't that right?"

Steven dropped the files he'd held. "I...uh, don't know what you're talking about, Hose Boy."

Chapter Sixteen

Thanksgiving was a nonevent, so far as Adam was concerned. He worked the entire holiday, and in more ways than at the clinic. He was tired, but he had plans, good plans.

Thanksgiving came and went, and he had no objections to that. Goodbye and good riddance. The holiday meant very little, although he admitted that if things worked out with Owen, he'd have something to be thankful for. But that was for next year. This year, someone had to take care of the animals, even if he did have to listen to T'Pau grouse that her new favorite human was nowhere to be seen.

She perked up considerably when Owen swung by Adam's house after visiting his sister and her family in the Bay Area.

When the doorbell rang that evening, T'Pau did as she always did. She hissed like all the hounds of hell had just crawled up out of the nearest sewer, and between that and the dogs' barking, it was enough to give him a headache. "You silly thing," he said, "it's Owen."

But when Adam opened the door, there was no one there. Probably some kids out doorbell ditching to ring in the winter holidays while their parents slept off the surfeit of food.

Then he looked down. He found nothing but a dead rat on the porch, its lower haunch apparently gnawed off. "Ugh."

"Fehhh," T'Pau opined from his shoulders.

He slammed the door, his heart pounding. Fumbling, he locked the door as fast as he could. They'd told him to report anything out of the ordinary. That was certainly weird, but reportable? Sure, dead, half-eaten rats didn't drag themselves to people's doorsteps, unless it was the zombie apocalypse, but he was pretty sure he'd have noticed something like that.

He slid to the ground, his back to the door, trapped in an agony of indecision. T'Pau jumped off his shoulders and raced for the relative safety of the space behind the sofa, where she continued to fume.

But how could he report this to Detective Cabot? It could've been something a stray cat left. But not the doorbell. That was the weird part. The doorbell. Well, that and the rat.

He'd just pulled his phone out to text the detective, and never mind that it wasn't Jordan's usual style, when he heard Owen's rolling wreck pull up. He pulled himself up and together. The last thing he wanted was for Owen to see something like that on the front step. Some welcome. He pulled the door open and kicked the rat into the bushes.

T'Pau must've heard their new favorite person because she raced out from behind the sofa, and only Adam's fast hands kept her from dashing out in the street. Traffic might've been light, but he didn't want to take chances. Putting his cat back together again wasn't how he'd planned on spending Thanksgiving evening, not when his boyfriend had just gotten there.

He wondered why Owen didn't replace his beat-up SUV, if not with something more current, then with something less dented. On the other hand, the 4Runner appeared to be indestructible, which was no bad thing, and its height off the ground made it easier to get in and out of, which was also a good thing since he insisted on reinjuring his left leg. How he managed the clutch with his leg in a brace, however, was beyond Adam's ken.

Adam watched Owen climb out and walk around the front of his SUV. He was comfortably dressed in jeans and a battered leather jacket. Really, was everything of his dented, scratched, abused, or otherwise put through the wringer? With a start, Adam realized he fit the bill, too, and thought maybe he wouldn't knock it, not if it brought that hot ginger sweetheart into his life.

Then Owen, his mobility hampered by the brace on his left leg, tripped on the sidewalk, but before Adam could reach him, he'd righted himself. "I'm okay," Owen said, sketching a proud little bow.

Adam had to smile. Somehow, Owen brought a style all his own to whatever he did.

"Mrrow?" T'Pau said in Adam's ear.

Adam couldn't wait. He hadn't seen Owen in a few days. He met him beside the 4Runner. "Hey, you."

"Happy Thanksgiving," Owen said, hugging him.

"It is now," Adam said, breathing in his scent, food and coffee and, under it, something rich and masculine and entirely Owen.

"I missed you today." Owen held on tight to Adam before reaching up to scratch T'Pau behind the ears.

"I missed you too. Let's go inside. All I have keeping me warm is you—ouch! Watch it, cat. I know how you're put together so I can take you apart," Adam spat. "Okay, I've got a living muffler around my neck, plus you, Owen."

Owen took Adam's face in his hand and stared into his eyes. "Adam, honey. You're standing on a sidewalk arguing with a cat. I want you to cut back on caffeine."

"Mrrrrow," T'Pau sniffed, sounding exactly like a huffy dowager as she crossed to Owen's shoulders and started digging at his jacket.

Owen sighed and unzipped it. "Look, I let you in, but I've got stuff to pull out of the car, so it's up to you to stay up there while I'm doing it, and watch those claws or you'll find yourself walking home."

"Now who's arguing with a cat?" Adam said playfully. *This must be what it's like when single parents meet someone who loves their kids,* he thought as the blood rushed to his head. And someplace further south. Suddenly he needed Owen inside now, before he made fools of them both.

Watching Owen bend over as he pulled something out of the front seat did not help Adam's growing problem. Neither did standing behind Owen, caressing that ass, so finely set off by the worn denim of his pants.

"Ooooh," Owen said. "Want something?"

"In the worst way," Adam said.

"Good thing for me I'm rested and well fed, then, isn't it? But there's just one little thing, boyfriend."

"What's that?" He loved this side of Owen, playful and fun. Between their discussion in his office and reestablishing their trust, plus his reinjured leg and dealing with his lawyer and the fire department, Adam hadn't seen a lot of that.

"If you don't back up, I can't stand up, and then we can't go inside and take care of things," Owen said.

Adam shuddered. Take care of things. Sounded like Owen was on the same page. He pushed himself up against Owen's ass. He couldn't help it. It was a good thing most people were away for the holiday, because he was tenting his scrubs in a big way.

"Easy there, stud," Owen rumbled. "You push me down you might never get me up."

"We can't have that," Adam said, but that didn't stop him from running his hands around Owen's belt, working his fingers into Owen's underwear.

"Adam, what's gotten into you?" Owen gasped.

"Nothing yet, why?"

"Oh ho! So that's how it's going to be?"

"Only if you stop dawdling," Adam complained. Damn, he had to get Owen inside right now.

Owen shoved back against him and finally! Adam thought he was getting somewhere, but it was only Owen with what looked like a brown paper grocery sack. "Here, carry this, maybe it'll keep those cold fingers out of my undies long enough for me to get inside, you horny little pest."

"Undies? How old are you, eight?" Adam asked.

T'Pau for once kept her opinions to herself, but she did snake a paw out from under the mantle of Owen's coat to take a shot at Adam.

"At least you don't deny that you're a horny little pest. That's progress."

"Hey, who're you calling little?" Adam said, kissing Owen's cheek.

Owen considered the matter. "I retract that word. Last time you fucked me I practically tasted you."

"What's in here?" Adam asked as they walked slowly to the front door. "And where's your cane? Don't think I can't see how carefully you're walking or that I missed that little stunt back there."

"At least I didn't go down," Owen sighed.

"Not yet."

"You're terrible." Owen rolled his eyes.

Adam grinned. "No, you called it. One look at you and I'm horny as hell and I'm willing to be a pest to get what I need."

"Okay then," Owen said. "Let me inside and let's get this put away."

"You didn't answer my question."

"What? Oh. Just some food. My sister apparently thinks anyone who didn't make it must be malnourished. The top layer is for you and your beasties, but there are some baked goods on the bottom for me to take to the firehouse."

"I like her already." Adam opened the door.

Owen nodded. "She puts on a good spread, especially when I bring what I can."

"You both cook, don't you?" Adam said as he shut the door behind them. He took a good look at Owen and his passenger. "You look like a hunchback with that stowaway under there, by the way."

Owen shrugged, earning him a muffled hiss, which for T'Pau passed as a mild admonishment. "Hush, love, or I'll turn you out. Come to think of it, I'll have to take my coat off anyway, but rude behavior means I'll hang it up."

Owen said hello to the small pack of dogs, throwing them treats from his pocket as they headed for the kitchen, but Adam wasn't paying much attention. He'd caught on the word "love" as it crossed Owen's lips. He knew his feelings for Owen had grown stronger and stronger, and as much as he really wanted Owen to dick him then and there, it wasn't just sex, not then and not for a while. Not for him, at any rate. But love? He didn't know what love was. Not anymore. Not after Jordan.

But Owen made him feel things no one else ever had. That was love, wasn't it?

"...but if we hadn't learned to cook, honestly, I think we'd have both starved with as hard as our mom worked when we were growing up," Owen was saying as he set foil-wrapped packages on the counter. "So, here's what Avril sent for the beasties. Since I know human food is supposed to be a big no-no for animals, it's pretty much just turkey—which I checked for bones—plus a tiny bit of stuffing for the dogs."

Abulafia conducted herself with a minimum of decorum, but Darwin and Huxley danced around their feet. Adam thought they were behaving admirably. He hadn't told Owen this, but they could easily jump five to six feet in the air. "I'll put it in the dogs' dishes while you get T'Pau settled on her perch."

In a few minutes they were both back in the kitchen, Owen minus cat and jacket. "You look amazing in that navy sweater," Adam said, "but not half as good as it's going to look on my bedroom floor."

"Wow, I bet that line worked really well on your frat brothers," Owen said with a smirk. That didn't stop him from pulling Adam closer.

"I was never in a frat. Crew kept me too busy."

Owen's smile broadened. "I was. I learned all kinds of interesting things."

"Did you, now? So, what do you have in there for me?"

"You think there's something in there for you?"

"I know there's something in there for me," Adam said, cupping Owen's groin and kissing him, but lightly, just touching his lips to Owen's.

"And you're right," Owen breathed. He kissed Adam back, light teasing kisses that did nothing to satisfy his need and only made his wanting stronger.

They stood there, kissing, exploring, enjoying each other, Owen leaning against the counter, Adam holding him there, and for that brief time, the world disappeared. It was just them. Adam felt like he'd never lived before Owen, as if somehow the man pressed against him had tapped him on the shoulder and pointed the way to a world he never knew existed, a world he'd been denied.

Adam broke free and rested his forehead on Owen's. "I don't know how you do it."

"Oh, that is simply not true," Owen said, breathless. "No one has ever done to me what you do."

"Yeah?" Adam kissed his way from Owen's full lips to his neck, sucking and nibbling. The sound of Owen's moan was both a goad and a distraction. He longed to do more and more to hear it grow, but he lost himself in the animal sound.

"Indeed, but—" Owen broke off. Adam felt him shudder beneath him, and so encouraged, reached down to caress him through his jeans. "But I'll be happy to give you pointers."

"That's what I'm hoping, and soon."

Owen worked his hands under Adam's sweatshirt and then tugged his T-shirt free of his scrubs and ran his hands slowly up Adam's abs. Not hard enough to wrinkle the material, not light enough to tickle, it felt just right. "Damn, you feel good."

"And you'd feel better with this," Adam said, pulling Owen's cock free of his boxer-briefs, "up my ass and soon."

"Sounds like someone's got a fire burning that only a blast from the Douglas fire hose can put out," Owen breathed, kissing Adam's neck.

"Can't believe..." Adam gasped. His leaned his head back, his eyes half-closed. "Can't believe you said that."

"Yeah, but you're not arguing."

"No, I'm not. Not with your finger on my nipple like that... Goddamn." Adam needed his boyfriend and now. "You ready...upstairs."

"I thought you'd never ask," Owen said even as he started working Adam's sweatshirt further up. He teased at the other nipple with his tongue.

Adam gasped as Owen took the nipple between his teeth and bit down carefully. "All you had to do was ask."

"A gentleman always waits for an invitation." Owen swabbed the nipple with his tongue to soothe the sting.

"Yeah"—Adam stroked Owen—"but you're no gentleman."

"I'll get you for that," Owen said before kissing Adam and then nipping his lower lip.

"Goddamn, I hope so."

"Then I guess I'd better get you upstairs and give you what you so obviously crave." Owen held Adam's hand and led him out of the kitchen to the c. stairs. He walked backward, smiling faintly and looking into Adam's eyes with his warm hazel ones. Adam saw something there, something that made him blush furiously, something he yearned for but was afraid to reach out and grab, something that gave him hope for a future different from his past.

When they came to the stairs, Owen paused, just for a moment, but Adam knew what it meant. Before his boyfriend could protest, Adam swept him into his arms.

"What! Put me down before you hurt yourself!" Owen said.

"Nope. I've got you," Adam said. He knew he could do this.

Owen flinched as they passed the second story, but Adam knew they were fine. No heads would be hit. He turned carefully at the landing to avoid running Owen into the wall.

"Okay, we're up here, you can put me down," Owen said.

Adam shook his head. He was enjoying this. "I've got you," he repeated, his voice softer.

"Okay." Owen rested his head on Adam's chest, and Adam felt his heart swell with more of what he'd seen in his boyfriend's eyes. This felt so right. This was what he'd wanted all these years and didn't know it.

Now came the tricky part, setting a man who weighed more than he did on the bed without dropping him or ruining his own back. Adam braced himself and gently lowered Owen down. He kissed him, forehead and then lips. He had to. He couldn't help it.

Owen had such a tender look on his face, like he was about to say something, but instead he sat up and pulled off his sweater, rewarding Adam with that view of muscles on muscles all wrapped up with ginger fur, just the way he hadn't known he liked it, how he hadn't known he'd needed it.

Adam didn't waste any time. He pulled off his hoodie and T-shirt in one fell swoop. "Pants or no?"

"They're coming off sooner or later," Owen said, watching with solemn eyes as Adam dropped his scrubs off his muscular legs. Adam met his eyes, and while Owen often seemed to joke, that night right then he looked so intent, so serious, so focused, as if Adam were the sum total of his world.

"So why am I the only one naked?"

"Because I was watching you." Owen hadn't buttoned up when they'd come upstairs, and he hitched his pants down his hips. "And because it's easier if I have help taking the brace off."

Adam nodded. "Of course, boyfriend." He started pulling the Velcro straps open. "How'd you put it on this morning?"

"I was a lot more flexible this morning before I made a round-trip drive to Petaluma."

"Why didn't you spend the night at your sister's?"

"Because it was important to me to be here."

Adam leaned forward and kissed him gently. "Me too." He hesitated. He could only imagine how the leg must feel. "If this is too much for you…"

"Help me get my pants off and I'll show you too much," Owen rumbled.

"Ooooh," Adam said. He'd lost much of his erection during and after their tender moments coming up the stairs, they both had, but now he felt it coming back. From the looks of things, Owen wasn't having any troubles either.

Adam eased Owen's pants the rest of the way down, enjoying the view the entire way. His boyfriend was turned on, by him and for him, and that just made him hotter too. He'd never known it could be like this, never known the emotional component could be just as important as the physical. He longed to share that with him.

"See something you like?" Owen sounded a little anxious to Adam's ears.

Adam smiled. "Yeah, I do. A lot."

He ran his hands gently up and down Owen's legs, both of them, trying to soothe the pain in the left leg without being obvious about it. Starting low, at the calves, he traced the muscles with his hands and his lips, kissing and kneading and loving on him. Owen groaned, and Adam spent more time on his boyfriend's quads, massaging them carefully, fanning his hands around Owen's groin, carefully avoiding his cock. His fingers edged closer and then danced away.

"Adam…"

Adam smiled. He loved hearing Owen whine with need. Then he lowered himself down next to Owen, still massaging close to what had to be a painfully hard erection, just close enough to tease. He exhaled on Owen's cock, focusing his breath so Owen would feel the hot, wet air.

"Aww, damn," Owen whined. "You're killing me here."

Adam looked up at him, trying to reflect with his own eyes what he'd seen in Owen's. "Never."

Then he licked the underside of Owen's cock from root to crown, smiling as Owen's shudder shook the bed. "Like that?" Before Owen could answer, Adam pulled the foreskin down, laving first the shaft and then the head, ending with the slit.

He lapped lazily. They were in no hurry, and the slower he played, the longer he drew Owen's pleasure out. They had all night, and Adam was happy to spend it making Owen feel good, making them both feel good.

When Owen laced his fingers through Adam's hair, it made him feel closer, somehow deepening the intimacy of their act.

Adam grinned as Owen's hips started bucking. "Hmmm, somebody likes this," he said before taking Owen in as far as he could. He couldn't deep throat the way Owen could, at least not yet, but he'd do what he could.

"A little too much." Owen grunted as he pulled Adam off.

"Why're you stopping?" Adam asked, a little hurt.

Owen exhaled long and slowly. "Because, as I recall, someone very much wanted some fucking, and that talented tongue of yours has me close."

Somehow, that was the magic word, because at the mention of it, the very thought of Owen using the cock he'd just been sucking on to penetrate him had his ass twitching. "Oh yeah, I don't want to do anything to ruin that."

Adam wasn't surprised when Owen lazily wrapped his right leg around him and used it to nudge him. He cooperated, turning over onto his belly. "You like me laid out, don't you?"

"I lo—like you anyway I can get you, boyfriend," Owen said.

Adam relaxed into his touch as Owen seated himself just below his glutes, and starting with his shoulders and neck, worked more of that scalp-massage magic like he had in the shower.

"You know what would make this better?" Owen said. "Massage oil. I'll bring some next time I come over."

"You're trying to enslave me through my body, admit it," Adam said. Somehow the need to breed, while there, had lessened as Owen's talented hands relaxed him as they traveled down his spine.

"Would that work?" Owen asked, rocking slightly. Adam felt Owen's cock sliding back and forth between his cheeks, which made him shiver. So lost in Owen's touch was he that he didn't answer, nor did he notice when Owen scooted off his legs and lay down next to him on the bed.

Adam definitely noticed, however, when Owen slowly rubbed his stubbled face across his glutes while teasing at his hole with a finger. "Yeah, do that some more."

Owen smoothed Adam's cheeks apart and moved his face closer, circling Adam's opening with his tongue instead of his finger.

"That, yes," Adam begged.

Then Owen stabbed his tongue into the tender opening.

"Jeez!" Adam barked.

Owen smiled, doing it again and again.

Then he smacked Adam's ass lightly. "Up."

Adam protested, but raised his pelvis just enough for Owen to snake his hand under him to stroke his cock. Then he licked from the taint back up to Adam's entrance to start the teasing all over again.

"Please," Adam whispered.

"Please what?"

"I need you in me."

Owen leveraged himself up next to Adam. "It's not the most romantic transition, but I'm afraid I need you to come up here and ride me like a cowboy. Tonight, my leg's just not going to handle me kneeling behind you. I'm sorry, Adam."

Adam sat up. He kissed Owen on the nose. "Don't be."

"But hey! I'm not totally useless. I can reach the supplies in the nightstand drawer."

That hurt to hear. "You're not useless, boyfriend, believe me. If you'd kept that up, I'd have made a real mess on the duvet. You're injured. Or reinjured, as the case may be." He swung one leg over Owen and seated himself over that lovely cock he'd been nibbling earlier.

"Thanks for being so understanding," Owen said, "it's just not the way I wanted tonight to go."

Adam took Owen's face in his hands and kissed him deeply. Then he said, "But it's the way tonight is, and I'm not complaining."

"I'm so lucky to have met you."

"Me too. Now fuck me."

"Yes, sir," Owen said, laughing.

Adam found Owen staring into his eyes as he rolled the condom on Owen's cock.

"What?"

Owen shook his head. "Nothing, I like to look at you, that's all. Your eyes are beautiful, just like the rest of you."

"Thanks." Adam ducked his head, suddenly embarrassed.

Owen reached out to touch his chin. "None of that now. But you certainly are the oddest combination of shy and balls of brass."

Adam almost said something about his past but didn't want to profane their moment together. And then he forgot all about it as Owen eased lubed fingers inside him, gently stretching him. Then more lube, and more still.

Then Owen guided his cock to Adam's hole and carefully breached him. Adam eased himself back onto Owen's cock with a sigh, shivering with pleasure as Owen filled him slowly, inch by inch, until his sac and its golden curls rested on Owen's dark-red ones.

But Owen still wasn't done with him. Just as he was about to reach for his own cock, Owen nudged his hand away. "Let me," he said, and tenderly, even reverently, took Adam's hard penis in his lube-slicked hands and started to stroke in time with the sensual, unhurried pace he set up with his own cock inside Adam. All Adam needed to do was feel.

He let his head drop back and his eyes close as sensation flooded his body and mind. Owen stroked him with one hand while the other caressed his chest, eventually finding its way to a nipple. "Owen," he gasped.

"Yeah, babe?"

"Not going to last like this."

"Then don't hold back."

"Never want it to end."

Then Owen shifted inside him and suddenly he was in flight as his boyfriend found his prostate, sliding over it with each stroke, still unhurried, still long and smooth, still pushing closer and closer to the brink.

Adam opened his eyes and looked down at Owen, who, although his eyes were glazed with pleasure, still looked up at him with the same steady gaze. His hazel eyes were filled with something that Adam wanted to name but couldn't, wanted to touch but was afraid to, wanted to seize but couldn't quite believe it was meant for him.

"It's okay, I've got you. Let go," Owen whispered.

With a howl, Adam did. He couldn't contain all the pieces anymore. The pleasure, plus something else he hadn't felt before, wouldn't let him. But he knew Owen would be there after the waves of blinding light had passed.

His first shot hit Owen's face, and Owen, his eyes half-closed, licked it off his lips as his thrusts grew jerky. Owen shuddered. "Adam!"

Owen smeared his hand through Adam's load cooling on his chest, as if somehow it were the most precious thing in the world and by doing so he could bring himself even closer to the man still impaled on his cock.

Adam bent forward to hold Owen as they rode out their climaxes. He knew his jism would be a real mess in Owen's chest hair when it dried, but so help him he just couldn't make himself get up to get a towel. Moving would break the spell, and right now more than anything, he needed to be with Owen.

They held each other as T'Pau cautiously peered over the edge of the bed.

"Mrow?"

"It's safe enough," Owen mumbled. "I'm done mauling your human."

"She probably wants to know what I was doing to you, the turncat," Adam muttered.

Owen slipped out as he pulled the comforter over them both. Lord knew where they'd find the condom in the morning, but since neither one wanted to move, that was the price they'd pay. He just hoped Owen knotted it off.

Adam snuggled down next to his boyfriend, whose muscular arms immediately closed around him. He couldn't think when he'd felt more secure or happy. Right as sleep claimed him, he realized he hadn't just been fucked. He'd been made love to.

Chapter Seventeen

Owen stretched out in the passenger seat of Adam's Honda Pilot. "So, where're we heading?"

Adam glanced at him and smiled. He'd waited long enough. "Point Reyes."

"Oooh!" Owen squealed. "I haven't been there since I was a kid."

Adam wiggled a finger in his right ear to clear it. For such a big macho stud, his boyfriend could sure shriek like a teenybopper. "Glad you're excited."

"So, what're we going to do?" Owen practically bounced in his seat.

"You'll see when we get there," Adam said. He sighed to himself. The interval between askings was shrinking, and they had a half hour until they arrived. Still, at least Owen was excited and trusted him to choose something they'd both enjoy, and with no questions asked beyond the "are we there yet?" variety. Adam was pretty sure Owen was doing that to tease him.

For all that going away for Christmas had been Owen's idea, it had quickly become something else, with each of them planning a surprise for the other, and after Adam insisted—rather firmly—he had almost two weeks off at the clinic. He wouldn't—couldn't—have done that had it not been for Owen's help and support, and he realized just how much he'd come to depend on the sometimes brash but always thoughtful man.

Owen shifted in his seat, almost lying on his side, to look at Adam. "So, how'd you do it? How'd you get the old bat to let you out? I mean, a week and a half? That's some serious time off there."

"I finally had to put my foot down," Adam said. "Dr. Endicott's been good to me, but enough's enough."

"See, you and I have differing definitions of good. You see it as a job when you needed one and a chance to buy the practice when—if—she ever decides to stop juicing you, oops! I mean, retire."

"I know." Adam sighed. "We've talked about this, you and I, and you're right. I went in there armed for bear, but first I just asked for the time off…"

"Oh, I'm afraid that won't be possible," Dr. Endicott had said. "Maybe when you're shouldering more of the work here at the clinic. Besides, I like to spend the winter holidays with my grandchildren, and they so love their Maw-Maw."

Adam had only snorted. "Elspeth, I'm taking a week and a half off, from before Christmas until after January second. Have you even looked at the books lately?" Despite the pain in his leg and his own battles with the fire department over worker's comp for the new injury to that leg, Owen had nonetheless spent quite a bit of his free time entering all of Adam's invoices so that Steven could crank out the bills. Those two bickered a lot but they worked well together.

"No, I can't say that I have," Elspeth had admitted.

"My work and the clients I bring in account for roughly sixty percent of this clinic's gross revenue. When you look at clients who pay their bills within thirty days, that figure jumps to almost eighty, which in turn means we're now paying our bills on time." Adam had looked up from the spreadsheet, satisfied to see her blanch. "After the new year, we need to sit down and assess how this clinic is run as a business, starting with how and when clients pay. But for now, I'm carrying this veterinary hospital, and I'm taking a break."

"You told her all that? With those spreadsheets I did for you?" Owen said.

Adam looked at him, wondering where this was going to wind up. Hopefully not with more damage to his hearing. He braced himself. "Yeah."

"Cool."

He'd never understand his boyfriend. "What I didn't tell her is that I've met with a lawyer about revisiting the terms under which I started there," Adam admitted. He didn't feel too great about this to begin with, but hopefully Owen would understand.

"Oh yeah?"

Adam squirmed. "I don't want this to sound like I'm disloyal or anything—"

"She's been taking advantage of you. Maybe not from the beginning and maybe not intentionally, but that's what's happened. I'm glad you're looking out for yourself. So, what're you thinking about?"

This was so not what Adam had thought he and Owen would discuss on their romantic Christmas getaway. "Uh...well, the billing, of course. Payment when service is provided. No ifs, ands, or buts." Owen nodded. "But given that I'm doing most of the work, I want more of the glory."

"I didn't know there was any of that in veterinary medicine."

"Be quiet, you. I want to be a full partner, not an associate. I also want to shift to an effort-based model of compensation. As it is, I'm keeping the clinic running and—"

"She's raking it in. You're nicer than I am. That'd have pissed me off a long time ago."

"I wasn't too thrilled at the time, either, but that was before I knew just how little work Elspeth was interested in doing and just how much she'd let the practice decay," Adam said, relieved that Owen had his back, but then, he'd seen Owen's face at Thanksgiving and after.

"If she wants to retire then she should just retire," Owen said petulantly. "She's wearing out my boyfriend, and that's my job."

Adam smiled. "Sometimes people just need a little push."

"Well, I've certainly been on the receiving end of your pushes..." Owen wiggled his eyebrows suggestively.

"Can we at least wait until we've checked in? I think you'll like the location." Adam grinned. "Nice and isolated. We can make all the noise we want."

Owen shifted in his seat and grinned. "So how much longer?"

"Someone's eager."

"When I went to the bathroom before we left your house? I put a plug in," Owen said.

His boyfriend was smirking again. Owen did that a lot, Adam noticed, and he loved it.

Then Owen's words hit him, and he dropped the pedal.

*

"Seriously? You brought a cripple to the beach?" Owen said as they rested in bed.

Adam had driven them the rest of the way to Point Reyes so fast Owen had held on for dear life, but then again, in the Honda Pilot, Adam couldn't go that fast or they'd have turned over. Their rental cottage right at the edge of Tomales Bay overlooked the Point Reyes National Seashore, sitting on stilts to keep it above the waterline at high tide, not that they'd cared right then. Owen had a few new bite marks and some scruff burn to enjoy.

Adam rolled his eyes. "You're not a cripple, as you just demonstrated quite ably."

"Sure I am," Owen said cheerfully. "With the brace and the cane? I'm practically RoboFireman."

"That doesn't get you out of your cooking duties, you know."

"Cruel!" Owen pouted. But really, they'd brought enough with them to feed a regiment and they were only staying three nights. If for some reason they didn't like anything they had, little dairies dotted the area and oysters and clams were farmed practically outside the cottage door.

Adam kissed him slowly, which Owen liked. A lot. Learning that Adam, his Adam, had another name, another identity, had thrown him. It was like he'd been in a relationship with a stranger, like he was back to fucking strangers. His boyfriend might've been a completely different person from the one he'd realized he was falling in love with, and that had hurt worst of all.

But Adam had been trying, he could tell. And to tell the truth, Adam or Alexander, he seemed like the same guy. A little naïve, incredibly sweet, a gentle giant, and yet a demon in bed. Owen wasn't sure how that particular combination had come about, but the more he was around it, the more he craved it. Adam's whole situation worried him, but Adam was the man he wanted in his life, so he'd have to make his peace with it.

They rested in each other's arms, and Owen snuggled in closer, breathing in Adam's scent. That he'd been with the same man long enough to know what he smelled like, and not only that, to become so familiar with it that he found it comforting, even needful, that...that was as good as the sex. He never thought he'd say that, and if anything ever happened to Adam, he didn't know what he'd do, because there was no way he could ever go back to hooking up. He pretended he wasn't a superstitious fool while crossing his fingers to ward off such bad luck.

But all good things, as they say. He pushed himself up.

"Where're you going?" Adam mumbled, pulling him back down.

Owen didn't mind. He wormed his way back into Adam's arms. "Since you're this great slave driver and all, I was going to start cooking, but now that I'm comfy again..."

Adam chuckled and held him, which Owen just loved. Even more so when Adam started stroking his hair. He wanted to purr like T'Pau did.

"Owen?"

"Yeah, boyfriend?"

Owen felt Adam inhale like he was about to say something, but Adam exhaled without saying anything.

He almost shifted to see Adam's face, but thought maybe he shouldn't. Whatever Adam wanted to tell him was hard for him.

"The last couple of months... they'vebeenreally specialforme," Adam blurted.

Owen smiled, his heart filling. He knew what he wanted to say but didn't feel that now was the right time. Closer to Christmas. He'd never said it to another man and wanted the moment to mean something.

He worked his arms around Adam and pulled him down on him. It might've been a bit awkward, but closeness was essential right then. "They've meant a lot to me too." *They've meant everything*, he thought.

They held each other until growling stomachs forced them apart, and then Owen wriggled out from under Adam and went to see about something to eat.

"So, what's on tap for tomorrow?" Owen asked.

Adam shrugged. "That's kind of up to you. If your leg's up for it, I thought we could go for a walk along Point Reyes, maybe see the lighthouse. That won't take all that long, so there's always just hanging out on the beach or even taking it easy here."

"I want," Owen said, pointing to a brochure, "to go sea kayaking."

"But your leg—"

"Don't need my legs for kayaking," Owen said smugly. "It'll be just like adaptive rowing, only with otters. Find me an otter, Adam?"

What Owen didn't mention was that he hoped kayaking would be very much like adaptive rowing. Something about rowing had helped his body recover. His PT, Deanne Lawson, speculated that the balance needed in the boat recruited a lot of little muscles, in addition to the more obvious bigger ones, and in so doing they laid down new blood vessels and created new muscle memory, all helping the recovery effort. It made him feel like the home front during World War II, but he didn't care. He just wanted to be able to walk without braces or pain. He wanted his old body back.

Adam reached out and ruffled his hair. "I'll do my best to find you an otter, but you know... It'll be cold out there."

"Yeah, but we can warm each other up afterward."

"Something tells me I'm going to need a vacation to recover from a vacation with you," Adam sighed, but he was smiling.

"We haven't even gotten to my part of our vacation yet," Owen said cheerfully.

This was what Owen wanted, and for the rest of his life.

*

Despite the pace Owen had demanded of him as they paddled around Tomales Bay and even out into the surf along the Pacific coast, Adam felt relaxed and rested as they headed into San Francisco.

"This is a nice car," Owen commented. "If mine ever dies, maybe I'll buy one of these."

He didn't even mind that Owen was driving his new SUV. "So, what're we doing? You'll notice that unlike some people, I haven't been badgering the planner of this part of our weekend with questions."

Owen smiled. "I was beginning to wonder if you had any curiosity in you at all."

"I trust you." The thing was, he did. Despite his only real experience with a long-term relationship (that week with Shelly Gardner in first grade didn't count), which should've ruined him for life, he knew Owen wasn't Jordan.

Sure, Adam knew he had all kinds of issues to work through, but he saw Owen as maybe helping him with them, not hindering him. Owen demonstrated on a daily, if not hourly, basis he was worth that kind of trust.

"I'm glad," Owen said. He interlaced his fingers with Adam's, and Adam let him. They were on the 101 into the city and the traffic was in no hurry, so neither were they. "Anyway, tonight I thought we'd clean up and have an early dinner, and then I've got tickets to the ACT production of *A Christmas Carol*."

"I've never seen it. That sounds like a lot of fun," Adam said. "What a great first night."

"Yeah?"

The look on Owen's face alone would've made Adam sit through just about anything. He snuggled down inside his coat, knowing that Owen was as safe a driver as they made, particularly after his accident.

He must've dozed off, because the next thing he was aware of was Owen shaking him gently. "Hey, wake up, sleepyhead. We're about to cross the Golden Gate and it looks to be gorgeous this afternoon."

Adam yawned and stretched, and damn, Owen was right. The late December day was gloriously clear and bright as only it could be on the Pacific coast, without a shred of the fog they sought to escape in the Sacramento Valley, and the sun shone down on the burnt-orange of the venerable Art Deco bridge as they drove across it, entering San Francisco.

"I'm told," Adam said, looking at Owen askance, "that when the bridge was originally under construction, some of the painters had a bit of fun and caught seagulls in little snares baited with their lunches. They then swabbed their heads with the same color they used to paint the bridge."

Owen grunted. "That long ago? Wonder what was in the paint and how long it took to kill the birds."

"It probably wasn't doing the painters any favors either," Adam conceded, "but then the gulls started showing up in the city. They caused quite a stir, even among zoologists, who were convinced they were seeing the emergence of a then-heretofore undescribed subspecies of seagull."

"Didn't anyone notice the color matched the bridge?" Owen asked, chuckling.

"Eventually, yes."

They laughed and drove into the city.

As Owen searched for their hotel, Adam's phone vibrated in his pocket. When he checked it, he found a text from Detective Cabot. "I'm almost afraid to read it."

"Only one way to find out, boyfriend."

"I bet you're the kind to rip bandages right off, aren't you?" Adam said sourly.

Owen nodded, paying more attention to the streets around them. "I'm a little hairy, so yeah."

Adam sighed and checked the text. "Huh. Apparently, Jordan was bluffing. He's been in his counseling and therapy programs all along. Everyone seems inclined to let this go."

"I'm not," Owen said.

"Detective Cabot's not, either, according to the text."

"Mike's a smart man."

Adam felt sick to his stomach. A part of him had hoped that Jordan really had fled the country. "I sure hope so."

*

"I still can't believe you did that last night," Adam said.

Owen shrugged. "The guy was ruining dinner for everyone. I made him stop."

"I know, it was just kind of embarrassing. I mean, some guy in a hotel window across the street from the restaurant exposes himself and then you stand up and expose yourself right back." Adam sighed. "Aren't you a little old for pissing contests?"

"I'm sorry I embarrassed you, I really am." Owen hunched his shoulders. This wasn't how he'd wanted their time in San Francisco to go. "Although I do have to say, I wouldn't have been able to do it if your foot hadn't been planted on my crotch. Please don't let this ruin our trip."

Adam took his hand. "I won't, I promise, and I must admit, it was pretty funny the way the guy just stared for a moment and then started crying."

"Don't forget the jealous looks you got." Some of the guys in the open-air restaurant really hadn't been happy with Adam after they'd seen what his boyfriend was packing. He hadn't thought he was *that* well-endowed, but apparently some of the other diners had.

"Those were a nice fringe benefit, yes," Adam admitted. He lifted their hands to his mouth and kissed Owen's hand, which made Owen feel warm and cared for.

"So, what're we doing today?" Adam continued as they walked toward Union Square.

"If you don't object, I thought we'd do a bit of shopping," Owen said. "I usually buy things for my niece and nephews, and since we're in the city, I thought it'd be fun to check out the mayhem at F.A.O. Schwartz. Plus, I like to buy a little something for Avril, little luxuries she'd never be able to afford raising three children by herself, plus intermittent child support from their jackass of a father."

"Oooh, great idea. I'd like to buy her something from me, as well. I hate arriving empty handed. You take good care of your sister, don't you?"

"I try. She'd never accept any help from me. Too proud. So sometimes I take the kids school shopping in the summer, buy them fun things at Christmas, be there for their birthdays, things like that."

"You're their father-substitute, the man in their lives."

Owen shrugged, suddenly embarrassed. Saying it out loud like that, he realized just how involved he was with his sister's family, maybe not the best message to send when he was trying to woo a boyfriend.

Adam dropped his hand and wrapped his arm around Owen's waist for a one-armed hug. When he was done, he didn't let go. "I love how involved you are with your family."

Or maybe not. Owen got a silly little smile on his face. Adam had used the l-word, too. Maybe not "I love you, Owen," but it was in same area code, and that set his heart to soaring. He knew he was in love with Adam and planned to tell him on Christmas Eve at his sister's house.

Tomorrow.

Not that he was scared or anything.

"I've hesitated to ask," Owen said, "but...you never mention your own family."

He felt Adam freeze up and pull away.

"Not every family is as shiny and happy as yours is, Owen."

"Given that my dad took off when Avril and I were kids and our mom worked herself into an early grave to support us, yours must be pretty damn awful. I'm sorry," Owen said quietly.

"They sided with Jordan," Adam spat.

Owen froze, unable to take another step. He could only stare at his boyfriend, his jaw hanging open.

"That not what you thought you'd hear?" Adam said bitterly. Owen put his hand on his shoulder, but Adam shook it off. "I don't want your pity."

"What about my comfort?" he said softly.

They stared eye to eye for a moment. Then Adam broke down crying. When Owen opened his arms, Adam rushed into them. "I'm so sorry, Adam," he whispered.

"Dad told me that since I'd 'chosen this lifestyle I could just take everything that went with it.' Mom just shook her head as I stood before her with a black eye. What kind of parents could do that?"

"Parents who'd better never meet me," Owen growled, steering Adam to one of the benches lining Union Square. "I'll destroy anyone who lays a hand on you."

"My hero," Adam said sadly.

They sat quietly while Adam regained his composure. "Sorry to go feral on you there."

"Sounds like you had a good reason," Owen said, still holding him. He pulled Adam in for a kiss. "Also sounds like you're holding a lot inside. Are you still seeing your therapist?"

"Um...maybe not so much lately. Still going to PT?"

"Good deflection, but this isn't about me. Save that for when I'm bellyaching about my leg."

Adam chuckled. It wasn't much, but under the circumstances, Owen was happy to get even that.

"You ready to face shopping for someone else's kids?" Owen said.

"Sure, why not? It's not my money," Adam said.

*

F.A.O. Schwartz, while indeed an experience, had also been a madhouse, one Adam would be just as happy not to repeat again in this lifetime. Catalogues and Kids R Expensive would be more than enough for him in the future. That said, he wouldn't have traded watching Owen shop and try out the toys for anything. In some ways, his big butch firefighter boyfriend was little more than an overgrown kid himself, and Adam swore seeing Owen in action had taken five years off his own age.

Adam and love were funny subjects. He admitted that. All those years with Jordan had warped and changed him in some fundamental ways. This he knew before his therapist even brought it up. Exploring that with his therapist could hurt, which was why he'd taken a break. Finding out just how badly he'd allowed Jordan to damage him was one more thing to feel bad about, and he had an awful lot of those as it was. But maybe Owen was right. Maybe it was time to go back.

Because Adam knew one thing. His relationship with Owen was coming to mean more to him than almost anything else. Somehow that gimpy redheaded lunatic had weaseled his way into the central spot in his life, and now Adam didn't know how he'd survive without him. This whole trip had been so special, the two of them spending time together, enjoying each other's company, doing things that couples do without it being a Big Deal. He was getting used to that so fast.

Did that mean he loved Owen? Love was such a complicated thing, and he just didn't *know*. He knew he had some loose screws, that there were things boyfriends did that he couldn't stand, and that things he saw as normal really weren't. Owen deserved someone who wasn't so fucked up, but he didn't seem inclined to look any further. Adam figured he'd just enjoy the ride and try to straighten himself out. Hopefully, Owen could be patient with him.

"You're quiet over there," Owen said as he drove them to the Castro.

Adam faced him and smiled. "Just thinking about how much I'm enjoying the trip with you."

"Yeah?"

Adam nodded. "Yeah."

Owen leaned over and kissed him, and Adam liked that just fine. They must've both liked it too much because Owen didn't notice the light had turned until someone honked.

"Oops," Owen said. "I'd say I'm sorry, but I'm not. I'm never sorry for kissing you."

Adam smiled and put his hand on Owen's thigh. Owen pulled it down to his crotch, but Adam laughed and pulled it back up to a less dangerous place.

"Killjoy." Owen pretended to pout.

"I'd prefer to make it to dinner in one piece."

"Fine. Be that way."

Owen parked and they walked to the restaurant hand in hand. Adam felt a few pairs of eyes on them, but it was the Castro and his boyfriend was hot. This was a good thing, because as mild as the winter day had been, with the sun setting, the temperature was dropping rapidly. Ambient heaters or not, he hoped they'd be eating inside tonight.

Adam felt more looks as they ordered and ate their dinner at their cozy table. He tried not to let it get to him, but apparently without much success.

"Are you okay?" Owen asked, his voice pitched low.

Adam hunched his shoulders. "It feels like people keep staring."

Owen put his napkin down. "They do stare, Adam. You're very tall, built, and damned good looking. How could they not?"

"You're biased." Adam was flummoxed. "I thought they were staring at you."

"Some of them may well be." There was a twinkle in Owen's eyes. "But I think you're the star of the show tonight."

"That's...that's just embarrassing. I'm not some celebrity. Can't they leave me alone to enjoy dinner with my boyfriend?"

"We're in the Castro, so I wouldn't hold my breath."

Owen's calm acceptance of this was just infuriating. Maybe even insulting. "I can't believe you're just sitting there."

"What do you want me to do, Adam?"

Adam sighed in frustration. "I don't know. I just don't like people staring."

"You could stare back. Make some faces or something. Or you could scoot over next to me and I could stick my tongue so far down your throat you feel it in your groin." Owen stuck his tongue out and licked his lips suggestively. Adam laughed despite himself.

"Would you be serious?"

"I am serious. I'm just not letting this ruin my dinner."

"Okay, point taken."

Just then, a younger guy of the frat-boy type who looked to Adam's eyes like he'd had a bit more to drink than he should've came up to their table, all but ignoring Owen. Adam looked at Owen as if to say "*See*?" But Owen just sat back and watched with undisguised glee as Frat Rat ignored him.

"Hey, dude."

When Adam didn't say anything, Owen said, "I think he's talking to you, Adam."

"Yeah, Adam. You're a good-looking guy," Frat Rat said.

"Thank you," Adam said in his coldest tone. What the hell was Owen up to? And where were the damn waiters? He looked around, but apparently the entire waitstaff had chosen this very special moment to hide in the kitchen.

"Why don't you ditch the old man? My friends and I'll show you a much better time. We can get you into MDNA. It's the best club right now."

"Go away," Adam said. "I'm too old for you."

Frat Rat leaned down and kissed Adam on the lips. "Don't be that way—"

Owen's arm shot out and caught the front of Frat Rat's shirt. Owen pulled him close. Adam had never seen Owen look so mean. Was he going to rip the kid's arms off?

But Owen stood up and topped the kid by a good six inches. "Pretty fast reflexes for an old man with a limp, huh?"

"Whoa, man! I didn't mean—"

"You think it's a good idea to kiss another man's boyfriend after you've insulted him?" Owen growled. "Guess what? It's not."

With that, Owen dragged Adam's struggling suitor to the restaurant's door. Then he grabbed him by the back of his shirt and the waistband of his pants and threw him out of the restaurant.

He beckoned to the maître d'. "This would never have happened if your waiters had stepped in. This restaurant was recommended to me as a good place to eat, but apparently not, not if you allow patrons to molest a couple trying to enjoy a quiet dinner together without intervening. The check—"

"Is on the house, sir."

Owen inclined his head, a little regally, Adam thought, but under the circumstances, not inappropriately. "That what you had in mind?"

Adam tried not to laugh. "My hero."

Owen reached across the table to caress his cheek but didn't say anything. He only stared into Adam's eyes. There was a softness there just for him, Adam recognized it now, and a message he couldn't quite make out. But he was getting closer.

*

Avril's Christmas Eve afternoon open house in her creaking Victorian in Petaluma was just like Owen remembered—noisy and packed to the rafters with her children's friends, plus her friends and their children, along with a few pets running around. She drew the line at the backyard chickens when her youngest tried to bring them in.

"But it's cooooold out," he whined.

"And there's a heater in the henhouse," Avril said. "The only chickens in this house are fried, baked, or roasted, so unless you're planning to do the dirty work yourself, they stay outside."

Once the kids were out of earshot, Avril said, "Well, there was that one kid you were dating…"

"You did not bring him up," Owen said, red as his fire engines.

Adam, grinning in undisguised glee, poked him in the side, and said, "Yeah, boyfriend, I think she did."

"I refuse to answer on the grounds that we weren't actually dating," Owen said.

"Then what were you doing with him?" Avril said. "Because I have to tell you, he was bone-deep stupid." She turned to Adam. "He really was, the kind of stupid that just doesn't wash off."

"Okay, I have to know, what were you doing with him?" Adam asked.

Fine, Owen thought. If Adam insisted on knowing, he'd tell him, but at just the right moment, like when he was taking a drink of the hot chocolate Avril apparently had on tap...

"Fucking him."

Adam coughed as he tried to aspirate his hot chocolate.

"Owen!" Avril ran to the kitchen to get a towel to clean up the resulting mess.

Adam coughed, but feebly, the danger of choking past. "Ass."

"Like you couldn't have figured out what I'd be doing with a stupid twink," Owen said.

"You didn't have to rub my face in it," Adam said sulkily.

Was he serious? "You *asked*!" Owen grabbed the towel from his sister's hand and started cleaning up Adam's face, carefully wiping away any trace of chocolate. "Egged on by *her*."

"He's kind of right," Avril said.

"Only kind of?" Owen said.

"I think I'll turn in, it's been a long day," Adam said.

Avril and Owen looked at each other, concerned that their old sibling games might've gotten out of hand. "Go after him," Avril whispered fiercely.

There wasn't room to walk next to Adam on the narrow wooden staircase leading to their room in the turret, and if he'd called out, Owen knew his niece and nephews, who probably weren't sleeping too soundly on Christmas Eve night to begin with, would've listened eagerly to their Uncle Owen's relationship issues.

But as soon as they were in their round room and clicked the area heater on...

"Adam, what's wrong?"

Adam sighed, his shoulders slumping. "I know you warned me, but there are a lot of you, and it can be hard to take."

"Can I hold you?" Owen was almost afraid of the answer, so he felt nothing but relief when Adam nodded.

Owen put his arms around him and just held him for a few moments. "Let's get ready for bed."

The bathroom was back down the stairs, and they did their thing in silence, partly to keep the kids asleep since it was after midnight and partly since they were both tired. Owen climbed into bed and then held both the quilts and his arms open for the man he loved.

"I'm sorry you felt... What did you feel, Adam?"

Adam turned his face to bury it in Owen's neck. "I don't know...overwhelmed? This is kind of embarrassing... Do I have to?"

Owen kissed the top of his head. "No, of course not, but I hope you can always feel safe and comfortable telling me what you think."

Adam didn't say anything for a few minutes, and as his breathing slowed, Owen thought he'd gone to sleep.

"I felt like between your relationship with your sister and all those children on the rampage there might not be any place for me here."

"Oh, Adam." Owen said. He wasn't going to argue him out of it. He knew he was close to his sister, and he wouldn't apologize for that. "It'll only be the three kids tomorrow, and only the three of us adults, as well. No open house or anything."

"I know," he said softly, "and they're your family. I get that. I'm just—"

"The man I love."

It wasn't when or how Owen had planned on saying it, but it was true, and it was what Adam needed to hear.

He let it sink in for a moment before he continued, "I know love is a complicated subject for you, and I don't want you to say it back until you mean it. But I love you, Adam, and I have since Thanksgiving."

"Owen…"

That he didn't hear it back hurt, but he still loved Adam. "Yeah?"

"No, I can't say it back right now, but I don't know what I'd do without you. What I feel for you… I've never felt for anyone else. I'm just so confused sometimes."

Owen held him tighter. "I'm not going anywhere."

"I know, and it's one of the things I love about you. Knowing you're there for me, knowing you'll be there for me… you have to know how important that is for me. But since Thanksgiving? Really?"

"Yep, Thanksgiving, although I think it started the moment I first saw you in the boathouse. Something clicked for me. At first it was just lust, you know? But when Brad interrupted us and my head cleared and I had a chance to think, I realized I wanted more with you. That was when."

"They used to talk about us at CCRC, you know."

Owen chuckled. "I bet they still do. When we're back on the water, we'll probably still disappear into each other the minute we're at the boathouse, even if we've spent the night together."

"Is this why you wanted to bring me here for Christmas?"

"One of the reasons, yes. The biggest reason, actually. I want my family to like you. I want you to like them, but you have to understand something. When I said I love you, I meant it. I'm ready to make my life with you. I'm ready to make you my family, and when you're ready, they'll have to like you because you'll be my family first."

He knew it was a lot to lay on Adam, but it was the truth, and once he'd said "I love you," it got easier, even though somehow, it didn't cheapen the words. Quite the opposite. Saying it only strengthened them and the feelings behind them, as if finally speaking the truth to the man he loved allowed the truth to grow faster and stronger.

"So the next time Avril and I get to be too much, just remember, she may be my sister and yes, she and I were as close as siblings could be without being *Flowers in the Attic* close when we were growing up—"

Adam dug his chin into Owen's shoulder. "I didn't need that visual."

"Okay, point taken. But she was my past, and while we'll always be close, you'll... I hope you'll be my future." Owen sniffed. His heart was so full right now, and if Adam didn't feel the same way, or wouldn't come to in time...it'd be a long, hard fall. He pretended his eyes weren't tearing up. "I think I'm starting to babble. Anyway, merry Christmas, boy—"

He couldn't say anything else, because Adam attacked his mouth just then, and he was busy kissing the man he loved.

Chapter Eighteen

In the end, Owen reflected, it was just as well he had a king-size bed, because he, Adam, Steven, Adam's two remaining dogs, T'Pau, who absolutely wouldn't let him out of her sight, and even Mike Cabot ended up piled on it, seeking comfort for what little remained of the night. No one seemed to have to be anywhere on Boxing Day and Owen didn't mind hosting.

What he'd found... He needed a Silkwood shower after that, and he'd never be able to unsee what he'd beheld when he'd first walked into the kitchen. To see his boyfriend's beloved dog lying there in her own blood, and then that note... Rationally, he knew it wasn't his fault, that it was all the product of a diseased mind, but part of him blamed himself because if he weren't in the picture, then Jordan wouldn't be doing bugnuts crazy stuff like that, right?

He said as much to Mike, who was in the kitchen helping him make breakfast for their men. Well, his man and the guy Mike threw wood for, since he hadn't made a move yet.

"No, I'd say you give him the strength to stand up to Jordan. Chances are otherwise pretty good he'd have gone back to him by now. Abusers like this are skilled at getting what they want."

Mike wasn't Owen's favorite person right now. Well, him and his whole department. As far as he could tell, Jordan had been and was still playing them. Shouldn't an entire department of law-enforcement professionals be smarter than a fucked-up psychopath? "So, what happened, Mike? You texted us—"

"I know," he groaned. "Jordan came back to his program like he was supposed to, so I was pulled off surveillance."

"Just like that? No follow-up to make sure he wasn't manipulating you? I thought you were doing this on your own time."

"Well, it was Christmas—"

The only reason Owen didn't scream was because it would've awoken his boyfriend. "And that might've interfered with your pursuit of the Boy Wonder in there?"

"How'd you know?" Mike said.

"Nice going," Owen said acidly.

"What's nice going? And could you two keep it down out here? I was trying to sleep," Steven said.

"Sorry for interrupting your sleep by discussing things with the detective assigned to my boyfriend's case in my own kitchen, *Princess*," Owen snapped. "By the way, the detective wants to fuck you, just so you know."

"Oh, okay," Steven said and stumbled back into Owen's bedroom.

"Owen!" Mike gasped.

Suddenly Owen was in Mike's face, right up in his grille. "You want a feud between badges in this town, you let a repeat of yesterday happen again. Got it?"

"Owen, please, police aren't perfect, and if you have to blame someone, blame the courts. They're the ones who diverted Jordan into a first-time offenders' program."

"Wait, what!" Steven yelled from the bedroom.

"Not now!" Owen and Mike yelled at the same time.

"Look, you were assigned here, and not only that, you gave me your word personally," Owen said. "Keep this creep away from us. How many more times does he have to do something like this before the police get him booted from this program, or better yet, arrest him?"

"I'll see what I can do. Hopefully, the CSI team can find something solid, like fingerprints."

*

Jordan Sanders sat in the group therapy room and tried not to strangle anyone. These meetings were so stupid. Actually, they were boring. The counselor was stupid. He was surprised. He'd have thought someone with a master's in family therapy would've been at least somewhat intelligent, but the tall but somehow roly-poly man who looked like Big Gay Al with silver hair spoke in nothing but the same clichéd affirmations to be found on page-a-day calendars. Every day after that first day had been sheerest torture.

Jordan was smart, super-smart, and he knew it. He also didn't have a problem, not like these poor bastards. No, what was wrong with his life was all the people in it, starting with Alexander. Jeez, that man was so damn infuriating sometimes. Alexander knew what he did pissed him off. He did. But he did it anyway, and then Jordan got mad and eventually hit him. But then poor little Alexander—all six foot five of him—would go sobbing off to the ER for some bruises and scratches and he'd look like the bad guy. The guy brought it on himself, so why the fuck wasn't Alexander the one sitting in these jack-off group therapy sessions, instead of him?

"So, Jordan. You were absent from group for a few days," Big Gay Al said. "Bit of trouble with the police. Can you tell us what happened?"

Right, time to pour it on. Jordan sniffled. "I just… I just missed my boyfriend and our dog so much. Ex-boyfriend, I guess. Since he's moved on." He made the tears come. These fools ate up the tears. In a minute, some sucker would hand him a box of tissue… Yep, right on time! "I just can't handle it, you know? Knowing he's out there. Without me. It brings out my worst impulses."

Now someone will chime in with some irrelevant remark, because hey! That's what group's for. All the mental midgets trying to compare themselves to me, thinking we have something in common when we fucking don't. "Yeah, that's a good point. You think I should send him a note telling him how I feel?"

Yeah, that's a great idea. That's called "evidence," dumbshit.

"That's very interesting," Big Gay Al said, one more reason he was a complete moron. "If this man matters to you, then you've got to fight for him. Otherwise I don't think you're going to resolve your issues."

"You really think so?" Jordan said. He made his eyes as wide as possible, so he looked all doe-eyed and innocent. Why not, it worked on the cops.

"Absolutely. You've got to show him that he means something to you."

I'll show him I love him too much to ever let him go.

*

New Year's Eve and Day had done their thing, and good riddance as far as Adam was concerned. The year looked like it had been all set to end on a sweet note, and then they'd returned from their Christmas trip to... He couldn't even complete the thought.

He'd always hated the phrase, but now he knew what it meant. Owen had been his rock, and without his boyfriend, Adam knew he'd probably have collapsed. Between the horror at what he'd seen combined with post-traumatic flashbacks to his own experiences at Jordan's hands...

Speaking of Jordan, the police had no leads, and he knew they wouldn't. Jordan was too smart. There were no clues, no fingerprints, nothing they could pin definitively on his ex-partner. The officers from the Davis Police Department who were now investigating, and were none too happy with the Sacramento PD for not telling them what was going on sooner, asked him to come with up with a list of any strange or threatening events that might've happened since he'd moved to town. Guess he should've reported that rat...

Oh well, there'd been one bright spot. Since the police couldn't definitely pin the crime on Jordan, the landlord had repaired the damage without charging him or breaking the lease. Adam was almost disappointed by that. He only felt safe when Owen slept there with him. Owen did that as much as he could too. Poor T'Pau practically lived in Owen's SUV, now. Adam was sad to let her go, but the one time he'd tried to take her home, she'd howled the entire way and then ripped his hands to ribbons for his troubles. The reality of their situation was that she belonged to Owen now, or more accurately he belonged to her, but he'd let Owen figure that out on his own. Besides, with as much time as he and Owen spent together, it wasn't like he never saw T'Pau.

And Owen. His Owen spent every moment with him he could, so Adam was never alone unless he wanted to be, or like that night alone at the clinic watching over a dog after surgery. Owen even escorted him to and from work, taking vacation time when he had to. It meant Owen logged a lot of miles, but he never complained. Adam smiled. He wondered if T'Pau had started her howling when Owen exceeded the speed limit like she'd always done to him...

Owen was even prepared to spend the night at the clinic with him, but Adam knew how tired they both were, to say nothing of the fact that the clinic roll-away, let alone the sleeping bag Owen offered to bring, would do no favors to Owen's healing leg. Adam didn't want to do anything to jeopardize that, and Owen was already way beyond boyfriend of the year territory.

Adam knew he was so lucky. Steven, who'd suddenly gone silent on the virtues of Detective Cabot for some reason, had regaled him with tales from the dating wars, and it wasn't like he didn't have the worst ex-boyfriend of them all to compare Owen to. He was grateful to have Owen in his life. He knew he loved Owen. What he didn't know was why he couldn't say it. Owen deserved to hear it. He deserved a lot more than Adam had to give. If only there were some way he could protect Owen from all this.

The sound of shattering glass and the alarm's shrill blaring forced him out of his reverie and set all the animals to stirring. Adam hit the police on his phone's auto dial and hit the floor.

*

Owen was already tired of associating flashing red and blue lights with his boyfriend. He was also pissed as hell, mostly at himself. He should've been there, never mind what Adam wanted. Not that he could've somehow stopped this unless he'd been lurking in the bushes outside with a shotgun. In his fatigue-addled state, he actually considered it for a few moments. "It's getting bad, isn't it, T'Pau?"

She lifted her head from where she'd nested in the blanket he'd placed on the front seat for her. "Mrow?"

"Just agree with me."

He parked on the street, since the clinic parking lot was cordoned off. He fired off a text to Steven, just in case. Not that he needed to be there right then and told him as much, but the kid needed to know.

"What is it this time?" Owen said.

"And you are?" the officer taking notes on the other side of the yellow tape said.

Mike Cabot looked up. "The vic's boyfriend. Let him in."

"What was it this time?" Owen asked him.

"Rock through the window with a note on it. *It's not over yet*," Mike said.

Owen ran a hand through his hair. "Great, he's a poet now."

"Sounds like a threat to me."

"Any prints?"

Mike shrugged. "Don't know yet. It'll have to go back to the lab, and which lab is the question of the hour."

"Please don't let this bog down in bureaucracy or jurisdictional jockeying for position. This is my boyfriend we're talking about, and possibly his life." Owen didn't want to think about that just yet, but knew he needed to. The stakes just kept going up and up...

"One question for you, my friend," Mike said. "Protective orders. Can you find out if Adam has one? He answered the bare minimum of questions, but then ran us out, said the commotion was too much for the animals. This is not the kind of cooperation we need."

Owen saw the Davis cops, who'd gathered behind Mike, nod.

"He had a surgery tonight, I know that. But yes, I'll ask him. Can I go in, now?"

"Beats the hell out of me," Mike sighed. "Knock on the door. See if the doctor will let you in."

"Thanks, Mike."

It took a few minutes of knocking, plus a rather firm text, to get Adam's attention. Even so, when Adam opened the door, he looked pissed. "I thought I told you, all this disruption—oh. It's you."

"Yeah, hello to you too. Can I come in?" Owen said. Adam didn't look good. The stress was eating him alive.

"Sorry. I didn't mean to bite your head off. The alarm, plus the cops... It's not good for the animals, let alone that poor dog I cut open earlier tonight." Adam pulled him in and then shut and locked the door behind them.

"Guess you didn't get my text if I'm a surprise," Owen said.

"No, sorry. It's been a hellish night."

Owen caught Adam from behind and held him. Only gradually did Adam relax into him. "What can I do to help?"

"Keep being you, I guess." Adam was quiet for a moment. "Owen, what did I do to deserve you?"

"You were you. That was all it took." Owen closed his eyes and rested against his boyfriend's broad back. The world felt better when he was in physical contact with

Adam, even with Adam's ex on the loose, a leg that wouldn't heal, and a fire department that was starting to demand more of its newest battalion chief, injured or not. "So, what do we do now?"

"I need to get back to the animals, I'm afraid," Adam said, "even though I'd much rather curl up somewhere with you."

"I'll help."

"I appreciate the offer, but you don't have to. Go home and get some sleep. I can calm them myself."

Owen smiled tiredly. "It'll be time to get up in an hour or so anyway. I might as well help you."

He felt guilty that he had an ulterior motive other than spending a little more time with the man he loved. But first, the animals. They'd developed a routine. Owen handled the boarders first. They needed food, water, and attention. That dark, cold morning he started with the two big dogs, turning first one and then the other loose in the clinic's "backyard," a large grassy area. Someone who was paid to do so could take them for a walk later. Maybe one of them could find and bite the perp. Who was he kidding? It was Jordan.

"Adam?" he said. No time like the present. "Do you have any kind of restraining order against Jordan? Because if you do, he's sure as hell violating it. It might help the cops."

Adam looked from the sick Dachshund he was coaxing to eat from a syringe filled with something disgusting-looking. From the look on his face, Owen knew he wouldn't like the answer. "No. When I left him, they told me I wouldn't need one because of that program he was in. I also didn't want to antagonize him."

He couldn't possibly have heard his boyfriend correctly. "Antagonize him? You're fucking someone else.

I think you've already done that. Promise me you'll call the victim's advocate today and get one."

"Will it do any good? We don't even have any proof he's doing this—no, let me finish—we have no proof, otherwise they'd have arrested him by now. A protective order is just one more thing to violate and won't actually do anything to make us safer."

Suddenly Owen was something he hadn't been in a long time. Furious. Mad at Adam for his seeming passivity and naiveté. Okay, he'd been a battered spouse. That was some serious shit, and he really didn't know how serious. He was grateful for that. But at some point, shouldn't Adam rear up on his hind legs and show at least some interest in self-preservation? Because right now, it looked like Adam was just rolling over and taking it, and Owen didn't understand how he could.

All that made him angry at himself too. So much for being a good boyfriend. He loved Adam. Shouldn't he be more understanding, more supportive? After all, this wasn't about him, although that seemed to be changing. But this scared the tar out of him and there was nothing he could do. He was a firefighter, not a cop, and even if he'd been in law enforcement, he'd have to go rogue to do anything himself.

Not that the cops were doing much. Law enforcement was apparently as useful as a eunuch at an orgy, from their absurd "first-time offenders" program that seemed to supervise dangerous abusers loosely if at all, to cops who couldn't watch a house and missed someone removing a kitchen window with a glass cutter and then torturing a dog. That the cop in question was a good friend of his only made it worse.

They were all helpless in the face of evil, and right then, Owen couldn't take it.

"You know what? I can't be here right now. Lock the door behind me."

Adam looked up, startled. "What?"

But Owen was already heading for the door.

Chapter Nineteen

Adam shut and locked the door behind him and reactivated the alarm immediately. Darwin and Huxley raced up to him, bounding and jumping and trying to lick his face. With all the changes, his two remaining boys had been extra clingy, and he couldn't blame them. He wanted to cling to someone who could make it all better too. He wondered if that was what he'd been doing to Owen. They hadn't spoken for a couple of days, not since Owen left the clinic the morning after the attack. Latest attack? That sounded so melodramatic, but that was basically what it amounted to. What was next, Adam wondered, mortar fire? Where Jordan was concerned, he wouldn't rule anything out. He had the uncomfortable feeling that if he went back to Jordan, all of it would stop immediately.

Almost all of it.

The honeymoon phase wouldn't last long. They never did.

He wished there were a way to make Owen understand. There was a cycle to Jordan's outbursts, a rhythm. Seeking a restraining order would only further fan the flames. It would be like putting out a grease fire with gasoline. The best thing to do was starve it of oxygen.

You didn't do that by jumping around and raising a ruckus. You did that by sliding a lid on it slowly so nothing got agitated, no burning grease got spread. Of the two of them, he was the one with the experience, after all. He'd tried explaining that to his therapist when he saw her yesterday, but she was on Owen's side, apparently.

This afternoon the clinic had closed early so he and Elspeth could meet with their lawyers and hammer out a new agreement. It hadn't gone nearly as genially as the last time they'd discussed details of Adam's employment. Was it the presence of the lawyers, or the fact that he and Elspeth didn't see eye to eye? He didn't know and didn't care anymore, but he was done funding her retirement at the expense of his own time and present income, as his lawyer had made clear. Every argument Elspeth and her lawyer had put forward was rooted in the past, because they could make no real claims about her contributions to the clinic's present. She'd about run it into the ground, and thanks to Owen, he had the hard data to prove it. As his lawyer had also made abundantly clear, it was entirely possible that without Adam, she'd be in bankruptcy proceedings now instead of reorganization talks. She had forty-eight hours to accept Adam's offer of him buying the practice on favorable terms based on his work turning it around this fall or he'd find work elsewhere. If she accepted his terms she could work as she chose as an "emerita veterinarian," otherwise she'd be a bankrupt one.

He admitted it was Hobson's choice, but he was fed up with the status quo.

Then something dawned on him. Darwin and Huxley. The alarm.

Groaning, he fetched their leashes and turned off the alarm. With the dogs bouncing beside him, he headed out into the January gloom.

He was almost home again when he got the text from Detective Cabot:

> *Owen's been assaulted. He's at the UCD Med Center.*

"Shit."

*

Mike Cabot met Adam at the ER.

"What happened, Detective?" Adam asked.

Mike looked up at him, his eyes dark and haunted. "He still hasn't forgiven me for not protecting you. Are you going to hate me too?"

"That depends on how quickly you get to the point," Adam said. "I've had a shitty day on top of a shitty few months, and you've just made it worse."

"Right. Like I texted you, he was assaulted this evening—"

"Where?"

"He was at home. Someone broke in and beat the crap out of him. Owen's assailant knew what he was doing too."

"What do you mean?" Adam demanded, steering Mike over to a row of chairs and forcing him down.

"Why're these always hard plastic? Just once, I want something comfortable," Mike muttered.

"They're hard plastic so they can be wiped with disinfectant after people bleed on them or cough tuberculosis all over them," Adam said. "Keep talking."

"Whoever he was, he broke Owen's left leg again. Went after it with a baseball bat, as a matter of fact. That's all I know, right now. Hopefully, we'll know more when he gets out of surgery. Do you have his sister's number? She should be notified."

"Goddamn, he was finally making headway on rehabbing it after the last setback," Adam muttered. "Yeah, I'll call Avril, and thanks for letting me know about Owen. How much longer will he be in surgery?"

Mike shrugged. "Another hour, maybe more, given what they're dealing with."

"Then I'd better call Avril."

After Adam called her, he tried to get some sleep, but as Detective Cabot had pointed out, the chairs and comfort were not well acquainted. He thought about stretching out in his Pilot, and he thought about offering the other front seat to the detective, but he wanted to be there when Owen got out of surgery, so plastic seats it was. He pulled his parka's hood over his face to block out the harsh fluorescent lights—or try.

"Adam? Wake up, honey, it's me."

"Go away, Mom. I'm wearing my retainers."

"Okay, that might've been funny when John Hughes wrote it, but you've got about five seconds to wake up before I pour my coffee down the neck of your sweater."

Adam blinked a few times to clear his eyes. "Avril?"

"Yes. What the hell's going on?"

"You're here." Adam struggled to sit up. He rubbed his eyes with his hands and then nudged Mike Cabot. "Detective? Wake up. Owen's sister's here."

"Of course, I'm here! You told me someone took a baseball bat to my brother!" Avril said shrilly.

"I didn't tell you he was in critical condition or anything. It's his leg, Avril. He'll be fine." Just what he needed, but that didn't stop Adam from getting up to give her a hug.

"Eventually maybe," she said, her voice muffled by his chest, "but again with the leg?"

"I know," Adam sighed. "Believe me, I know. So, who's watching the kids?"

"My oldest is old enough, and I let my best friend know what was up, so she's on call. Hopefully, I'll be back in time for breakfast. If a few people get weird haircuts today, it's not the end of the world. Other than my kids, Owen's all I've got in the world," Avril said.

Adam made the appropriate introductions and they settled back into the waiting.

Fortunately for Avril, she didn't have to wait very long, because while the estimate given to Detective Cabot was wildly off, the surgeons finally finished putting Owen's leg back together—again—not long after her arrival.

A tired-looking woman came out of the OR. "I'm Dr. Singh. Is one of you family?"

"I am," Avril said.

Dr. Singh frowned. "Then who are the rest of you?"

"I'm the detective handling Mr. Douglas's case," Mike said.

"And I'm his boyfriend," Adam said.

"Was this a bias crime?" Dr. Singh said.

Mike sighed. "No, at least not in the way you're thinking. He wasn't bashed because he's gay."

"Well, thank goodness for that," Dr. Singh said, "but that doesn't explain why he had a testicle clenched in one fist."

"A what!" Adam gasped.

"Oh, don't worry, it wasn't one of his. We checked."

Avril started laughing. "I'm sorry, but this is too much."

"It is kind of funny, especially since I have an idea whose it might be," Adam said.

Dr. Singh looked at him strangely. "I think we'd better go sit down."

She led them to a room, dark and unused at that hour of the night. "All right, the damage to Mr. Douglas's leg. As you all know, he's had quite a bit of damage to that leg already. I was on the original surgical team when he was brought in last summer, and I have to admit I'm not pleased at whoever did this to my patient and handiwork." She looked at Adam. "Am I correct in thinking that the testicle belongs to the person who did this?"

"I'm pretty sure it does," Adam said. He bit his lip to keep from laughing. If Jordan attacked Owen, and he had every reason to believe he did, then Owen's last act of defiance was the best thing ever, something he and his boyfriend would share a chuckle over forever.

"As a healer, I can't condone this sort of thing, but as Mr. Douglas's surgeon, I'm going to allow myself an exception just this once," Dr. Singh said primly. "Now, as to his recovery, which is what you want to know... Unlike the last time, there will be lasting permanent damage. The trauma from the attack was too great given the underlying state of the leg. His leg will be an inch or so shorter, and depending on how physical therapy and rehabilitation go, the knee may have a bit of a bend to it. Whether or not he requires a brace or cane depends on too many factors to guess at this point, but you, boyfriend and sister, need to make sure he goes to PT."

"Can we see him?" Adam asked.

"Briefly," Dr. Singh said. "It's late and he needs his sleep. We all do."

*

Owen lay back on his bed. Dr. Singh had just left, and she didn't look any happier to deliver her news than he was to hear it. Left leg one inch shorter and that was if he was a good boy and haunted Deanne Lawson's PT office. He'd haunt it all right; he'd haunt the fuck out of it so he could stand on his own two feet and kick the shit out of Jordan Sanders himself. Goddamn punk, breaking into his house while he was in the shower and coming after him with a baseball bat. The little bastard had seemed surprised when the aluminum bat went *clang!* on one of the titanium plates in his leg, and that surprise had given Owen a fighting chance.

And fight he had, Owen recalled with a grim smile. Whatever else happened, Jordan Sanders would never forget him.

He hated hospitals. He'd seen far too many of them since last summer. Those had been due to an accident. Sure, it had been carelessness on the part of another part of the fire department—and he was still trying to make up his mind about a lawsuit—but an accident, nonetheless. This? This was assault, pure and simple, and as soon as Mike Cabot got his happy ass down here to take his statement, he'd make sure charges were filed, and none of this diversion program crap.

There was a knock on the door and Mike stuck his head in. "You awake?"

"Yessir, come on in. We have things to discuss," Owen said.

"At least you're happy to see me, for once."

Owen grinned. "Because I got a very good view of the man who attacked me."

"You think it was Jordan Sanders?"

"Yep. Get a picture from Adam, and we can find out for sure. And in the meantime, I've scored my own trophy. All you have to do is start checking the ERs for people who came in with one nut ripped out and you may have your perp."

Mike chuckled. "The doctor couldn't quite bring herself to condemn the maiming."

"She's not real happy about the damage to my leg. Neither am I," Owen said flatly.

"I don't blame you."

Owen glared at him. "Maybe if you wankers had done something about him…"

"The criminal justice system works slowly, Owen," Mike sighed.

"Or maybe it's more about justice for criminals and not their victims," Owen fired back. "I never used to believe that crap but going through what Adam and I have for the last handful of months, I have to wonder. We've been prisoners of Jordan's terror, and he's been free as a bird. He should've been locked up last summer when Adam left. Or when he pretended to disappear from his program. Or—"

"Is this going to come between us, Owen?"

"I think it already has, Detective. Now you need to take my statement and start calling ERs, because this? I'll make sure this case won't go away." Owen thought about the media attention he had while he was out cold last summer. "'Firefighter injured in last summer's crash stalked by psycho cops won't jail' has a nice ring to it."

"Fine, tell me what happened," Mike said wearily.

Owen did. "So, when his bat hit one of the plates in my leg, I grabbed a pair of scissors out of the drawer and started stabbing at him to make him drop the bat. I was in a lot of pain, but I didn't want him to brain me. This guy's nuts. You have no idea if you haven't looked into his eyes."

"Did he? Drop the bat, I mean?"

"Yeah. I got a couple of good jabs at his wrists. You might check ERs for that too. Then I yanked his sweatpants down and made my grab."

"Damn, are you serious? He was already down."

Owen held up his hands. They were huge. "This man's inflicted terror on me and mine for months. So, I grabbed, and I squeezed as hard as I could. Turns out, it doesn't take all that much pressure to detach testicles from the body. The one I got popped through the skin of his sac. We were both pretty shocked. He shrieked and got away from me."

"Did you chase him?"

Owen shook his head. "I hurt too much, and I couldn't stand. Leg hit with a baseball bat, remember? I had to drag myself to my bedroom to call 9-1-1 as it was. Then I passed out."

"All right, Mr. Douglas. I have to inform you that if my investigation shows it, you may face assault charges, possibly felonious."

"Yeah, good luck with that," Owen muttered.

Mike put his notebook down. "Owen, it doesn't have to be this way."

"Then how does it have to be? You come charging in with talk of owing me and fumble everything. Jordan needed to be behind bars a long time ago, and you know it. If not that, he needed a bullet and a shallow grave."

"Jordan still has a lot of friends. People like him, they're good at hiding their crazy. Only the people they hurt see it."

"Adam told me his parents sided with Jordan," Owen admitted grudgingly.

Mike shrugged. "It happens. I need to get going. Even if you're being a jackass, you're right. Wrists stabbed with scissors and missing a nut are great leads. There's no way he could not seek treatment, given what babies we men are about our 'nads. I'll also see if I can't get a warrant issued for his arrest. Even the judge who put him in that diversionary program has to be sick of him by now."

*

After hearing about the attack on Owen, Adam did something he never thought he'd do again. He called Jordan. His hands shook and he wanted to vomit, but he still made the call.

It was a little different from the other times he'd run away from Jordan. For starters, he was smart about it. He bought a cheap, disposable phone with some random number he'd never use again. He asked to meet his ex in a very public place, and he didn't agree to come back. He was also furious, angrier than he could ever remember being. He could never prove that Jordan had killed Butterscotch, the same with Abulafia. The whole point with both was only to arouse suspicion. But with Owen, he knew damn well who had assaulted his boyfriend, and if Jordan thought he could bowl Adam over with his swagger this time, he was in for a very rude awakening.

And just look at that. He was swaggering. This was going to prove interesting.

"I knew you'd call," Jordan said as soon as he was close enough not to be overheard. He leaned in for a kiss.

Adam intercepted Jordan long before he was near enough to kiss, his hand on Jordan's throat an unmistakable message. He hoped.

"Did you, now." Viewed dispassionately, Jordan Sanders caught the eye. He was muscular, if a bit overbuilt, but then, he didn't work all that hard and spent a lot of time in the gym. Some guys liked that; Adam wasn't one of them anymore. Jordan took good care of himself, so his brown hair had a healthy sheen to it and his green eyes were clear. But Adam knew the truth about pretty packages and ugly contents.

"Sure, just as soon as the collateral damage to your pets was enough. They were always your weak spot. You know I don't care what I damage, so long as I get to you."

Hearing Jordan say it—no, confirm it—made Adam want to vomit. He put his hands in his lap to hide their shaking. He smiled, but it held no warmth. "Get yourself all patched up?"

"He'll pay for that."

Adam rolled his eyes, playing as best he could the part of an ex who'd moved on instead of a scared man facing his abuser. "You started it, you fucking fool. Why'd you attack something that has opposable thumbs? Two-paws smarter than four-paws, remember? Except in your case, apparently."

"If you come back to me, I'll forget it ever happened."

"That's all you've got, Uniball?"

Jordan's face darkened like a thundercloud, but for an instant his anguish and pain were naked and exposed. "He unmanned me."

"He did not. You've still got one left unless you've gone and done something—else—stupid." When Jordan didn't say anything, Adam swallowed his bile and continued. "What I want to know is why you're doing this? Really, why're you doing this? When they catch you—"

Jordan laughed. "I'm too smart to get caught. Hell, after you ran crying away, I convinced them I'm just some poor misunderstood creature and they put me in that first offenders' program. Fools."

Adam couldn't tell if Jordan meant the court system or the people in the program, but it didn't matter. "But you're getting sloppy in your arrogance. Answer me this— where'd you get yourself patched up, smart guy? An emergency room? What'd you pay with?"

Jordan didn't say anything, but Adam could see the wheels turning, perhaps for the first time since he left. That gave him strength. "The point is, however you did it, when you tangled with Owen you left clues. Did you know his best friend is the police detective on your case?"

Jordan's eyes widened, and that more than anything gave Adam hope that somehow, he and Owen might come out on top. "You thought I was just fucking around with some older guy, some dumb firefighter with his brains in his biceps, didn't you? You don't have to answer that. I know how you think."

Adam sat there and eyed Jordan speculatively. "You know what I think? I think you're a scared little animal. You haven't changed one bit since we were in school, but I have. So, you're there with whatever nasty things are going on inside your head and you can't bear to see me go because then what will you do, you sick fuck?"

Jordan stared at him, hatred burning in his eyes. "He did this to you. You were never like this before."

"Or maybe I was, and you never thought to look. Maybe when—if—I come back you should be careful about what you put in your mouth. I own—or am about to—

another practice. I don't hit people. I never have. But all those drugs I work with can be poisonous in the wrong dose."

"You're coming back?" For the first time, Adam saw hope in Jordan's eyes. Owen thought he was psycho, but Adam wasn't so sure. An abuser, yes, and probably amoral, but true sociopaths were rare, and in any event, Adam wasn't a psychiatrist and he was too tired to speculate. "Why?"

"For my own reasons, but on this condition: all scores are settled. Agreed."

"I have what I want."

And I've all but sealed my death warrant, Adam thought, *but it's the only way to pull Jordan away from seeking revenge on Owen for the nutcracking. Because knowing Jordan, he'll keep after him until he's satisfied and that might mean Owen's dead. But now I have to break our hearts. I just hope Owen understands.*

Jordan never saw it, but Adam almost made it to the restrooms before he threw up.

*

Adam couldn't bear what he had to do next, and no matter what he told himself about saving Owen's life, he hated himself and couldn't stand what he saw when he looked in the mirror, both his fear and his betrayal. Was this really what he'd become?

It appeared that yes, it was.

Owen had been home from the hospital less than twenty-four hours, and Adam was about to shit all over him, the man he loved. He'd never even told him that. Did that make it better, or worse?

It didn't matter. He was still shit.

He led Darwin and Huxley up the walk. He carried a bag with their stuff in it over his shoulder. There was no way he was taking them back to Jordan's house. It would never be "his" house, and he was keeping his rental, at least through the end of the lease. He didn't think "going back to his abuser" was a good reason to break a lease. Jordan could just do what Owen did—had done, Christ that hurt—and come to him. Knowing Jordan, that'd be most of the time. It wasn't like Jordan didn't know where he lived.

He let himself in. "It's me!" he called.

"I'm in the bedroom," Owen called. He sounded groggy. That made this easier...and harder.

He settled the dogs in the kitchen, although knowing them, as soon as he left, they'd run straight to Owen. Hmmm. He'd have to hire a dog walker to come in, at least until Owen was more ambulatory. He was about to owe the man that much.

His eyes filled with tears as he went to see Owen. He knocked on the door.

Owen looked up. His eyes were a bit glassy. Painkillers. This ought to be interesting. "Where th'hell were you earlier? When I was released, I mean. Mike Cabot had t'bring me home, and we're not friends anymore. Was awkward."

"I can imagine." Adam tried to keep the fondness, the love, from his voice. "Listen, Owen, there's something I need to talk to you about."

"Yeah, like where my boyfriend was," Owen said crossly.

"I was at work, okay? I have to work for a living."

"*I* work for a living. I would've been there today, e'sept your ex-boyfriend broke my leg with a baseball bat."

Adam was sick to his stomach. This was it... "He's not my ex anymore. I'm going back to him."

"The fuck you say!" Owen reared up in bed, his voice clear.

"I... I just can't take this anymore, Owen."

"But...why? What about what we have?"

"Had, Owen." Adam tried to keep his tone level, tried to keep his heart from flying apart into a million little shards.

"But I love you," Owen said sadly. The devastated look on his face was more than Adam could bear. He had to turn away.

"I know you do, and I cared for you, but Jordan and I were together for a long time. I can't just get over that."

All Adam could think about was the witch from *The Princess Bride* who shouted "Liar!" at Princess Buttercup, because she was shouting it at him. "Liar!" He could hear it ringing in his ears.

"...I can't stop you," Owen said. "Thanks to your boyfriend, that's lit'ral."

Then Darwin and Huxley ran into Owen's room. They yipped and launched themselves onto his bed, executing perfect little arcs. They licked his face, and he automatically put his arms around them. "And you're leaving me your last two pets. Nice. I can't even walk them."

"I think it's best," Adam said levelly. *Please, let him understand it all when his mind clears,* he prayed.

"Get this straight, Adam or Alexander or whatever your name's going to be for the rest of this week. I'm not dropping my case against Jordan. Once they catch him, that is. That fucker's permanently crippled me. I'm not quitting rowing either. If anything allows me to walk at all normally again—or as normally as you can walk missing a chunk of bone in your leg—it'll be PT plus rowing. If it's awkward at the CCRC boathouse, that's just too damn bad. If anyone asks me what happened, you can bet I'll tell him. You made this bed, you sleep in it. You know where the door is. You can leave your key on the mail table."

Adam kept his sobs quiet and did as instructed, but in his SUV, he cried for twenty minutes before he was able to drive away, because every word was deserved and every word cut him like one of his own scalpels.

Chapter Twenty

Owen allowed himself to cry for the rest of the night, but no drinking. He needed his painkillers too much. He sent Brad and Drew a quick e-mail to let them know but hadn't been in much contact with them all winter. He'd see Brad when they were back on the water. He e-mailed Nick Bedford to let him know about the assault and to request more time on an adaptive erg, if that was even possible since the adaptive rowing program had been an experiment and he didn't know if CCRC wanted its equipment tied up, but Nick assured him it'd be fine. That was a relief.

But to Mike and Steven he sent texts, and the subject was much more honest. So, the night after his heart was unceremoniously stomped into the dirt, he hosted a pity party in his bedroom. Drinks were nonalcoholic and he served pizza on his best paper plates. He fed T'Pau ham right from his own plate. He knew he wasn't supposed to give pets people food, but then, T'Pau thought she was people, so that counted, right? He wasn't going to be the one to tell her otherwise. Her coat was damp with his tears, and besides, she lived around his neck, and her claws were sharp.

Darwin and Huxley were welcome to whatever anyone felt like giving them, because they were family and you didn't starve family. That was just rude, especially when you were all huddled under the same blankets.

"So, what's all this?" Steven said when he let himself in.

"Adam dumped me. He left me his pets, at least the ones his current boyfriend hasn't already murdered," Owen said. "Pizza?"

Steven shook his head. "That all went by me rather fast. Can we back up a few spaces and start over?"

"We might as well wait until Mike gets here so I don't have to go into it twice. I'm not sure my nerves can handle that."

"Detective Cabot's coming?" Steven's voice cracked, Owen noticed.

"Yes, will that be a problem?"

"No," Steven squeaked.

Owen smiled. "It's okay, you can admit it. He thinks you're hot too."

"I'm too young for him." Steven sat on Owen's bed, deflated.

Owen pulled back the covers. "Climb in. The self-pity's better under the duvet."

Steven looked at him and looked at the covers. Then he kicked off his shoes and climbed under.

"Huh. You're right. Pass me a dog." Owen complied, and Steven said, "Which one's this? I can't tell them apart."

"I think it's Huxley, but I can't be sure without checking their tags."

Steven sighed. "I should've thought of that."

"No worries. It's a pity party, so it's a recrimination-free zone."

"I could get to like that."

"Me too."

They waited in silence for Mike to get there.

"Owen? Steven? Anyone here?"

Darwin and Huxley threw themselves off the bed, barking up a storm, and Owen wondered why he didn't have dogs before this.

"We're back here," Steven called.

Mike poked his head in the bedroom door to see the man he was crushing on and his former best friend in bed together. "Oh. Well. This is cozy."

"Climb in. It's a pity party," Owen said.

Mike squinted at him. "Have you been drinking?"

"No, and I figure I've got about five more minutes before I start blubbering again, so if you want all of what I'm about to say to make sense, take off your shoes and get into bed."

Steven nodded encouragingly. "It's okay, Detective. We're both clothed."

"I'm not sure that helps." But Mike did as he was told as Steven scooted closer to Owen.

T'Pau opened one eye. "Mrrrow?"

"Hello to you too. Guess I won't be seeing you at the clinic much," Steven said.

She put one paw out and rested it on his shoulder.

"That's really uncanny," Mike said, frowning.

Owen shrugged. "You get used to it."

"So, what happened?" Mike said. "And does this mean we're friends again? I mean, I'm sitting in your bed listening to you...whatever."

"I guess. It was too much trouble staying mad anyway." Owen took a deep breath. "The short version, since that's all there is, is Adam went back to Jordan. I don't really know why. I thought we had something good, even if I was frustrated with what I took to be his inability to stand up for himself. But he was the only man I've ever loved, and he took that and wadded it up and threw it back in my face."

Owen started crying again. He turned his face into T'Pau's side, and she began licking his hair, grooming her baby. "He never even said he loved me."

"I can't even guess what the hell he was thinking," Steven said, "but he left you his pets, Owen. You may not realize the significance of that, but I do. Those are his children. Laugh if you want, but he'd die to defend them. I think that's why Jordan was always careful about when he killed them. Adam may not be as muscular as you, but he's tall and he loves his fur kids. If he knew for a fact that Jordan had been responsible, he'd have ripped Jordan apart with his teeth. That he gave them to you means he trusts you more than anyone else on earth."

"That's not love," Owen said, curling over on his side.

"It is in my book," Steven said firmly. "No, think about it. You just dumped someone. Do you then leave your kids to that person? Especially going back to *that*?"

Mike frowned. "Walk me through the breakup, Owen. All of it."

"Oh Christ, Mike, do I have to?"

"This is both personal and professional, so yeah, I'm afraid so."

It was painful for all three of them, but Owen did. "Thanks, Owen. You were in no condition to note this," Mike said, "but unless you left something out, think about what else he left you. His keys. You told him to leave his keys on the mail stand, which he did. Did you give him back the keys to his place?"

Owen shook his head.

"And did he ask for them, then or since?"

Again, Owen shook his head.

"Then something else is going on here," Mike said. "His words may have said, 'breakup' but his actions, to my way of thinking, said something quite different. If I had to guess, I'd say he wants you to keep an eye on him."

"Can you blame him?" Steven snorted.

"You think so?" Owen said, raising his head from his tear-stained purple cat, who immediately set about fixing her fur. "And no, I don't. The thought he might voluntarily go back to...that gives me nightmares."

"I doubt Adam was aware of this, but Jordan should've been. I've found no record of any kind of protective order, but it's a violation of the terms of Jordan's diversionary program to resume any kind of relationship with the person he abused," Mike said. "It's basically like violating parole. I know this is cold comfort right now, but each little thing like this is another piece of evidence I need, and when I get enough to have an airtight case, I can go to the DA and get this bastard put away, because right now? Someone higher up the food chain's dragging his feet, possibly even protecting that asshole. I have to make our case against Jordan overwhelming."

"I just hope it's before he kills Adam," Owen whispered.

"That's where you come in, Owen. You've got to do what Adam wants you to do. You've got to be strong for him, even if you're not his boyfriend anymore," Mike said. "You've got to keep an eye on him."

Owen eyed Steven speculatively.

"What?" Steven said. "You're making me nervous."

"You work with him. You feel like helping?"

"You think I'm going to let you fight Adam going back to that asshole by yourself, you're crazy," Steven said hotly. "Of course, I'm going to help you, Hose Boy. I'm your spy at the clinic."

"You're mine too," Mike said, making Steven blush. "Owen will need Adam's schedule, but I'll need a record of any bruises, cuts, any physical problem you think is the result of abuse. Don't worry if you're wrong. If there's a pattern, it'll emerge from the observations soon enough."

"He talks to you," Owen said, rallying to his own cause. "I don't want you to betray confidences, but try to remember, we're all on his side, even if he doesn't know it."

"You know what else might work?" Steven said, his eyes afire with the possibilities. "Nanny cams!"

"Okay, I so didn't hear that," Mike said. He swung his legs out of bed. "I'm going to go order more pizza while you two discuss—or not—that subject. I brought the mail in with me, and when I come back, Owen, we'll open that registered letter from the fire department. And then, Steven? You and I can go back to holding hands."

Somehow, despite being lovelorn himself, that only made Owen smile.

*

After doing some research online, Owen did not in fact buy nanny cams. He ended up spending a fair amount of money on much higher quality surveillance equipment that broadcast images to a scrambled Internet address. Even if the cameras were found and reverse-engineered, without the encryption keys possessed by Owen, they were useless.

Thanks to Steven's connivance, he now knew exactly when Adam worked, when he didn't, when he took his breaks, and when he left the clinic. The only wild card was Jordan, since no one really knew what he did, but Mike bent the rules and came through with his therapy schedule. It was the best he could do, and Owen recognized it as such.

Thanks to all the time he'd spent with Adam in the past, the neighbors thought nothing of his presence around Adam's house, so one day in late January when Adam was at work and Jordan allegedly in therapy, Owen made his move. Despite the cost of the bugs, he planned on two per room, excluding the bathroom. He included the bedroom, figuring that even if Adam and Jordan had sex it was more likely to be rape than making love, and regardless of whether he could bear to watch, it might help Mike build his case. Kitchen, dining room, bedroom, study, living room.

On his way out, he bumped into the coffee table in the living room, jarring it slightly. More worryingly, he knocked something over. He remembered what Adam had said about Jordan sneaking into his dorm room and turning something over that no one else would notice, the sick fuck. He'd better make sure he got everything back exactly right. He just had to do it quickly, because for some reason being in Adam's house now made him extremely uncomfortable, maybe because he knew Jordan would do drive-bys and would punish Adam if he caught Owen in the act.

He got out of Adam's place as fast as he could and made it home with only one incident. Three fire trucks passed him, running hot. Instead of just pulling over temporarily as required by law, he ducked down a side street where he practiced breathing deeply until he could get his hyperventilation under control along with his racing heart. The sweating lasted a while longer.

All of this gave him something else to think about besides that letter. It seemed the department had finally gotten tired of his disability and sick leave claims. There was to be a disability hearing in two weeks to determine whether and how disabled he was.

So charming. Never mind one leg now had more metal in it than Iron Man's. They'd decided that since he couldn't handle the physical fitness test he was disabled, but since it was due to an assault it wasn't the department's fault. Too bad, so sad.

*

"Ms. Kim will see you now," her assistant told Owen.

Cute kid, and if he weren't still aching for Adam, or just aching period with his leg back in another plaster and fiberglass cast, he'd be drilling him by now. Except he was trying to be better than that. Even if the love was lost, the lessons remained.

"Thanks, Edward."

Owen gimped his way in on his crutches. They hurt, but he refused to retreat into the wheelchair. It felt too much like capitulation. Besides, he was saving the chair for the hearing. He wasn't stupid.

Pearl looked up from her desk. "You've still got the wheelchair, right? I want you looking as crippled as possible the day of the hearing. For that matter, you have to assume they're watching you. Edward's going to help you back to your car when we're done and you're going to use your chair until the hearing."

"Isn't that a little paranoid?" Owen said.

"Just because you're paranoid doesn't mean you're wrong. Have a seat."

As Owen eased himself into the chair, he said, "The wheelchair's in the back of my SUV, as a matter of fact."

Pearl's hand shot out. "Keys. Edward!" Almost instantly her assistant appeared. "Please take Mr. Douglas's keys and get his wheelchair. Have it set up and ready for him when he leaves. Thanks." She turned her attention back to Owen. "Now, as you surely must have muttered to yourself, two weeks is bullshit."

Pearl was an elegant woman a few years older than Owen, and while her looks might suggest a certain well-bred gentility, Owen knew those looks belied a tongue and temper to shame a Teamster. She was also worth every penny of her billable, and then some.

"They're doing this to catch you unprepared and to try to intimidate you. Tough titties for them such juvenile tactics don't work on me." She read the letter again and then looked over the documents he'd brought. "It's a good thing you're so anal retentive," she said, looking over her reading glasses at him. "I like that. It saves time.

"Now, the fact that you weren't exactly compliant early in your convalescence won't help you, but they're going to have a tough time with their claim that if you can row you aren't disabled, since your rehabilitation only really took off once you went through this Nick Bedford's adaptive rowing program, and thank you for getting letters from him, from his supervisors, and from your physical therapist attesting to this. I don't know who told you to be one of Bedford's test subjects in the lab—including a muscle biopsy!—but you owe him a blowjob at the very least."

Owen snorted. He was pretty sure Brad would object to that, since it was Drew who told him to go help Nick out in the lab, although the irony wouldn't be lost on any of them.

Pearl took off her glasses. "One of their main arguments is that rowing is strictly recreational, but we're going to hand them the science that it's both. That you're now back to rowing and begging Bedford for more of his adaptive magic is also a stroke of genius."

"I'm just desperate to walk as normally as possible after the assault."

"And I am so sorry about that, Owen. I hope they find the motherfucker who did that and cut his balls off."

"I already got one of them," he said blandly.

Pearl's eyes bulged as he told her the story. "You son of a bitch. I knew I liked you. Now, back to this nonsense.

"I wish the psych part of your defense was stronger, but at this point all we can do is run you before one of my stable of experts and hope for the best. The department will have its own expert who'll also examine your files and possibly you before the trial. You're not going to have much fun in the next two weeks and you're going to be busy being poked and prodded by our experts and theirs, and there's no help for it. Neutral examiners will review our conclusions and theirs."

"So, what do you think? Assault aside, what're my chances?" Owen asked.

Pearl leaned back in her chair. "Before I answer, let me ask you: what outcome do *you* want? Do you want to remain a firefighter? Do you want permanent disability? Something in between?"

Owen thought about it. "To be honest, for a long time, fighting fires and helping people was my life. Then I was promoted—"

"*Was* promoted. Interesting. Go on."

"Then I *made* Battalion Chief and was injured in short order. I'm not fighting fires and I'm not helping people. I can't hear sirens without hitting the deck feeling like I'm having a heart attack. My psych file isn't thicker because the therapist I saw didn't think there was much point. A fire truck killed my driver and almost turned me into pâté. Sometimes, my shrink said, there are perfectly logical reasons for the psychological reactions we have. Since then I've done a lot of thinking. It's time to go. I've never thought about the department owing me a living for the rest of my life."

"Start, because they do. They'll piss and moan and try to make you feel guilty by playing the 'we're all brothers behind the fire hose' card, the sexist pigs, and I'll be reminding your union that you've been paying dues for a reason and could they please get behind you and push for this, but the cold, hard reality is that you were almost wiped off the face of the earth because these jackasses couldn't coordinate the trucks from their different damn departments. If that engine hadn't been where it was when it was, none of this would've happened. End. Of. Story." She pounded on her desk with her fist.

This was why his first lawyer recommended her and talking to her about his case was the only time Owen ever really felt that optimistic about it. Too bad he couldn't camp out in her office until the hearing.

"So," she said. "Any more questions for today? Otherwise, I've got a letter to draft to their lawyers letting them know we'll be there, along with a number of discovery demands with an absolutely ridiculous deadline, just because I can."

"No, but you've set my mind at ease as much as you can at this point. I almost feel like I have a chance," Owen said.

"Careful there, Owen. You almost sounded optimistic there for a moment. Believe it or not, people have fought city hall and won before, and I have a very good track record. I know the fire department's legal counsel. They're nice guys, but the last time I faced one of them in court, he pissed himself. Something to think about if you decide to sue."

Owen smiled. "I'm leaning in that direction."

"Oh good. I get a third of anything we get out of them, you know." Pearl rubbed her hands together. She scared him a little. "Say the word and I'll go for the jugular. I live for that."

Edward knocked on the office door and stuck his head in. "Mr. Douglas's wheelchair, Ms. Kim."

"Get it on over here, Edward. He can't sit in it if it's all the way over there."

*

Adam found himself working more and more of late, and not just because he'd pushed Dr. Endicott out of her own practice. Like a cowbird, he thought, laying its eggs in another bird's nest so the baby cowbird could push its foster nestlings out of the nest to their deaths while it grew fat. Or something. He was tired. It didn't have to make sense. He was working hard so he didn't have to go home to a house that was no longer a refuge. He was working hard so he didn't have to see Jordan, just like the old days.

Except now, he was also working hard so he couldn't miss Owen. But that was impossible because everywhere he turned in his clinic, he found some trace or other of his boyfriend...former boyfriend, and by his own words and deeds. Owen's blocky, masculine handwriting on a chart. Towels folded Owen's way in the clinic's OR. Bottles of drugs turned upside down in the dispensary to indicate they needed reordering, Owen's innovation. Steven's apparent amnesia where his romantic life was concerned. He'd thought Steven found Owen irritating, but suddenly his assistant couldn't sing his praises loudly enough. If Adam hadn't agreed wholeheartedly, it would've pissed him off.

Instead, Adam knew Owen's last words and the look of anguish on his face would be cemented in his memory and imagination for the rest of his life. He saw them every time he closed his eyes. Every time he looked in the mirror to brush his teeth or shave, he saw Owen next to him, T'Pau draped across his broad shoulders, only instead of smiling in pleasure at shared company, his eyes were full of accusation and hatred. He didn't *know* Owen hated him, but how could he not? Adam hated himself, so how could Owen, whom he'd wronged, not hate him all the more?

So, when Adam got home and found Jordan's car parked in the middle of the driveway, it was just the smelly icing on the shit cake of his day. In the past, he'd have parked somewhere else when he couldn't put his car in the garage due to his alleged boyfriend's entitlement issues. This time, he parked so he blocked the entire driveway. Two could play that game, even if Adam had to force himself not to cave, swearing it'd be different this time.

Adam went ahead and hit the button on the garage door opener but let himself in the front door. He barely had the key in the lock before Jordan opened it. "What're you doing coming in the front door?" he demanded.

"You took your half out of the middle of my driveway, so I couldn't get my car in my garage," Adam said, putting just a bit of emphasis on it. "This isn't your house, Jordan. You don't live here."

"Nice attitude. I thought we were trying to make a new start here, but I feel like I'm the only one trying. Could you make a little effort?"

"Save that for your therapist, Jordan. He might buy it, but I don't. Are you going to move? And how did you get in? I don't remember giving you a key."

Jordan shrugged. "I made wax impressions of yours since you didn't give me one. Pretty rude of you. What kind of message are you sending with your actions? Have you thought about what they say?"

"Move, Jordan."

Jordan wasn't short by any means, but he wasn't nearly Adam's height, and while Adam had never hit anyone in his own defense, he wasn't defending himself, he was defending Owen...

"Fine," Jordan said, stepping aside like he was doing Adam a favor letting him into his own home. "And next time, you should choose alarm codes that're harder to figure out."

"What do you want, Jordan?"

"I'm just here to spend time with my boyfriend. Jeez, don't have a cow."

"Did it ever occur to you to try calling to see if it was a good night for me? I've worked all day and I'm dead tired."

"You know, Adam, it's not all about you."

"Poor Jordan. You really don't know how to handle it if the focus isn't on you at all times, do you?"

Jordan's face creased in confusion. "You really must hate me. Why did you call me to get back together if you hate me so much?"

Good question. Adam sighed. "I don't hate you, Jordan, but I don't share your conviction that you're the sole reason for the creation of the universe either."

"What did he do to you, anyway?" Jordan demanded.

"He didn't hit me, did you know that? Not once. Something to think about, isn't it?"

"Aw, babe, don't be like that. You just made me so mad sometimes, but it won't be like that this time. I promise. I'm different now. I've been to therapy and everything."

"Don't 'aw, babe' me. We both know you're snowing those people. I didn't 'make' you mad, and I'm not responsible for your emotions." It felt good to say these things, and maybe he should've said them years ago. Come to think of it, he couldn't have said them years ago, because it had taken intensive therapy of his own to realize it. And none of it meant anything, because Jordan would respond with his fists as soon as he got angry enough.

Jordan looked baffled. "That's what I said."

"Whatever. I'm going to eat dinner."

"Great! I'm starving. What're you ma—"

Whatever shut him down, Adam was grateful to it. He might even nominate it for sainthood or set up a shrine to it or something. Little bronze bowls, incense, offerings of fruit, the works.

"Who is he?" Jordan demanded as he stormed down the hall toward the kitchen.

Adam leaned against the counter. It was late, he was hungry, and one of Jordan's tantrums was the last thing he needed. "Who is who?"

"Someone was here! Who the fuck was he? You're cheating on me already. Goddamn, that didn't take long, did it? No wonder you didn't want me to come over. You were probably planning on meeting him tonight, weren't you?"

"What're you talking about, Jordan?"

Jordan shook a small paperweight in his face, a dandelion head encased in Lucite. "This! It was upside down on the coffee table. It wasn't the last time I was here," Jordan screamed.

"I haven't invited anyone over...yet," Adam said, trying to stay calm. It was already starting. They'd only talked a week ago.

"Fuck that shit! I'm just watching out for what's mine, and this is why." Jordan's face was red, and his entire body shook with rage.

"Nothing I say will satisfy you, but for the record, there's been no one here but you, apparently." Adam felt his heart speed up, his breath come in ever shorter gasps.

"Don't lie to me. Someone's been here," Jordan hissed. "You fucking, two-timing slut. You won't give it up for me, oh no, but some guy you found, sure, you'll let him fuck you."

Adam didn't fight as Jordan shoved him across the kitchen. He could've. But he didn't. He was already sliding back into the old patterns. Both of them. They both were.

When Jordan's fist struck him, he wasn't even surprised.

Chapter Twenty-One

Owen, mindful of Pearl Kim's admonition about being watched, assumed the CCRC boathouse would be prime spying territory and used his chair to get in. It wasn't as if he'd be out in a boat. He planned to use the modified erg until the orthopedists downgraded his cast to something more manageable, which would also play well at the upcoming disability hearing. The thought of that made his stomach clench. *Deep breaths, Owen, deep breaths.*

He'd barely made it in the door when Brad shanghaied him by the simple expedient of grabbing the wheelchair's handles and pushing him into a quiet corner. "Drew and I were really sorry to hear about you and Adam. You seemed like a great match," Brad said softly. "If there's anything we can do…"

"Keep me from blubbering or making a fool of myself when he walks in is all I can think of," Owen said.

Brad smiled sadly. "I think that one's up to you alone, Owen."

"Oh well, thanks anyway. Can you get the modified erg down as long as you've dragged me over here? I can't go out in a single until I get this latest indignity a little more healed."

"Yeah, buddy, sure thing." Brad pulled down one of the ergs with a fixed seat. Brad also hovered, from what Owen could tell from where he carefully stretched. He was limited in what he could do by the chair, so he decided to hobble from the chair to the erg and get to it. He'd give it a rest as soon as Nick started his Welcome to the Spring Racing Season patter.

"Whoa, dude, nice shiner!" Brad said.

Owen's head whipped up from where he was stretching, and all his carefully rehearsed disinterest flew right out the door. He had to look. He had to see what had become of his one love.

He heard Adam make some excuse or other, but it didn't matter. Even five seconds later, he couldn't have told anyone how Adam had explained it away.

He gasped—a reflex—and stared. He'd promised himself when he saw Adam at the boathouse that if he couldn't yet manage true friendliness, he would at least be collegial since they were still teammates. All he wanted to do was rush up to Adam and demand to know who had done this, but he knew, just as he knew it was because of Adam's own actions.

That didn't mean Owen had to like it.

Then Adam met his eyes, and they were now the eyes of a much older man. Just as before, the boathouse faded from his awareness, but that morning there was nothing of joy in it, only sadness and a terrible realization. Everything Owen suspected about Adam's motivations was true. He didn't know how he knew, he just knew.

Owen looked away. He couldn't stand it any longer. Brad. Where was Brad? "Brad!"

In a second, Brad was at his side. "Owen?"

"Get me out of here," Owen said thickly.

Brad grabbed the handles at the back of the chair and started pushing. "Coming through! Outta my way!"

Brad had his faults as a person and a friend, but excessive questioning wasn't one of them. They might come later, but when action was needed Brad was right there, which was a damn good thing.

They were out of the boathouse door, nearly mowing down Nick in the process, and almost to a strip of grass.

"Stop, stop," he cried. Then he threw himself onto the grass and vomited up what little was in his stomach.

The beautiful Adam, beaten like that, marked by someone's fists and anger, and...he threw up again.

"What's wrong?" Nick asked Brad.

"Adam is here with a bitch of a shiner," Brad answered softly, "although how anyone even reached his eye in the first place... You know they broke up?"

Nick nodded. "Owen told me when he told me about the assault." He knelt next to Owen. "I'm not sure practice is in the cards for you this morning. Why don't you go home and rest?"

Owen shook his head. "He won't let me."

"Okay," Nick said uncomprehendingly. "Go ahead and take a few minutes to pull yourself together and then come back in. We're just erging today anyway."

"No, I'm going home." Owen blinked. Then he grinned sheepishly. "Sorry, Nick. I know I'm not making much sense right now. Seeing Adam beat up like that... I can't do it right now. I've got an erg at home and I'll use it this morning, I promise."

"Sure, Owen. See you next time," Nick said.

Brad helped him back into his chair, and then Owen wheeled himself back to his SUV. It was a small adventure, climbing into it with a cast on one leg, but he managed. If anyone from the department was watching, let him marvel at his resourcefulness. Or not. Right now, he didn't care.

Somehow, he made it home and managed to wash out his mouth before collapsing into bed. So much for being the big macho firefighter, but he got to have emotions, too, didn't he? Seeing Adam like that... He wasn't prepared for it. Such a beautiful man.

A beautiful man.

He thought about the knowledge that passed between them, that his friends' every guess was right. He wasn't prepared to accept that, yet, but assuming it was so, what did it mean? Steven said Adam still loved him, which was why he had a bed full of animals right now and no longer turned the heater on at night. And Mike, he thought maybe Adam wanted Owen to keep an eye on him.

Was that what Adam's look meant? Everything you thought was true, is? And even if it were, was he, Owen, bound to respect it? Should he respect Adam and his stated wishes, or read between the lines around Adam's eyes?

Because instead of facing danger together, Adam had taken this decision out of his hands and broken his heart. Sure, assuming all guesses were right, and it was to protect him, Adam had never asked him, and he thought he ought to have a say. Personally, he'd rather face a threat head on with his man at his side. He'd rather deal with Adam's ex, and he'd rather face his disability trial, together with Adam.

With that thought on his mind, Owen drifted off to sleep, Adam's fur kids hemming him in. When he woke up after a few hours of fitful sleep, he realized he'd never checked the cameras he'd placed in Adam's house. As long as he felt this shitty...

"Sorry, boys, but I keep telling you that if you curl up against the cast, I wouldn't have to move you. Besides, the warmth feels amazing. This way? Scoot over."

He hopped on one leg to where his crutches leaned against the wall. In his own home with the blinds drawn, he'd use his crutches and screw the department.

A few minutes and several collisions with poorly situated furniture and walls later, he was at his computer and logged into the site that registered the cameras' telemetry. The process was time-consuming, as each camera had its own URL. That, plus the learning curve, meant Owen spent the better part of an hour on the first camera's first hour alone.

T'Pau strolled in and leaped onto his shoulders. He hardly noticed the pinpoint sting of her claws anymore. Each time was a momentary reminder to clip them, quickly forgotten as she purred her sweet nothings in his ear. He leaned his head against hers for a moment, enjoying the closeness and warmth. He'd liked her well enough when he and Adam were together, but after the dumping, T'Pau in particular had become his link to the complicated man he still loved.

"Mrrow?"

"I miss him too," Owen said. He barely noticed that he was talking to a cat. It helped that she was smarter than some of the firefighters under his command, at least based on the distressingly short amount of time it had taken her to figure out how to open the freezer door and liberate a frozen salmon filet. She was patient. A little gymnastics in the morning meant she dined well at night. It was spooky.

It was while he was resting his head on her, however, that he noticed the link reading, *Thumbnails*. "What's this? Why, T'Pau, I do believe you're a genius."

She butted her head against his, purring.

He clicked on it, and sure enough, there was the first of many pages of thumbnail screen caps at five-minute intervals. Most were pictures of an empty house, some few were of Adam alone, but those containing people usually featured Adam and a man he recognized from the assault in his bathroom, what he called the Testicle Incident. Inevitably, those contained violence.

At first, Owen only stared at the grainy images of the man he still loved being yelled at, being pushed around, being struck. None of it looked real at first, just screen caps. They could've been anyone. Until he clicked on one. Then his screen filled with a large, detailed image of Adam, his Adam, reeling back as a fist connected with his face.

Owen wondered if that was where that morning's black eye came from. He wondered how Adam would explain that to his clients; if he'd use whatever excuse he used at the boathouse. The animals wouldn't care.

Owen stared at it. He didn't know how long. He didn't even know he was crying until he felt T'Pau lick the tears off his cheek with her raspy tongue.

"I'm sorry, sweetheart. I'm soaking your fur again." He reached up and rubbed from her chin up around her ears, just the way she liked it.

He made himself look away, and then view the images as dispassionately as he could. This was why he'd bugged Adam's house, after all, why Adam had left him with keys and hadn't changed the alarm codes. He was doing this for Adam, and he couldn't afford to be sad, not right now.

He called Mike on his cell phone, his personal one.

"Mike Cabot."

"Hi, Mike, it's Owen."

"How're you doing?" Owen hated the concern he heard in everyone's voice these days, like they all thought he was made of bone china. One wrong move and he'd shatter. He was made of stronger stuff and it was time to act like it.

"I've been better, but that's not why I'm calling. Those nanny cams you don't know anything about? Theoretically speaking, let's say I struck pay dirt. This stuff seals the theoretical deal in terms of an arrest warrant, since the last time I checked, assault was still illegal. What should I do? Theoretically speaking, of course."

"Well, speaking strictly in the most abstract of terms of course, you'd want to copy those images, ideally onto a hard drive you wouldn't mind giving to a law-enforcement agency. You'd want a hard drive you could live without for a long time since it'd be evidence. Speaking in the abstract of course."

"Of course. We should have dinner soon. Catch up, because I want to know more about that hand-holding you and Steven were doing."

"Of course, you do. How's tomorrow?"

"Sounds perfect. It's the night before my disability hearing and I'll need a distraction."

"I'll pick you up after work then," Mike said before he hung up.

"Well, I guess you heard all of that, T'Pau. We need a hard drive we don't mind not getting back."

A quick trip to an office-supply store and Owen was in business, downloading clips and stills into folders by date. Adam would need it organized for whatever he had planned. Owen had to trust, to believe there was a plan.

*

"So how do you feel about the outcome?" Pearl asked him.

Owen was in his dress uniform, apparently for the last time in his life, or at least the last time he could foresee. It'd been a bitch getting it on over his cast that morning too. A few more days and he'd be downgrading his cast to something more manageable. Oh well. At least rowing would be a possibility, which was just as well. He was already heartily sick of erging.

"I'm not sure I can answer that right now," Owen replied. "I've been a firefighter practically since I got out of college and now, I'm not. It's going to take a while to work through that, let alone decide what I'm going to do with the next half of my life. But I'll say one thing. I expected something more trial-like from a disability hearing. This was just us on one end of that conference table and them on the other end."

"Yes, but there were only two of us and a lot of them," Pearl pointed out. "And as you quickly figured out, their 'We're all friends here' was the second biggest lie on earth, right after, 'I won't come in your mouth.'"

Owen choked on his water. Hearing her filthy mouth in her office was one thing but hearing it at lunch in a five-star restaurant was quite another. No doubt people eavesdropping from nearby tables thought so too.

He thought for a moment. "For me, hearing myself and my medical and work records discussed like I wasn't even there was weird. Yeah, hi guys, I'm right here in the room. It was kind of rude."

"I can see that," Pearl said, "but then again, some of it was intentional. This is a game. They were trying to throw you off, but that's why you had me."

"True, and you were right. They really went after rowing. If I can row, I can work and never mind the fine print. Even before my assault, my leg wouldn't bear the pressure of racing. I was never going to be more than a recreational and fitness rower with a lift in my shoe and a brace on my leg. Now, who knows, but given that I was injured twice on my job, the worst and most significant time due to their negligence, you think they'd be a bit more contrite or something."

Pearl leaned forward. "But Owen, that's why they kept hammering on the rowing. They were trying to distract you. It's also why they tried to slip a no-litigation clause into the settlement contract, and why I ripped them new assholes. It was your disability hearing, and for them to do that was pretty despicable. I really think you should sue the shit out of them for that reason alone, by the way.

"So yes, they think if you can row, you can work, but never mind you've been injured twice on their watch through no fault of your own in or on department property. Yes, you can function normally—in everyday life. You can't fight fires, and due to your first accident that is absolutely their fault, you really can't even stand being around fire departments. Even their tame psychologist agrees that your reaction to the sound of sirens is a normal response under the circumstances and one you may never get past even with long-term therapy."

Owen laughed, but it was devoid of humor. "Hooray for that. So, explain how they arrived at the disability score. The shrinks all agree that I'm one hundred percent disabled psychologically because I can't hear sirens without tripping out, which I guess means I'm crazy or something, so go—"

"It does not mean you're crazy, so get that out of your head right now," Pearl said. "It means you have a perfectly understandable neurosis and unlike a lot of people, you know exactly where yours came from. It also means that while you function perfectly well in virtually all areas of life, you can't do your job, since that's where your neurosis came from, so... One hundred percent psychological disability to do the job they're paying you to do.

"Now, your physical disability. This one was harder, as you can guess from the divided decision. You assault complicated everything. You would've had some physical disability before it, of course, but that toilet licker who took exception to you dating his ex whacked your leg again, causing you to lose bone. If it hadn't been for that, and hadn't been for your issue with sirens, the department argued it could've found a desk job for you. There's some justification for that. Not a lot, in my opinion, since they didn't come into the hearing with an offer in hand and didn't produce one when I demanded it."

"That was a bad sign, wasn't it?"

Pearl nodded. "It certainly wasn't a good one. So. You asked about calculating the disability. It's a combined score, psychological and physical, one hundred plus seventy-five divided by two, or eighty-eight percent disabled. In other words, given your present salary, enough to be comfortable on, which is a relief. Too often I see people who're disabled out of a job reduced to penury. Under the circumstances, while flipping out at sirens is inconvenient as fuck, it's a small price to pay for financial security. Now, have you thought about—"

Owen held up one hand. "Not now. Right now, my ex-boyfriend has gone back to his abusive ex, I think to protect me. With his covert blessing, I bugged his house with surveillance cameras and caught the little bastard in the act. The thing is, Adam didn't ask me if I wanted protecting, but he's definitely in need of rescuing himself. Let me get this squared away and then I'll let you know. Because right now? All I've got is an exchange of agonized looks at practice three times a week."

Pearl's eyes had grown progressively wider as he'd sketched his situation. "Damn, Owen. You don't fool around, do you? Are the cops involved?"

He shook his head. "Not officially."

"Good. If it blows up in your face, call me. I know some truly evil criminal defense attorneys. If it comes down to it, at the very least I may be able to keep them from representing your sweetie's abuser."

"He's not just my sweetie; he's the only man I've ever truly loved."

Pearl reached across the table and took his hand. "Then go home, get out of that uniform, put on something that can get blood on it, and prepare to fight dirty."

*

Owen planned to do that right after lunch with Pearl but was derailed by the simple fact he was exhausted. All that bone didn't just come from nothing, he guessed. Or maybe T'Pau just wanted her favorite pillow back home and cast a spell on him. At this point he wouldn't put anything past her. Darwin and Huxley didn't strike him as the type, but then, wasn't it always the ones you least suspected?

He thought by now he'd be familiar with the ups and downs of the recovery process, since he'd been at it more or less continually since the previous summer, but these random power outages still surprised and annoyed him.

Oh well, they'd pass. They always did. Besides, he had PT later and needed to rest.

When he felt better, he texted Steven.

So what's Adam's schedule like for the next few days?

The same, came the reply. *Early to work, late to leave. Of course, that means I have the Asshole underfoot a lot. Do something about him, Hose Boy.*

Fuck, I'm sorry. Also, not Hose Boy anymore. Hearing yesterday.

Damn, I forgot. My bad. :-(And???

Disability retirement.

And???

Still processing.

Shit. Asshole's here. Gotta work. Do something about Asshole PLEASE xoxo

Owen was amazed at how quickly he and Steven had gone from being mildly antagonistic toward each other to allies. Grateful, but surprised.

Midmorning the next day sounded like a safe time to head over to Adam's then. He had another bout of PT first thing in the morning, but so be it. After his indifferent adherence to the regimen the last time around, he'd insisted on double physical therapy. Deanne thought he was crazy, but she didn't turn him away. She just cautioned him that in a way it was like training for a marathon or one of those insane endurance races where you wallowed in mud and dodged burning obstacles with electrical current running through them—part of the regimen was giving his body a chance to adapt to the changes they were working on, so that meant rest. He could live with that, so long as he saw results too.

"You're driven this time around," Deanne said that afternoon.

"I have a goal," Owen said before returning to the exercise bands.

He watched her like a hawk as she demonstrated each exercise. "That's different from last time."

"Your injury's different from the last time you were here," Deanne said, nodding.

With demonic intensity, Owen bent to it, toning, stretching, strengthening. There had always been a certain machismo around the firehouse, but one thing physical therapy taught him was that low resistance strategically applied under skilled guidance could produce significant results.

She handed him a bottle of water. "You're done, Owen."

"Are you serious? We've only just started." How on earth was he going to regain whatever use he could salvage if she kept making him stop?

"Owen, you've been at it for forty-five minutes. I shouldn't have let you go even this long. The only reason I have is that you were in good condition before the assault so your body can handle more stress. Take a look at yourself. You're soaked in sweat."

Owen looked down at his shirt, surprised to see she was right.

"I want you to cool down properly, and then go home and eat," she told him. "Then take a warm bath and put the brace back on your leg. Then, if you need it, take an anti-inflammatory or a painkiller."

Owen nodded. "Now that you mention it, I'm a little hungry."

"I don't doubt it. I should make you wear a heartrate monitor next time just so you'll take me seriously about how hard you're working. And speaking of tomorrow... If you're more than a little sore, we're cancelling. Got it?"

Owen laughed. "Yes, boss."

"But Owen? Good job. I'm proud of how much ownership you're taking of your recovery this time."

It was amazing, Owen thought on the drive home, how a little recognition went a long way. He wondered if his recent work would show up on the next X-rays...

*

In fact, Owen felt up to PT the next morning. As he told her, he had a goal, and that goal was what he saw as the emancipation of the man he loved. He couldn't call him his boyfriend, not anymore and not yet. But he was working on that, oh yes, he was working on that.

He sent a text to Steven

> *Is he at work?*
>
> *He's in the next room.*
>
> *What about the Asshole?*
>
> *No sign.*

That worried Owen, but according to information received from Mike, Jordan was supposed to be in therapy. If Jordan knew what was good for him, then he'd be there. When it came time to assess compliance with those court-ordered diversion programs, the judge overseeing the programs would probably like to know just how compliant participants were before he passed them out of the program. Minimal compliance sometimes meant prison.

Text me ASAP if Adam leaves work for any reason, k?

Always.

Owen found it much easier to get around now that he had a brace rather than a cast. He still couldn't run, so he just had to pray Jordan was where he was supposed to be. If he was caught, he was screwed, but he was doing this for Adam. Besides, the longer he left the cameras there, the greater the chance Jordan might find them. He'd risked it long enough as it was.

Twenty nervous minutes later, he was back in his car, his hands shaking as he put the key in the ignition. He drove to a nearby gas station and texted Steven:

Brace yourself, I'm about to shock your boss.

Then he texted Adam, their first contact since Adam had left him:

Meet me in the singles house at CCRC tomorrow morning at 9:00 AM. You owe me that much.

Then Owen, his heart finally calming, drove home.

Despite all of Owen's precautions, he never noticed the man in the beat-up truck on a side street watching Adam's house.

Chapter Twenty-Two

Just as Pearl had advised, Owen was dressed in jeans and a tight-fitting technical fiber top that kept him warm but allowed him to move, clothes designed for work and metaphorical blood. He wasn't there to work out, after all, but a part of him admitted he dressed to show off his assets. It never hurt to show Adam what he'd thrown away, right?

He paced up and down the boathouse until his leg reminded him that was a stupid thing to do. Then he forced himself to look at the single rowing shells, some owned by the club, some owned by individual members. Someday, he thought, maybe he'd own one. He still had no idea what he wanted to do with the rest of his life, but then, he'd been distracted.

He started pacing again, back and forth across the boathouse, measuring the steps. It wasn't all that wide, but it didn't have to be since the boats weren't much wider than even the chunkiest rower's hips. He checked his watch compulsively and then sighed. It was two whole minutes later than the last time he'd checked it.

What if Adam didn't show? What if this entire time he'd been laboring under one delusion after another, and

Adam really had meant goodbye? What if he, Mike, and Steven had been wrong, and Adam hadn't meant any of those things, and had only wanted Owen out of his life?

Someone coughed in the boathouse's doorway.

Owen jerked his head around.

Adam.

"I'm here," he said softly, eyes downcast.

Owen could only stare. He'd only seen Adam at a distance since they managed to stay away from each other at practices, a neat trick considering the men's team at CCRC wasn't all that large to begin with.

Owen tried to speak, but the words stuck. He coughed. "Thanks for meeting me."

Adam looked up. He wore dark sunglasses. They didn't hide his black eyes very well. "You didn't give me much choice."

"That was more than you gave me!" Owen couldn't help the bark of cynical laughter that escaped him.

"I'm sorry about that."

"So am I." This wasn't how he hoped it'd go. "I miss you. You'll never know how much."

Adam started to speak and then stopped. His shoulders slumped in defeat. "I miss you, too, Owen. I'm not sure you'll ever know how much either."

Owen blinked away a tear. "I see you at practice. I've seen you look at me."

"And you look at me," Adam said. It sounded like an accusation.

"How could I not? You blindsided me. No warning, no hint that there were problems, you just abandoned me." Owen didn't accuse, but he didn't have to. The facts alone were accusation enough. Blinking wasn't cutting it anymore. He had to wipe away the tears.

"I did what I thought was best." Adam lifted his chin defiantly.

"For who?" Owen demanded. "For who? For you? For Jordan? Because it sure as hell wasn't for me."

"You didn't know what was going on. You don't know now!" Adam yelled.

"Of course not! You didn't talk to me. If you knew something I didn't, you sure didn't fill me in," Owen said bitterly.

"He wouldn't have stopped with the leg," Adam rasped.

That wasn't what Owen expected. "What!"

"You heard me. He wouldn't have stopped with the leg. After what you did? Sooner or later, he'd have come back for more. He wouldn't have stopped until you were dead, Owen."

Owen shook his head. Adam broke his heart over a testicle? "I can protect myself."

"What if he killed you, Owen? What if he killed you, and I could've prevented it? I'd never be able to live with myself." Tears ran freely down Adam's cheeks.

"This is living? He's destroying you. Have you looked at yourself lately? I mean really looked?" Owen demanded. "What do you tell your clients?"

Adam didn't say anything.

"You never asked me if this was a price I was willing to pay. You never asked me if this was something we could face together. I thought we were boyfriends heading toward more. You were my guy, the man I loved," Owen said, his voice low. "The man I still love. Do you hear me, Adam? I love you. I would've protected you or died trying."

Adam looked at the floor, his breathing ragged.

"Look me in the eye, Adam. Look me in the eye and tell me honestly that this is what you want, that what we had together wasn't good, and I'll leave and I'll never bother you again."

Owen looked at Adam, pouring all his love into that look, everything he felt. All the hurt, all the pain, all the suffering, none of it meant a thing compared to what he felt for the man standing before him.

Adam looked back at him, anguished, even tormented by what he saw, a man at war with himself.

"I'm right here, Adam. Look me in the eye. That's all you have to do."

Adam raised his head, and it broke Owen's heart all over again, the thought of that beautiful face and the gentle soul beneath it under the fists of a monster. With a wordless cry, Adam hurled himself toward Owen.

Owen opened his arms and caught him, barely standing up under Adam's onslaught, but he held him. He could only hang on to Adam while he sobbed into his shoulder, rocking him back and forth, while Adam whispered, "I'm so sorry" over and over.

"You are the only man I've ever loved," Owen said, "the only man I'll ever need. Together, we can face anything, d'you hear—"

"I knew it!" Jordan screamed, advancing into the boathouse. "I *knew* you were cheating on me with him, you fucking whore!"

Jordan pulled on the boathouse doors until they moved and then slammed them closed until all three were shut in the singles house.

Owen realized too late that he'd just missed what was probably his one opportunity to rush Jordan, because when Adam's ex turned around, he had a gun.

"I never cheated on either one of you," Adam said numbly.

"Liar!" Jordan screamed. "He was in your house at least twice while you were at work. If you weren't cheating on me, what was he doing there?"

Owen had long thought Jordan was unbalanced based just on Adam's reports, but standing before him, apparently his hostage, he realized Jordan was outright deranged. He and Adam were trapped in the boathouse with quite literally a raving lunatic, and—Owen sniffed.

Smoke.

Jordan had set fire to the boathouse and then trapped them in it.

"You want to know what I was doing?" Owen said, stalling. "I was planting bugs. Surveillance cameras, really. I was trying to catch you in the act."

"Fucking liar."

"Seriously, Jordan, why would I lie to you? These were tiny, military-grade cameras that communicate with my computer wirelessly," Owen said. No sense in giving him all the details. "What they sent me is enough to get you out of that bullshit program of yours and into jail where you belong, because no matter how many times Adam tells people he tripped down the stairs and fell into a doorknob, the film shows you beating him up. Different times, different days, different rooms, but the same pathetic little man striking his boyfriend over and over."

"What're you doing?" Adam hissed. "He'll shoot us."

"Trying to keep him off-balance so he won't. Smell that?"

Adam sniffed. "Shit."

"That's right. He's set fire to the boathouse," Owen said, coughing. He looked around, automatically starting calculations about where the fire started, how long it had been burning, fuel source, but then he stopped himself.

The only thing that mattered was getting Adam to safety.

He dropped to the floor. "Get down here," he hissed to Adam, tugging on his hand.

Adam, coughing, dropped to the floor next to him. "So, what's your plan, Battalion Chief?"

"Right now? Stall for time. There are sprinklers in the ceiling, and when they kick on, I rush him in the reduced visibility while you get out and get help," Owen whispered.

Owen squinted through the thickening haze. He could only see Jordan up to his neck.

"Should be any moment now."

"But—" Adam protested but he started to cough.

Owen kissed his cheek. "Don't argue with me. This is my world, remember? If you can find a bottle of water while he's threatening us, soak the front of your shirt and breathe through it."

"Get up, fuckers! I'll shoot you if you don't get up!"

Owen motioned for Adam to roll away to the other side of the boathouse, away from where Jordan last saw them, while he did the same in the opposite direction.

The fire alarms went off and air turned into water.

"What the hell!" Jordan screamed, apparently surprised by the turn of events.

But Owen grinned savagely. Even injured, he was still in his element and his reflexes still catlike. While Jordan was off-balance, he sprang, letting his body weight carry them to the floor.

"Adam! Find some rope!" Owen bellowed as he grabbed for Jordan's wrists.

While the water cleared the air and killed the visibility, it also made them both slippery, allowing

Jordan to partially wriggle out from under Owen. Then the contest began in earnest.

Owen went right for Jordan's eyes, but Jordan dodged and made for Owen's injured leg. Owen jerked his leg out of the way and brought it up into Jordan's groin as hard as he could. He connected. "How's that feel, you ballless shitsucker?"

Jordan, crying in his fury, clawed his way toward the dropped gun, and Owen perforce had to as well, scratching at Jordan's wrists along the way. It was street fighting at its dirtiest, but Owen was fighting to win, not to make the Marquess of Queensberry proud.

Just as Jordan reached the gun, Owen found a stray hand weight that had rolled under a boat. He grabbed it just as Jordan took hold of the gun and cocked it. Before he could think, Owen smashed it into the gun, and then smashed it into Jordan's hand. He kept smashing, hand, wrist, and not even the crunching of tiny bones registered.

Owen saw Jordan's face through a haze of red as he straddled Jordan's chest. "You fucking son of a bitch," Owen breathed as he reared up, the hand weight held high overhead. "This is how it feels to have your face pummeled. Enjoy it. You won't be nearly so pretty once I'm done."

Owen slammed the weight down and Jordan jerked his head to one side at the last second.

"Hold still!" Owen screamed.

"Owen, no!"

Owen slammed the weight down again, and Jordan jerked his head away.

This time something held Owen's hand. "Let go! No, Owen! You're too pretty for prison!"

Owen's vision cleared and he relinquished the weight to Adam. His shoulders slumped. "You're right, Adam."

"I've got the rope you wanted," Adam said. "I'll help you hogtie him. That should hold him until the police get here."

Adam helped Owen stand as the adrenaline left him. They rolled Jordan over, but he was cooperative, still staring at Owen in absolute terror.

"Where'd you learn how to hogtie?" Owen asked.

Adam grinned. "Vet school. Large animal rotations."

When he was done, Adam handed Owen a small foil packet. "What's this?" Owen asked.

"Mylar blanket. As soon as the sprinklers turned on, I ran out of the boathouse. I got into the main boathouse and called 9-1-1. Then I got some rope and two of the blankets out of the emergency bags that go in the safety launches. I made it back in before you took Jordan out permanently."

"Thank you," Owen said as he opened the blanket and wrapped it around himself. "And you were right."

"About what?" Adam said.

Owen nudged his boyfriend's shoulder. "I am too pretty for prison."

Shoulder to shoulder, Adam helped Owen out to sit and wait, but they wouldn't have to wait long, for they could hear sirens in the distance.

*

"What've you done to my dogs?" Adam demanded as soon as he walked in the door to Owen's house. "They're fat."

"They're not fat," Owen said, sounding injured.

"Fat? They're practically round."

"Wait a minute... *Your* dogs? I think you mean *my* dogs. You dumped them on me, as I recall, and when I was in no condition to protest. Dick move there, Lennox. Dick move."

Then Adam had to be close to Owen. He just had to be. Driving him home had been nice enough, but just hadn't cut it. With one quick step, Adam was up in Owen's face. He held it in his hands, smoothing his thumbs under along his cheeks. He kissed Owen's lips, tasting the smoke as much as smelling it, but then, he reeked of smoke too.

He kissed and drank his fill, denied Owen for so long by his own cruel plan. But Owen, brilliant Owen, had figured it out, with a little help from their friends. There were all kinds of things to sort out, but for now, they were together and that was all that mattered.

He ran his hands down Owen's chest. How he'd missed that chest, and Owen, the tease, had worn that sinfully tight Under Armour top. If it hadn't been to tease him, it had done that, nonetheless. He'd sported a semi as soon as he'd rushed into Owen's arms, and not even impending death had killed it. If anything, it only made his need stronger. Talking to the police for the rest of the morning hadn't changed that. Thank God Owen had had the presence of mind to text Steven to warn him something was up ahead of time. He had to figure out just how long his senior intern and his boyfriend had been in cahoots, but for now, he wanted into Owen's pants.

"Bed?" Adam asked hopefully, palming the front of Owen's jeans.

"Bath," Owen said firmly.

"Works for me."

They stripped as they walked, but Adam scooped it up.

"Just leave it in a pile outside the bathroom. I'll put it on to wash after we clean up. Today will catch up with my leg soon enough, but for now, I want us to get clean and into each other before that happens," Owen said.

Adam kissed his neck, biting and nibbling as much as kissing. He grinned as great shudders shook Owen's body and his breath hitched.

"I missed you," Owen rasped. "There wasn't anyone."

"Jordan didn't get anything but a blowjob," Adam said, "and I refused to swallow."

Owen turned around. "Adam... I want us to get tested, then retested in six months. If we're clean I wanna fuck you without anything in the way."

That Owen was fingering his ass while he said that took away his power of speech, at least temporarily. "Uh-huh."

Smiling, Owen turned on the water, and when it was warm, they stepped in together. At first, they just kissed, no roaming hands, no nothing, but it didn't last. They'd been denied each other too long, and Adam still had so much loving to express.

Owen picked up the bar, but Adam said, "Please, let me."

So, Adam soaped him gently, started with his face, washing the ash from his cheeks and neck and then moving onto his shoulders and back. But when he began to wash Owen's chest, things ceased being about hygiene. Adam couldn't help getting a hard-on. Somehow Owen's chest was even more developed, or maybe he'd lost fat. It didn't matter. It was Owen. And when he glided the slick and slippery suds from the soap across Owen's nipples, Owen sucked in his breath because hello? Someone was playing with something sensitive. Adam knew Owen was a tit pig. He was too.

It seemed like the most natural thing in the world for him to lock his mouth down over Owen's, and this time he didn't kiss him chastely. He had to be in contact with as much of his man as he could be, because a physical passion he'd never felt for anyone else, once banked, now burned high and hot after the threat to their lives. Hands on his man's chest and a tongue in his mouth weren't and couldn't be enough, so he brought his leg up and hooked Owen around the waist. He pulled him closer, holding him tighter, the soap somehow bridging the distance between them. That satisfied his need.

For a moment.

But it sparked other needs, more urgent needs, for wait, what was that poking at him? He reached a soap-slick hand down and wouldn't you know it, his man was harder than a steel piston and so was he. Soap didn't work so well for that, so he felt around, and his man, now moaning, obliged him with something else. It looked like conditioner. He put it on their cocks and stroked, and they moaned into each other's mouths. He stroked them lazily for a time, content to drift in the warmth and the near-bliss. It was Owen. It was him. They were together.

But he wanted more. He needed more. He needed to fuck. He took the hand that wasn't on their cocks and slowly opened his lover's entrance. Owen rested his forehead on his shoulder, and that was good. He would hold up Owen forever if he had to, just as the thought of Owen had sustained him through his own dark time. "Is this... Can I?" he asked, suddenly shy about things that had once been so natural to them both.

"Don't make me beg," Owen whined into his shoulder, "because I will. I'm not proud."

They both knew that was a lie, but it was good that when it was just them, Owen didn't have to be.

"Please tell me—"

"Cabinet over the toilet."

He loved how organized his man was. "I'm going to have to let you go for a minute."

Owen nodded and managed not to look too miserable, he noticed as he leaned out of the shower to fetch supplies. Moments later when he returned, the sight that greeted him took his breath away.

His man was up against the shower wall, legs spread, his ass out and ready. Adam stood behind him for a moment. He kissed Owen's neck, loving on him. Then he bit it, marking him. Owen cried out, but he shoved his ass back into Adam's crotch, too, seeking his cock.

"Soon," Adam whispered, licking and nibbling, making Owen shudder.

He ran his hands down the broad planes of Owen's back, marveling anew at their musculature and the way they tapered to a trim waist. It was what made it such a pleasure to see him walking away without a shirt on, so long as he planned to come back, of course.

Adam knelt, just to watch the water run down Owen's back and into the cleft between his cheeks. He ran his fingers down the crack, teasing the pucker, making it flutter beneath his touch.

Owen was ready, but he wanted a taste. He loved his man's freshly cleaned ass, so pink and perfect. He spread Owen's cheeks and brought his face close. He smelled of soap rinsed clean, of man, of Owen. He flicked his tongue against the pucker, just a bit, just enough to touch, but it was enough.

Owen gasped, startled by the sensation. That was all it took for Adam. As with the mouth, so with the ass. With one hand loosely on Owen's cock and the other holding the cheeks apart, he flicked his tongue all around the entrance and then stabbed it into the opening before flicking again. It drove Owen to begging in no time.

"Please, Adam…please."

He stood up and slicked up his own cock with lube before rolling a condom down over it. Lube for his cock, plus more for his man, all shielded from the shower by his own body, and then he was lining his cock up at Owen's entrance. "Ready?"

For an answer, Owen impaled himself in one swift move. "Goddamnit! Fuckfuckfuck, yes!" he bellowed.

Adam couldn't say anything. He was in heaven. He shook his head, clearing it enough to move. He put his hands on Owen's shoulders and started moving slowly, but it didn't last long. He couldn't go slowly.

"Faster!" Owen said through gritted teeth.

Owen fell forward. Adam grabbed Owen around the chest with one arm, his cock with his other hand. He didn't hold back. He fucked him hard, reclaiming him like he longed to. He bit down on Owen's neck, and Owen threw his head back, moaning and gasping.

Then Adam realized in six short months, long before the holidays, they'd be doing this again, but he'd be fucking Owen bareback. Then he'd finally mark him in all ways. That was all it took. "Owen!"

Adam came and came as hard as he ever had. He shook with it, grateful for the shower rod to brace himself against.

But he wasn't done, his man hadn't come yet. He draped himself over Owen's back, nipping and biting Owen's neck, holding him, pinning him the way he knew Owen sometimes liked. He could tell by Owen's breath it wouldn't be long.

"That's right, Owen. Give it to me."

Then Adam pulled out and swung down and under, and between one stroke and the next, he put himself in the way of his man's cock.

"Wa—?" Owen looked down to see his dick sliding in and out of Adam's mouth.

Adam looked up at him, filling his eyes with everything he hadn't been able to say, all the love, all the joy, all the comfort, he held in his gaze and gave them to Owen.

"Adam!" Owen roared, and then Adam felt his lover's essence filling his mouth. It spilled out the corners of his lips, but he didn't care. He swallowed and took more, whatever Owen had to give. And that's when he knew he always would.

But even as Owen's eyes cleared, Adam could see the pain there. "Step over me," he said softly.

"What?"

"Trust me," Adam said.

When Owen had, Adam rotated, a neat trick in a cramped space, but then his back was against the tub wall. He beckoned. "Now you can lean against me and have a soak for that leg."

"It's okay," Owen said.

"Dearheart, it's hurting. Some hot water, a bit of a rub, and then I'll take you to bed."

The tension seemed to flow out of Owen's body. "Okay."

Owen lowered himself down, and then Adam reached around him to kill the shower diverter. With the two of them in there, it didn't take long to fill the tub.

Adam reached forward with long arms and gently rubbed Owen's left leg. He was very careful, but still, Owen hissed when he hit sensitive spots.

"So how do I taste?" he said.

Adam leaned over Owen's shoulder and kissed him. "Like that."

"Mmmm, like heaven then."

Adam rested his head on that muscular shoulder. "Like home."

When the water began to cool, which wasn't long, Adam helped Owen to stand, and then dried him off before he dried himself off.

"Painkiller?" Adam asked.

Owen nodded. "I'm afraid so."

"That's what they're for."

Wrapped in the big thirsty towels Owen stocked and Adam approved of, they found three animals waiting outside. It may have been early for bed, but they were both tired, and their companion animals liked their humans inert and under the covers.

So, with one arm around Owen's waist, Adam helped him to bed. He pulled the covers back for Owen and then slid in after.

"Owen...there's something I want to say. Are you up for it?"

"Sure...boyfriend," he said with a tired smile.

Adam blinked back tears that hadn't been there a second before. He brushed damp hair back from Owen's forehead. "Owen... I love you so much. Will you marry me?"

Owen couldn't speak, but he nodded. Adam leaned in and sealed it with a kiss. Then, as Adam held Owen in his arms, they both drifted off, with T'Pau and the dogs settled around them.

*

Later that evening, when Owen was still asleep, Adam got up to lock the doors and put their smoky clothes on to wash. He had to have something to wear to work tomorrow, after all, and practice would be interesting, assuming they both made it.

As he locked up for the night, T'Pau greeted him in the hallway. "It's good to be home, isn't it, girl?"

She looked up at him. "Mrrrow."

He picked her up and carried her back to bed, purrs filling the air as they went.

Epilogue

Owen sat on his front porch with Drew and drank coffee. They pretended to direct traffic and the others pretended to listen to them, but mostly he and Drew talked.

"See? It's not all bad," Drew said.

"Yeah, but they're calling us the Cripple Contingent," Owen grumbled.

Drew shrugged. "Not anyone who wants to get laid in the near future."

"Truth." Owen sighed. "It just makes me feel kind of itchy to have all these people crawling all over my house without me in there to supervise."

"But you trust Adam." The way Drew said it, it sounded like a question.

Owen nodded. "I trust Adam. We talked about this a lot before we decided which house to move into, but in the end, it wasn't much of a question. I own, he rents."

"You're talking to a real estate agent, remember?" Drew laughed. Then he stopped. "Besides, isn't his place kind of tainted? I mean, that poor dog? The abuse?"

"Exactly. Neither of us wants to live there." Owen barely stood setting foot in Adam's place after the smoke cleared. In every room, his imagination summoned horrible images of Jordan beating Adam.

They sat in silence for a while, enjoying their coffee and their token protests about how much they wished they could help. "Still struggling?" Drew said after a while.

"Like you said, good days and bad." Owen looked out over his front yard, where the dogs played on leads carefully measured to keep them out from under the feet of the CCRC's men's team, who were providing most of the labor for the move. "It's gotten better since I quit the department."

"I'm glad." Drew looked around. "Is it me, or are there children underfoot?"

Owen laughed, happy to get away from the toys in his attic. He no longer felt like a broken man, even though he still felt like all the pieces of his life didn't fit together like they should. Midlife crises—gotta love 'em. "Adam's best intern—that's him over there with the guy with the half-sleeve tat—brought a few undergrads with him. Apparently, they helped him move when he escaped Jordan and he couldn't resist the symmetry."

"And the one following your fiancé around like a lovesick puppy?" Drew pointed to a sturdy man with the corn-fed look of someone raised on a farm.

"Joey?" Owen said. "Adam thought Joey was over him. Guess not. Maybe some of the rowing beef will distract him."

"Or," Drew said, giving him a sly look, "you and Adam could make it perfectly clear which way the wind's blowing."

"You're a cruel man, Drew. I knew I liked you." Owen checked his watch. "I'm going to go pick up the pizzas and beer necessary to feed these animals. Want to come?"

"I probably should, if only to make sure you ordered enough. Have you seen how much these people can eat? Besides, Brad's got a thing for handcrafted microbrews and they're not cheap. It's only fair if I buy some of them." Drew stood up, but he walked with a bit of a limp. "Like you said I said, some days are better than others. I ran yesterday and appear to be paying for it."

Owen signaled to Adam they were heading out, but when Drew saw Owen's 4Runner, he said, "I'll drive."

Owen rolled his eyes but went along quietly. After all, Drew drove a new BMW X5, so being gracious wasn't exactly a burden. They continued to talk as they rode, and Owen was glad Drew had put his earlier animosity aside, because talking things out with someone whose life had been turned upside down helped as much as his therapist did. They had support groups for abusers like Jordan, but not people whose lives had been dramatically rearranged without prior consultation.

"Hey, look at that, perfect timing," Drew exclaimed as they pulled up in front of the house to cries of "Food!"

Owen smirked. "You know rowers. I know how much is going into that house and where they're putting it."

They toasted their coffees. "To gimping! May we get over it quickly."

No sooner had Drew raised the back gate on his SUV than the rowing horde descended and bore the pizza and beer away.

"Well, that didn't take long, did it?" Owen remarked.

Drew shrugged as they exited the car. "They're like locusts, really. We had a BBQ for the men's team last summer. They cleared the buffet table in what felt like no time, and Brad couldn't even keep up with the grilling."

"They sure seem to burn it off," Owen said as he surveyed the field. "Isn't that right, Joey?"

The younger man stood less than an arm's length away. He looked like he wasn't listening, but Owen knew faking it when he saw it. He also knew staring after his fiancé.

"Yes, sir," Joey said, gulping.

Owen engaged him in chitchat for a few minutes until Joey made good his escape.

Drew watched the entire thing with undisguised glee. "That was cruel."

"How would you be acting right now if Brad and I had scored more than once and if I kept slobbering all over him?" Owen said, fixing Drew with an intent look. "If I were still looking to bone him with you standing right here?"

"You think that's what's going on?"

Owen shrugged. "Maybe not consciously, and I trust Adam, but..."

"Gotcha," Drew said, nodding slowly.

"Watch this," Owen said with a wink. He walked up where Adam sat on the front steps with Brad and Morgan.

Owen put his fingers to his lips and whistled so loudly it set Darwin and Huxley, who'd slipped their leashes and were busy sneaking toward the remains of the pizza boxes, to howling. When all eyes were on him, he said, "Thanks for helping me and Adam out today. We—"

"We help our own!" one of the rowers called.

Owen inclined his head. "And Adam and I are grateful. There's no way we could've done this ourselves, not with my leg and not with the furniture."

"Speaking for myself, I'm glad to help out, and I count you two as friends and great additions to the team," Brad said. He started clapping and fortunately he didn't even have to glare at the others before they started clapping too.

Adam stood up. "He's right. We'll help when it's our turn."

Then Adam pulled Owen to him. Owen expected something sedate, but not himself almost completely swept off his feet. "What're you doing?" he whispered.

"Putting on a show for Joey. Kid needs a lesson in manners," Adam said.

Owen wrapped his arms around Adam's neck and kissed him in a way that made him glad he was a man. Adam responded, pulled Owen's lower lip into his mouth, biting and sucking on it. Owen didn't even have to fake his moans.

It looked like it went on forever, and Joey said as much to the guy next to him, a lean man with dark, curly hair. "We've got great lung capacity."

"Damn, I'm going to have to check out rowing," Joey breathed.

The lean rower with the dark curly hair looked at him speculatively. "I'd be happy to take you out sometime. In a boat, I mean."

"Yeah?" Joey said. He blinked, as if he'd only just noticed how handsome the man next to him was.

"Are you at UCD?" the rower asked.

Joey nodded. "I'm majoring in Animal Sciences."

"Really? I studied Plant Sciences, graduated last year."

And like that, they were off and running.

Later, on the front steps, Owen stuck close to Adam to continue his hosting duties as people left, called away by other duties or even just because the party seemed to be breaking up. Soon it was down to Brad and Drew, Nick and Morgan, and Owen and Adam.

"Hey, guys, want to take it inside?" Adam said. He'd just come back from stuffing a stack of pizza boxes in the trash.

"Good call," Morgan said. "It's getting cold out here, spring or not."

Brad stood. "I'll be in as soon as I clean up the beer bottles. Is the recycling around back?"

"Blue bins next to the trash cans," Owen said.

"I'll help," Nick said.

Adam went to retrieve Darwin and Huxley, back on their leads, which they'd tied into knots, while Owen led Morgan and Drew inside.

"Have a seat, guys...wherever you can find one," Owen said.

As soon as she heard his voice, T'Pau emerged from behind her current favorite hiding place and source of roughage, a large and now somewhat worse for wear fern atop a bookcase. "Mrrrow."

It wasn't a question. Owen reached up for her and deposited her on his shoulders. "It's okay, sweetheart. The bad people have gone."

He scratched her chin for a few moments while Drew and Morgan made themselves comfortable.

"That's uncanny," Drew said.

T'Pau ignored him, finally relaxing enough that Owen could coax a quiet purr from her.

"That's nothing," Adam said as Darwin and Huxley bounded in ahead of him. T'Pau didn't deign to acknowledge their existence. "She has an opinion on everything to which we're all entitled. Funny thing, once Owen and I became serious, it took her about five minutes to decide he belonged to her."

"This is nice," Morgan said. "We don't get together often enough."

"Busy lives, busier schedules," Drew said, nodding. "And now that you and Nicky aren't the only students anymore..."

"Nicky?" Owen said.

Morgan rolled his eyes. "They've known each other for years. Drew's the only one he'll take that from. Except for me, of course."

"And I'll take all kinds of things from him," Nick said, grinning as he walked in. He sat down next to Morgan, who lifted his legs up and then put them down in his partner's lap.

"If you're not taking pictures, don't tease us," Brad said, shutting the door firmly behind him. He settled on the arm of Drew's chair. "I think your yard's pretty much clean, now."

"Thanks, Brad. That was really nice of you," Adam said. He settled on the floor, and when he noticed Owen looking for a place to sit, he crossed his legs and patted his lap.

Owen lowered himself down into Adam's lap, a bit awkwardly, but he quickly settled in. Damn, it felt nice to lean back against his fiancé's chest and let Adam hold him. T'Pau didn't seem too happy, based on the tail lashing, but contrary to her opinion, they didn't live to serve.

"Did I hear someone say something about me and Morgan not being the only ones in school?" Nick said.

Owen nodded. "Yeah, now that I'm a man of leisure, I thought I'd take some classes at City College to see what I'm interested in, with an ultimate eye on studying library science at one of the local universities. It's either that or make a nuisance of myself down at the clinic."

"That ought to keep you out of trouble," Drew said.

"You'd think," Owen said.

Brad leaned forward. "So, how's it really going?"

Owen looked at Adam, who nodded slightly. "I've decided to sue the fire department and the city. Injuries in the line of duty are one thing but being mangled because one engine hits another is something else altogether."

"And then there's Jordan Sanders," Adam said. "A whole different can of worms."

"Yeah, people think, 'brave Owen beat the crap out of the arsonist while clever Adam ran to call the fire department and saved our boats' and that's the end of it, but it's not, is it?" Morgan said.

"Not by miles, I'm afraid," Owen said, sighing.

"I'm afraid we're both going to be on and off the witness stand in the coming months," Adam said.

Owen made a face. "And for some time to come, starting with his sanity hearing."

"He's copping an insanity plea?" Drew said.

"Don't they all?" Morgan laughed.

"Is he actually crazy?" Nick asked.

"I think he's nuttier than a fruitcake," Owen said.

But Adam shook his head. "He's not insane. Whatever his problem is, it's not simple insanity, and whatever that problem is, I don't care. That's up to the courts, and we've got a lawyer representing us this time."

Owen growled. "I intend to make sure he doesn't weasel himself into another chickenshit 'diversion program.' I've got all those pictures from those cams I planted to prove he's a batterer."

"And I'll tell anyone who asks that Owen planted them with my knowledge, and that I used myself as bait to catch Jordan in the act," Adam said, "since it was what I was hoping he'd do anyway."

Owen pulled Adam's head down and kissed him gently. "You have no idea how much that killed me," he said softly.

Owen and Adam didn't notice, but the other four made "time to go" motions.

Nick pulled Owen up, the usual rounds of "See you soon" and "Let's have dinner sometime" were exchanged, and then it was just Adam and Owen, their animals, and the boxes representing the integration of their two lives.

Adam held Owen. "Here we are."

"I'm glad we're here," Owen said, resting against Adam.

"And I'm glad you'll be there with me tomorrow when I resume therapy," Adam said quietly, so quietly it was almost a whisper.

"I'm your fiancé."

Adam kissed him softly. "And I'm yours."

"And now you're home. We both are."

Acknowledgements

It's been said many times by many people, but while writing's a solitary profession, it's rarely an entirely independent effort. I finished the first draft of the first edition of *Burning It Down* in a Herculean push while on vacation at South Lake Tahoe with my parents, at the resort that was the model in my imagination for Alpenglow in *First Impressions* (forthcoming, NineStar Press). But I never would've been able to do that without my parents' help and indulgence. They took over all care of their grandson for that week, allowing me to write for eight to ten hours a day in a way that I cannot at home. Thanks, too, to my son, who was finally old enough to understand that if Daddy's allowed to work undisturbed, he'll be done and available that much sooner. So thank you, Mom, Dad, and the Man Cub.

I also want to acknowledge with gratitude everyone at NineStar Press for their help in bringing this story to press: Rae, Elizabeth, Natasha, and everyone else who might've had a hand in it. Their work has made this a better story.

I also gratefully acknowledge the support of my husband. His support for my writing means the world to me.

About the Author

Christopher Koehler always wanted to write, but it wasn't until his grad school years that he realized writing was how he wanted to spend his life. Long something of a hothouse flower, he's been lucky to be surrounded by people who encouraged that, especially his long-suffering husband of twenty-nine years and counting.

He loves many genres of fiction and nonfiction, but he's especially fond of romances, because it's in them that human emotions and relations, at least most of the ones fit to be discussed publicly, are laid bare.

While writing is his passion and his life, when he's not doing that, he's a househusband, at-home dad, and oarsman with a slightly disturbing interest in manners and the other ways people behave badly.

Christopher is approaching the tenth anniversary of publication and has been fortunate to be recognized for his writing, including by the American Library Association, which named *Poz* a 2016 Recommended Title.

Email:
christoarpher@gmail.com

Facebook:
www.facebook.com/Christopher.tells.stories

Twitter:
@christopherink

Website:
www.christopherkoehler.net/blog

Other NineStar books by this author

CalPac Crew Series
Rocking the Boat
Tipping the Balance

Coming Soon from C. Koehler

Settling the Score

CalPac Crew, Book Four

Randall Sundstrom's trial proved to be every bit as grotesque as Philip thought it would be when he'd set his plan in motion. Not that Philip intended to let the Grand Guignol that was Randall in high dudgeon stop him.

Randall had tried to make a mockery of the justice system, ensuring he'd be enjoying the dubious hospitality of the California Department of Corrections for a long, long time. Philip supposed he was lucky they had room for him at Folsom, because otherwise he'd be driving up to Susanville, or worse, down to Corcoran. Randall was an asshole, but not actually the kind of hardened criminal who ended up on death row, which ruled out San Quentin or Pelican Bay. Through his long-suffering lawyers—his third legal team, since he'd fired the first and the second had quit in frustration—Randall had fought every bit of evidence presented against him, even when it overwhelmingly pointed to him.

Even when Alex Beltran, the man Brad referred to as their father's evil henchman—and really, were there ever good henchmen?—took the stand and laid it all out in sickening detail, Randall blustered and argued and protested. Even when Beltran confessed to ordering several of his less seemly builders to maul Drew St.

Charles in an attempt to permanently shutter his efforts to renovate the Bayard House. Philip's jaw clenched at that. They'd almost succeeded in shuttering Drew permanently, all to get Brad to toe the family line and come to work the job with the family firm that was killing him.

For Philip that was the last straw, the absolute last fucking straw. Randall was a monster and a loose cannon, and this sort of thing could ruin Sundstrom Homes, if only because Randall was the sort to take SunHo down with him, and that Philip would never allow. He had endured far too much at Randall's hands to let Randall destroy his inheritance, and if Philip had to remove his father from the company Randall had created out of nothing, then Philip would do exactly that.

He had another, purer motive too.

The thought of Brad's boyfriend dying in a pool of his own blood because their father, like some third-rate mafioso, ordered him beaten to a pulp, filled Philip with quiet rage. Age separated the two brothers, along with the lack of a real sibling relationship, but this much Philip could do for his little brother and the man Brad was making his life with. He could make sure Randall paid for his homophobic arrogance.

What Randall didn't know, what Alex Beltran didn't know, was that he, Philip, Randall's quiet, dutiful eldest son, ever the loyal lieutenant, groomed to take over Sundstrom Homes, had set all this in motion.

He had located Beltran's daughter, a lesbian, and told her what their fathers had done. He had struck a bargain with her too. If she made sure her father turned state's evidence and testified against his, he'd pay Beltran's legal costs and do everything possible to keep him out of prison. Packaged right, it would look like Beltran, stricken by a crisis of conscience, had come forward on his own.

When Serena Beltran asked him why he was doing this to his own father, all Philip had to say was his brother was gay and the man attacked was his brother's boyfriend.

"Damn, that's messed up," she'd said.

But that was all it took.

Also Available from NineStar Press

Connect with NineStar Press

www.ninestarpress.com

www.facebook.com/ninestarpress

www.facebook.com/groups/NineStarNiche

www.twitter.com/ninestarpress